I0561240

Murder at the Midsummer Feast

A Vale & Stone: Consulting Detectives
Mystery
J.P. White

Ink &
Aether
Studios
Literary Press

Ink & Aether Studios, LLC

For my grandmother, Brenda — thank you for the countless hours we spent curled up together watching *Murder, She Wrote* and *Matlock*, solving mysteries before the detectives did (or at least trying). Those moments didn't just spark my love for cozy crime—they built some of my happiest memories. Thank you for always encouraging me to be unapologetically myself, for believing in my stories before they were even written, and for filling my world with laughter, warmth, and wonder. I carry you with me in every chapter, and I know you've been my guardian angel from above throughout this whole writing adventure.

This book is for you.

CHAPTER ONE

THE WINDING MOUNTAIN ROAD unfurled before Cressida Vale like a ribbon of gray silk, each hairpin turn revealing another slice of Blue Ridge majesty. She cranked the volume dial on her 2018 MINI Cooper's radio, letting the Billie Holiday track wash over her. The engine's purr harmonized with the brass section as she rounded another bend, the guardrail to her right the only thing between her and a spectacular drop into fog-thick valleys below.

"*The difficult I'll do right now,*" Cressida sang along, her voice surprisingly steady considering the altitude. "*The impossible will take a little while.*"

Her fingers tapped against the steering wheel in time with the music, nails painted a defiant shade of crimson that matched her lipstick. *You're doing the right thing,* she told herself for what must have been the hundredth time since loading the last box into her car that morning. *Absolutely the right thing.*

The mantra had lost some of its conviction somewhere around mile marker forty-seven.

Ahead, a weathered sign announced: BLACKVALE - 12 MILES. EST. 1873. WHAT THE SHADOW KEEPS, THE VALLEY REMEMBERS.

Cressida's throat tightened. Twelve miles to Vale House Inn. To Aunt Sylvia, to the sprawling Victorian house that had been in the family for three generations, to the town where she'd spent every childhood summer but never truly lived. She hadn't been back for any extended time since her best friend left for college—years ago now.

The song shifted to something slower, more melancholic. She didn't turn it down.

Blackvale held good memories. Summers from age six onwards, running wild through Aunt Sylvia's gardens, learning to identify bird calls and poisonous plants with equal enthusiasm. It was there where she'd learned how to see—really see—the world around her, to notice the details others missed. A *photographer's eye*, her dad had once called it, though she'd been more interested in solving the mystery of who'd been stealing strawberries from the kitchen garden. (It had been the neighbor's ancient beagle, wearing guilt like a red bandana.)

Cressida had always thought she'd need something bigger, louder, more *substantial* than a Blue Ridge mountain town of 3,200 souls.

And yet.

Here she was, her entire life packed into a MINI Cooper, driving toward the very place she'd once thought she'd outgrown. After quitting her job at the Charlotte Observer—the fifth iteration of a journalism career that had slowly calcified from calling to compromise—she'd finally accepted what had been staring her in the face for months: she had no idea what she was doing with her life.

Aunt Sylvia's offer had arrived like a lifeboat tossed to a drowning woman: stay at Vale House Inn, help out around the place, figure out her next move. *You need quiet, darling girl*, her aunt had said in that way of hers that made it sound like a decree from the universe itself.

So: quiet. A few months at Vale House Inn. Some freelance photography work to keep her portfolio active and her bank account from complete desertion.

The road dipped lower. The valley opened before her.

Blackvale spread out below like a watercolor painting someone had left out in the rain—all soft edges and muted colors, church steeples rising through morning mist. The dark thread of Hollow Creek cut through the town's heart. In the distance, she could just make out Blackvale

Manor, the old Black family estate, its Gothic towers piercing the fog like accusations.

Vale House Inn would be on the eastern edge of town, where the old families had built their summer retreats back when Blackvale had been a destination for those fleeing the lowland heat. Three stories of honey-colored stone and dark wood. Wraparound porches, gardens that Aunt Sylvia tended with the dedication of a high priestess.

Her phone buzzed in her purse—a slightly faded chocolate brown leather from the '70s currently residing in the passenger seat. She ignored it. Probably her mother, calling to deliver one more lecture about throwing away perfectly good opportunities. Or possibly her sister Rosalind, checking to make sure she hadn't chickened out and turned the car around.

Through the windshield, Blackvale waited, patient and inevitable as gravity.

"*The impossible will take a little while,*" Billie Holiday promised.

Let's hope so, Cressida thought, pressing the accelerator as the road curved downward into the valley's embrace.

The descent continued. Each curve revealed more: old farmhouses with tin roofs catching morning light, orchards climbing hillsides in neat rows, wooden fences mended by the same hands for generations. The fog burned off. The white spire of First Baptist emerged, then the copper-green dome of the old courthouse, Main Street following the creek like a loyal companion.

The road leveled out as Cressida approached the valley floor. Billie Holiday gave way to a crackling advertisement for Hollow Creek Tavern's Friday fish fry. She reached for the dial—

And nearly rear-ended the pickup truck that materialized around the bend like a rust-covered apparition.

"Jesus Christ." The brakes slammed beneath her foot. The Mini's anti-lock system engaged with a stuttering pulse.

The truck ahead—calling it a truck was generous; it looked assembled from parts salvaged from three different vehicles and held together with prayers and baling wire—puttered along at what couldn't possibly be more than twenty-five miles per hour. The speed limit sign she'd just passed clearly stated thirty-five.

Cressida's nails bit into her palm. *Okay. Fine. It's fine. Maybe they're turning soon.*

They were not turning soon.

The truck continued its glacial progress, exhaust pipe belching black smoke that probably violated at least seven EPA regulations. Through the grimy rear window, she could just make out the shape of someone's head—a baseball cap, maybe, though it was hard to tell through the accumulated filth.

Are you kidding me right now? Her internal monologue shifted from philosophical to murderous in approximately thirty seconds. *Three hours. Three. Hours. I'm literally twelve miles from Vale House Inn and hot coffee and Aunt Sylvia's lemon cake, and this—this automotive disaster is going to make me late because apparently we're now traveling at the speed of continental drift.*

She checked her mirrors. The road was still too winding, the shoulder too narrow, the drop-off too severe. Passing would be suicide.

So she followed. And seethed.

Twenty-four miles per hour now, according to her speedometer. The truck's left taillight was out. No, wait—there was no left taillight, just a hole where one should have been. The bumper sticker was too faded to read, but she thought it might have once said something about fishing.

Of course it did. Of course he's a fisherman. Probably has all day to get wherever he's going. Probably thinks twenty-four miles per hour is speedy. Probably—

The road straightened. Not much, but enough. She glanced in her mirrors again—clear behind, clear ahead for maybe a hundred yards before the next curve. The centerline was dashed rather than solid.

She didn't give herself time to reconsider.

Her foot hit the accelerator and the Mini responded with the eager enthusiasm of a dog let off its leash. She swung into the left lane, engine revving as she pulled alongside the truck—

Confirmed: yes, baseball cap, yes, approximately ninety years old, yes, oblivious to her existence—and shot past with maybe fifteen yards to spare before the next curve.

"Unbelievable," she muttered, settling back into the right lane. Her pulse hammered with the particular cocktail of righteousness and adrenaline that comes from a perfectly executed passing maneuver. "Absolutely un—"

Blue and red lights exploded in her rearview mirror.

She blinked. Once. Twice.

"Oh, you have *got* to be kidding me."

Her eyes darted to the speedometer—already dropping, but there was no denying she'd been doing at least forty-three in that thirty-five zone. Maybe forty-four. Her mouth went dry. She signaled and pulled onto the narrow shoulder, gravel crunching under her tires.

The patrol car settled in behind her, lights still flashing their accusatory rhythm. In her mirror, the door opened. Not the unmarked black Bronco, thank god—that would have been Sheriff Stone himself, and while she'd known Dan Stone since she was six years old, she doubted he'd look kindly on her speeding on her very first day back in town.

No, this was one of the county's aging Ford Explorers. A deputy, then. Maybe Pete Burress? She'd gone to summer camp with Pete's youngest son. Or—

Cressida rolled down her window. Arranged her face into what she hoped was an appropriately contrite expression.

Found herself looking up at a woman she'd never seen before in her life.

"You're not Pete Burress." The words escaped before her brain could stop them. "Wait, who are you?"

Smooth, Cressida. Really smooth.

The deputy's expression didn't flicker. "That's my line." One hand extended, steady and professional. "License and registration, please."

Cressida fumbled for her purse, fingers catching against a mini notebook as she extracted her wallet. The deputy waited with a stillness that could only come from military training or exceptional patience—probably both, given the ramrod posture and the way her weight distributed evenly on both feet in spite of the uneven shoulder.

Handing over her license and registration, Cressida used the moment to study the woman properly. Late thirties, maybe. Bronze skin caught the morning light—warm undertones that suggested mixed heritage, though specifics remained elusive. Different from Cressida's own copper-brown complexion, but close enough that she wondered if they'd ever face the same assumptions in a town like this.

What she *could* catalog: the sharp-eyed assessment of someone who missed very little, a gaze that indexed details the way Cressida herself did, though probably for different reasons. Dark hair pulled back in a bun so tight it had to be giving her a headache. The uniform stayed crisp in defiance of mountain humidity, nameplate gleaming, boots polished to an almost aggressive shine.

Most notably: her expression suggested she had precisely zero interest in hearing excuses, explanations, or anything resembling charm.

The deputy examined Cressida's license with deliberate slowness usually reserved for diffusing bombs. Her eyes moved from photo to face and back, a slight furrow appearing between her brows.

She looked up. One eyebrow climbed toward her hairline in a gesture that conveyed both skepticism and expectation. "Want to tell me why you were doing forty-five in a thirty-five zone?"

"Technically," Cressida said, unable to stop herself, "I was doing forty-three. Maybe forty-four at most. Eight miles over, and only for the fifteen seconds it took to get around the hazard—" She gestured toward the road ahead, where the ancient pickup truck was *finally* puttering past at its glacial pace. "—of *that thing*, which poses more danger on these roads than me going eight miles over for less than a quarter mile."

The deputy's expression remained unchanged. If anything, it calcified further.

"And by law," Cressida added—because apparently her mouth had decided this morning was a great time to be technically correct rather than strategically silent—"you have to identify yourself when asked."

A muscle twitched in the deputy's jaw. The only sound: the distant rumble of the pickup truck's failing exhaust, the soft tick of the Mini's cooling engine.

"Deputy Carla Jensen." The woman's voice was flat as hammered steel. She tapped the nameplate on her uniform—polished brass, perfectly aligned—with one precise finger. "And eight miles over is still over, Miss..." A glance down at the license. "Vale."

Weight settled on the name, as if she were testing it. Her eyes returned to Cressida's face, sharp and assessing.

"You visiting, or passing through?"

Cressida's shoulders straightened. She hated this part—the small-town calculus of connections and reputation, the way a name could open doors or close them before you'd even said hello. She also hated the idea of another speeding ticket, of watching her insurance rates climb when she was already on what could charitably be called a fixed budget.

"Neither." She forced pleasantness into her voice. "I'm coming to stay with my aunt, Sylvia Vale. And my older sister, Rosalind Vale."

The effect was immediate. Deputy Jensen's entire posture shifted—not relaxing, exactly, but recalibrating. Her eyes dropped to the license, then up to Cressida's face with an intensity that felt almost physical.

"You're related to Ms. Vale." Slowly. Not quite a question. Then, with more emphasis: "Ms. *Rosalind* Vale?"

There it was—the Rosalind Effect. Her sister had been in Blackvale for years now, had somehow made herself indispensable to the town's power structure despite being what the old guard probably still thought of as "new money" and "from away." Mountain town politics weren't that different from Charlotte boardrooms, apparently.

Cressida pulled off her sunglasses—60's cat-eye frames, naturally—and offered Deputy Jensen her most winning smile.

"I know. It still surprises me too, sometimes."

The statement had layers Deputy Jensen couldn't possibly understand: how strange it was that she and Rosalind had taken such different paths, how their mother still couldn't quite hide her disappointment that Cressida hadn't followed her sister's trajectory, how coming back to Blackvale felt simultaneously like failure and relief.

Deputy Jensen studied her. Morning light caught a small scar at her temple—old, barely visible. Military service, maybe. Or just a hard childhood.

Her radio hissed static, then fell silent.

"We have a speed limit here in Blackvale, Ms. Vale." The deputy's voice carried practiced neutrality—the kind reserved for people who thought their last name should mean something. "We expect everyone to observe it."

She turned toward her patrol car, boots crunching gravel. Then stopped mid-stride and glanced back, satisfaction flickering in those sharp eyes.

"And for the record"—she tapped Cressida's license against her palm—"Nelson Sawyer drives this route every day at this time. Hasn't had an accident in over a decade."

Cressida's eyebrows shot up. "Nelson Sawyer?" The name reeled her back through summers at Vale House, Aunt Sylvia's exasperated complaints about the man who'd fixed her porch at geological speed, the ancient jack of all trades who'd seemed impossibly old when she was twelve. "You mean Old Man Sawyer is still kicking around?"

The static crackled again. Longer this time.

Deputy Jensen turned fully to face her, a frown creasing her brow. Not quite disapproval—something adjacent to it. Cressida had just confirmed whatever private suspicion the deputy had been nursing.

"Mr. Sawyer, yes." Weight on the title. "He'll probably outlive us all at the rate he's going."

She tapped the license once—sharp against the mountain air. Behind them, a bird called out. Something local, something Cressida couldn't name but whose song felt oddly familiar. Muscle memory for the ears. The kind of sound that should have been comforting but instead felt vaguely unsettling in the heavy stillness.

"Sit tight, Miss Vale."

Deputy Jensen strode back to her patrol car, posture ramrod straight, every movement economical. Cressida watched her go in the rearview mirror—the way the deputy's hand rested naturally near her radio, the way she scanned the road even as she walked. Still alert. Still cataloging. Still on duty in a way that seemed to run deeper than the uniform.

Well, Cressida thought, slumping back against her seat as the adrenaline drained away. *That went spectacularly.*

Through her windshield, the Blue Ridge mountains rose in layers of blue and gray, each ridge softer than the last until they faded into mist. Beautiful, certainly. Peaceful, even.

But Cressida had spent enough time in small towns to know that peace was often just another word for secrets kept quiet.

She'd been back in Blackvale for approximately twenty minutes and had already managed to insult a local institution and antagonize law enforcement.

Rosalind is going to love this, she thought grimly, already composing the conversation in her head. Her sister's cool, assessing gaze, the slight tightening around her mouth that meant disappointment delivered with surgical precision. *Welcome home, Cressida. Try not to burn all your bridges before you even get to the inn.*

Behind her, Deputy Jensen's voice murmured into the radio, too quiet to make out words but rhythmic enough to suggest she was calling in the stop. Running the plates, probably. Checking for warrants, outstanding tickets, anything that might turn this from a warning into something more serious.

Cressida drummed her fingers against the steering wheel. Counted her breaths. Tried to remember the meditation techniques her therapist had insisted would help with her impulsivity.

Breathe in for four, hold for seven, out for eight. Or was it in for seven? God, I'm terrible at this.

The mountains watched, impassive and ancient. Somewhere in the distance, water ran—a creek, probably, swollen with recent rain. The air smelled of pine and damp earth and something darker. Decay, maybe. Or autumn pretending to be death. The kind of smell that lingered in places where secrets grew roots.

A prickle traced the back of Cressida's neck—that old familiar sensation, the intuition that said *pay attention, something's shifted.* She'd felt it three months ago when a routine insurance fraud case had turned into something darker, the same electric awareness that had made her pull court records on a hunch that cracked an embezzlement ring wide open.

The bird called out again—that same unfamiliar song—and this time it sounded less like welcome and more like warning.

Twelve miles from Vale House, she reminded herself. *Twelve miles from Aunt Sylvia's lemon cake and a hot meal. You can make it without doing anything else stupid.*

Probably.

Behind her, Deputy Jensen's voice murmured into the radio, words she still couldn't catch but whose rhythm felt oddly final, like the closing of a door she hadn't known was open. The mountains kept their vigil, holding whatever truths Blackvale preferred to keep quiet in the spaces between their ancient ridges.

Chapter Two

Deputy Jensen's boots crunched back across the gravel. She stopped beside the Mini's window, and Cressida could see her own distorted reflection in the deputy's mirrored sunglasses—looking significantly less put-together than she'd felt twenty minutes ago.

"Well, Ms. Vale." Deputy Jensen held out the license and registration with careful precision that somehow felt like a reprimand all on its own. "I'm letting you off with a warning this time. Consider it a welcome-home courtesy." The emphasis landed with surgical accuracy. "Just remember we have a speed limit here in Blackvale, and we expect everyone to observe the law. Everyone."

A pause. Cressida could have sworn she saw the ghost of something—not quite amusement, but maybe its distant cousin—flicker across those stern features.

"Your sister speaks highly of you. Try not to make me regret this decision."

"I—thank you, Deputy Jensen." Cressida accepted her documents with what she hoped was appropriate contrition. "I appreciate it. Truly."

Deputy Jensen gave her one last long look, the kind that suggested she was filing away every detail for future reference, then tapped the roof of her car twice.

"Drive safe, Ms. Vale. And remember—we're a small town. Word travels fast."

It sounded like advice. It felt like a warning.

Fifteen minutes later, Cressida was still replaying the encounter as she navigated the winding descent into Blackvale proper. Embarrassment and residual indignation crept up her neck like ivy climbing old stone. The way Deputy Jensen had said it—so calm, so absolutely brooking no argument—made Cressida feel about twelve years old and caught sneaking cookies before dinner.

You're thirty, she reminded herself firmly. *You've once talked your way out of a very awkward situation involving a stolen Picasso sketch.*

You can handle one small-town deputy with a badge and an attitude.

Except Deputy Jensen hadn't had an attitude, exactly.

She'd just been implacable. Like a mountain that had decided to take human form and enforce traffic laws.

The road curved sharply. Cressida slowed to a crawl—suddenly there were *people* everywhere. On the sidewalks, crossing the street, clustered outside shops with ice cream cones and shopping bags and that relaxed summer contentment that came from being on vacation.

"Oh," Cressida said aloud to her empty car. "Oh no."

She'd forgotten about the summer crowds. In all her careful mental preparation for returning to Blackvale, this detail had escaped her entirely. The town in her mind was the quiet, almost melancholy place from winter breaks—shops half-empty, streets silent enough to hear the creek's ice cracking, locals bundled and nodding to each other by name.

This was *tourist* Blackvale. The carefully curated postcard version. Sidewalks packed with visitors in hiking boots and expensive athleisure, cameras dangling, children darting between adults, like schools of brightly colored fish. Every parking space along Main Street was full. The shops—those beautiful restored Victorians with their gingerbread trim and hand-painted signs—had lines spilling out their doors.

Then she saw the banners.

Deep purple fabric hung from every lamp-post, gold lettering catching the afternoon sun: **Blackvale Midsummer Feast & Fair**. Some featured illustrations of dancing figures silhouetted against a full moon, others showed tables laden with food, still others depicted the Ferris wheel rising above the buildings at the far end of town, its cars painted in jewel tones that seemed to glow against the mountain backdrop.

Perfect.

The Midsummer Feast & Fair was Blackvale's biggest summer event—bigger even than the Winter Gala Rosalind complained about. A week-long celebration that managed to be equal parts county fair, music festival, and slightly pagan summer solstice party, complete with craft vendors, local musicians, carnival rides, and enough food to feed a small army.

As a kid, she'd loved it. *Loved* it. She and Miles Stone—God, Miles—would spend entire days there. Riding the Scrambler until they were dizzy, eating their weight in funnel cakes and candied apples and corn dogs dripping with mustard.

Pure, uncomplicated joy.

Simpler times. Before college applications became blood sport. Before "*What are you going to do with your life?*" started every family conversation. Before she and Miles had drifted apart the way childhood friends do—slowly, imperceptibly, until one day the realization hits that you can't remember the last time you actually talked to each other, not really.

Traffic crawled. A family crossed the street—parents, three kids, a golden retriever on a leash—taking their time because why wouldn't they? They were on vacation. The youngest child skipped with an enormous blue teddy bear clutched under one arm.

Something twisted in Cressida's chest. Not quite nostalgia. Not quite regret. Something between.

A car horn honked behind her. She eased forward. No parking spaces. The Fair must be in full swing; she could hear music now, something with fiddles and drums, the rhythm carrying over the crowd noise and general summer chaos.

Vale House Inn was still about three miles away. Three miles through this crowd, through streets she half-remembered and half-didn't, through a town that seemed determined to be both exactly as she remembered and completely transformed.

The ache of it surprised her.

She found a spot near the edge of the festival grounds—not really a parking space so much as a stretch of grass trampled flat by dozens of other vehicles with the same idea. The Mini's tires sank slightly into the soft earth as she pulled in beside a dusty pickup truck with a peeling "I ♥ Blue Ridge Mountains" bumper sticker.

The moment she opened her door, the smell hit her: fried dough sweet and greasy, barbecue smoke thick with hickory and char, the sharp tang of vinegar-based slaw, and underneath it all, that indefinable carnival scent of hot metal and sun-warmed grass and too many people in too small a space.

Her stomach growled audibly, reminding her that the granola bar she'd eaten four hours ago wasn't quite cutting it anymore.

She locked the car—unnecessary in Black-vale, probably, but Charlotte habits died hard—and turned toward the festival. The music was louder here, fiddles and banjo joined by what sounded like a washboard played with genuine enthusiasm. A child shrieked with delight somewhere to her left. The Ferris wheel turned lazily against the mountain backdrop, its jewel-toned cars glinting in the afternoon sun.

Getting to Aunt Sylvia's can wait an hour, she decided, heading toward the main thoroughfare where vendors' tents created colorful corridors.

When was the last time she'd let herself just *be* somewhere?

The answer, she realized as she joined the flow of festival-goers, was embarrassingly long ago.

She wove through the crowd, searching for a corn dog vendor. The sun beat down with that particular intensity summer afternoons in the mountains achieved—not oppressive exactly, but insistent. Sweat prickled at her hairline.

There—tucked between a booth selling hand-carved walking sticks and another offering "Authentic Appalachian Honey"—she spotted it: *Corny's Corner*, complete with a hand-painted sign featuring a corn dog with a smiley face and sunglasses.

The line was longer than she'd hoped but shorter than the BBQ place. Maybe eight people deep. Cressida took her place behind a couple debating the merits of mustard versus ketchup with the kind of passion usually reserved for political discourse, and pulled out her phone to check messages.

Three texts from Rosalind, each more tersely worded than the last:

ETA?

Cressida.

You better not have gotten lost. Dinner is at 7.

Cressida typed back: *Got caught in festival traffic.* Close enough.

The line crept forward. The couple in front of her had reached an impasse on condiments and were now expanding the debate to include relish. Behind them, someone's phone played country music, competing with the live band two tents over. Heat and grease shimmered in the air, mixing with the particular chaos that came from hundreds of people all trying to have a good time in the same square footage.

By the time Cressida reached the front, her stomach was making noises that could probably be classified as threats. The vendor—a woman in her sixties with "Corny" embroidered on her apron and the weathered face of someone who'd spent decades working outdoor events—looked up with a weary gaze that said she'd probably been asked if they had vegan options approximately forty times already today.

"What can I get you, hon?"

"One corn dog and a large Cheerwine, please." Cressida reached for her wallet.

"Make that two of each."

The voice came from directly behind her—deep, warm, edged with amusement that made something in Cressida's chest flip.

She knew that voice. Knew it the way you know a song you haven't heard in years but whose lyrics are still written somewhere in your bones.

She spun around.

And had to look up.

Miles Stone had always been tall, even at fifteen when gangly had been his default setting. Somewhere in the intervening years, gangly had resolved itself into something else—broad shoulders in a dark gray henley, sleeves pushed up to reveal forearms that suggested he'd taken up something more strenuous than the chess club, dark jeans that hugged a trim waist and legs in that way truly good denim did. His hair was shorter than she remembered, dark brown and perfectly cut, and those eyes—God, those eyes—black enough to unsettle—crinkled now with barely suppressed laughter.

"Miles!"

The name burst out louder than intended, drawing looks from nearby festival-goers. For a second, she just stared—caught between the impossibility of him being here and the sudden, disorienting rush of familiarity.

Something in her chest loosened, just slightly, and she let herself smile.

His grin widened, transforming his face from handsome to something dangerously close to devastating. "Hello, Cressi." The old nickname rolled off his tongue like he'd used it yesterday instead of a decade ago. "Still causing trouble, I see?"

The easy warmth in his voice should have been comforting. Instead, it sent a flicker of something defensive through her—a reflex, maybe, against how *effortless* this felt when it shouldn't.

Not after so much time. Not after so much silence.

"Wait, what are you doing here?" The words came out sharper than she meant, confusion bleeding into wariness.

His grin took on a slightly sheepish quality as he raised one hand in a gesture that managed to be both apologetic and entirely unapologetic. "Well, Deputy Jensen called in your speeding to Aunt Marnie, who called and told your sister Roz, who called and told your Aunt Sylvia, who told me." He paused, letting that *ridiculous* sentence—somehow exactly how information traveled in Blackvale—, sink in. "And I figured once you saw it was Midsummer Feast & Fair, you'd stop for a corn dog. This is the closest seller to the entrance."

Cressida stared at him.

The gossip chain was one thing—she'd grown up with that. But Miles *predicting* her moves with that kind of precision, after years of radio silence? That was something else entirely. Something that felt both unsettling and oddly... reassuring.

Like maybe some things didn't change, even when everything else did.

"Still got it," she said, allowing herself a small smile disregarding the surreal absurdity of the moment. The sun caught the edges of his hair, turning it almost bronze where it wasn't quite as dark. Behind him, the Ferris wheel completed another rotation, children's laughter rising and falling like a tide. "Naturally you're paying for this. I've had a hard morning."

Warmth and knowing crossed his features—the look of someone who understood *exactly* what kind of morning involved getting pulled over by small-town law enforcement and having your every move reported up the social chain before you'd even hit city limits. "Naturally," he agreed, reaching for his wallet. "Though I'm going to need to hear about this hard morning. Especially the part where you apparently made enough of an impression on Deputy Jensen to warrant a phone call."

Corny watched this exchange with the barely concealed interest of someone who recognized good gossip when it was happening right in front of her.

"So that's two corn dogs and two large Cheerwines?" she confirmed, her tone suggesting she was mentally filing this entire interaction away for later discussion with whoever Corny discussed things with.

"That's right," Miles said, then offered Corny a warm smile. "I appreciate you keeping this operation running. Can't be easy in this heat."

Corny's weathered face softened, something like surprised pleasure crossing her features. "Well, aren't you sweet. Most folks just bark their orders and move on."

"Not much point in rushing through a good thing," Miles said, handing over his credit card.

Cressida watched the exchange with quiet amusement. This was the same old Miles Stone who even at the age of seven had the kind of presence that made people feel *seen* rather than flattered.

The same quiet attentiveness that had gotten them out of trouble more times than she could count when they were kids. The same sincerity that had earned them impromptu slices of apple pie from Mrs. Walton at the diner, that had convinced Principal Morrison to give them a second chance after the unfortunate incident with the school's chemistry lab—*who frowned upon learning even during summer break, anyway?* Miles had always had a way with people. Especially those who'd been dismissed or overlooked. Judging by Corny's expression, he hadn't lost his touch.

"Tell you what," Corny said, turning to the deep fryer with noticeably more care than she'd shown for the condiment-debating couple. "I'll throw in an extra. You seem like the type who appreciates good work."

Miles stepped up beside her, close enough that she could smell his cologne—something clean and understated, cedarwood, with notes of citrus. The proximity made her suddenly, acutely aware of how travel-rumpled she must look after hours in the car. Her crown braid had started its inevitable journey toward chaos sometime around the Cleveland county border, and she was pretty sure there was still granola bar residue on her cardigan.

"So," Miles said, his voice dropping to something more private, meant for her ignoring the crowd pressing in around them. "Welcome home, Cressi."

A beat.

"It's been a while."

The understatement of the century, delivered with that particular Miles Stone brand of wry observation that made it both acknowledgment and gentle accusation. Yes, it seemed to say, *it has been a while, and whose fault is that exactly?*

Fair question.

One she didn't have a good answer for, standing here in the late afternoon sun with the smell of fried food thick in the air and the ghost of who they'd been to each other hovering between them like something that had never been laid to rest.

Chapter Three

Miles held out one of the corn dogs—golden-brown and glistening—and as Cressida reached for it, her gaze snagged on his hand.

Paint.

Not just any paint, but a green—deep and muted, the kind that might be moss in shadow or aged copper oxidized by time. It caught in the creases of his knuckles and smudged along the edge of his thumb, accompanied by flecks of something lighter, a warm cream or off-white that dotted the inside of his wrist where his sleeve had been pushed up.

The colors themselves weren't particularly distinctive—nothing bold or unusual—but something about them together made a ping go off in the back of her brain. That shade of green reminded her of something she couldn't name, some half-remembered detail that hovered just out of reach. A recognition she couldn't quite place, like a word on the tip of her tongue.

But heavier somehow. More *important*.

She accepted the corn dog, keeping her expression neutral even as her mind cataloged this new information with the same automatic precision she'd use to note a misplaced book in a crime scene photo. Miles Stone. With paint on his hands. The same Miles who'd once produced a finger-painting at summer camp that their counselor had diplomatically described as "abstract" and Miles himself had called "a crime against art." The same Miles who'd stuck to chess club and debate team and activities that required zero artistic talent whatsoever.

That was then. And she hadn't seen him—hadn't even *talked* to him—in years. People changed. Found new passions. Discovered hidden talents in the space between who they were and who they became.

Still. Interesting.

She filed it away, taking a bite of the corn dog instead of commenting.

The taste was exactly right—salty, slightly sweet, the kind of processed perfection that could only be achieved at a small-town festival. Around her, the crowd flowed and eddied like a tide, families with strollers navigating the narrow pathways between vendor tents, the eternal Ferris wheel turning its slow circuit against mountains and blue skies.

"So," Cressida said, once she'd swallowed and taken a sip of the aggressively sweet Cheerwine, "are you just here for a quick visit, or did you actually move back?"

The question came out more casual than she felt, but that was fine. Casual was good. Casual didn't reveal that she'd been doing mental calculations about Miles Stone's presence in Blackvale ever since he'd materialized behind her in the corn dog line.

Miles laughed—a real laugh, warm and surprised. "Depends on your point of view, I guess." He gestured with his corn dog toward the main thoroughfare, and they fell into step together, moving with the crowd. "Been back about a month. Calling it a visit makes it sound temporary, which... maybe it is. The length of the visit is... up in the air."

Something in his tone—not quite evasion, not quite full disclosure either. The verbal equivalent of a shrug that suggested complicated circumstances he wasn't ready to elaborate on to someone he hadn't seen in a decade, even if that someone was currently walking beside him eating fair food and pretending this wasn't the weirdest convergence of past and present she'd experienced in recent memory.

"What about you?" Miles asked, turning those dark eyes on her with the kind of attention that made her suddenly aware of every part of herself—the way her braid had definitely started its journey toward chaos, the granola bar crumbs she was now certain were visible on her cardigan, the fact that she probably had mustard on her chin. "How long are you gracing Blackvale with your presence?"

"Staying with Aunt Sylvia for at least the summer," Cressida said, sidestepping a group of children who were engaged in some kind of running game that involved a lot of shrieking. "After that, well. Hopefully the universe will tell me what comes next."

She paused, then turned to him with a grin that was pure mischief. "Speaking of which—you know if the Great Esmerelda still has her tent up?"

The effect was immediate and gratifying. Miles's entire face transformed, that composure cracking to reveal something younger, more playful. "Oh my God. *Mrs. Matthews.*"

"The one and only," Cressida confirmed, warming to the memory. "Blackvale's premiere psychic, dispenser of mystical wisdom, absolutely zero percent Romani but one hundred percent committed to the aesthetic."

The Great Esmerelda—really Mrs. Chloe Matthews—had been a fixture at the Midsummer Feast & Fair for as long as Cressida could remember. For just as long, she and Miles had made a game of trying to sneak close to her tent, only to be intercepted by Sheriff Stone with uncanny timing.

"Your dad had a sixth sense for whenever we were within fifty feet of that tent."

Miles's smile took on a fond, slightly melancholy edge. "He claimed it was training and good situational awareness. I'm pretty sure Mrs. Matthews just called him the second she spotted us lurking."

Cressida pointed her corn dog at him for emphasis. "Conspiracy. The whole town was in on it."

"Probably."

Miles went quiet, his gaze distant—somewhere else, some other summer, some other version of themselves. Then he shook himself back to the present, and when he looked at her again, that mischievous spark had returned in full force.

"Let's go find out if she's still here. Funnel cake to whoever can get the most outrageous prediction."

Something in Cressida's chest expanded—lightness, possibility, the echo of a friendship that had somehow survived a decade of silence and distance.

"Oh, you're *on*." She was already scanning the festival grounds for any sign of Esmerelda's distinctive tent. "But I'm warning you, I've gotten *very* good at asking leading questions. I'm going to get a prediction so wild it'll make your chess club trophies weep with envy."

"Chess club trophies don't weep. They maintain dignified silence in the face of all provocations."

"We'll see about that."

They moved deeper into the festival, corn dogs in hand, the midday sun bright and warm overhead.

The air had grown hotter and stickier by the time they left the cotton candy stall.

Cressida was pouting.

It was an undignified expression, one she'd perfected somewhere around age eleven and hadn't needed to deploy in years, but watching Miles eat his funnel cake—powdered sugar dusting his fingers, that insufferably satisfied smile playing at the corners of his mouth—brought it roaring back with a vengeance.

"You *cheated*," she said, not for the first time since they'd left the Great Esmerelda's tent.

The afternoon air pressed warm against her skin, the sun still high and bright. Around them, families drifted past—children sticky with cotton candy, their energy somehow inexhaustible despite the heat.

Miles tore off a piece of funnel cake, chewing with the deliberate slowness of someone

who knew exactly how annoying they were being. "You're going to need to be more specific
about your accusation."

"I don't know *how* yet," Cressida admitted,
falling into step beside him as they navigated the
thinning crowds. Her corn dog was now a distant
memory, and the funnel cake—*her* funnel cake,
the one she should have won—was torturing her
with its existence. "But I will figure it out. I always do. And when I prove it, I expect *two* funnel
cakes before the end of the festival."

"You remember the rules." Miles's tone was
maddeningly reasonable. "You can't make an accusation without proof. Didn't work when you
were fourteen. Doesn't work now."

The reference to their childhood investigations—elaborate theories about who'd stolen the
last of Aunt Sylvia's lemon bars, byzantine con-
spiracies involving the disappearance of Miles's
favorite chess set—made something warm unfurl in Cressida's chest.

They'd fallen back into this so easily. Best
friend mode, activated like no time had passed
at all.

It had always been like that with them. Every
summer, as soon as her parents dropped her
and Roz off at Aunt Sylvia's house, Cressida
would run—not walk, *run*—down to their secret hideout spot in what the locals dramatically
called the Haunted Forest. Really just old growth
woods that bordered the Stone property, their

"secret hideout" the treehouse Miles's dad had built him one summer, complete with a rope ladder and a No Girls Allowed sign that Sheriff Stone had made Miles take down after approximately forty-five minutes.

Miles would already be there waiting, as if the whole school year—her in Charlotte navigating prep school politics, him at the local Blackvale public school—hadn't happened at all.

The parking lot stretched ahead of them, grass trampled flat from hundreds of feet, the air thick with car exhaust and residual deep-fryer oil. Miles headed toward the far corner where overflow parking had started.

She followed, still mentally cataloging evidence of cheating that she *knew* existed.

Then she saw it.

"Oh my God," she said, stopping dead. "You're not still driving that death trap."

The Ford Bronco sat there like a relic from another era—because it *was* a relic from another era. Forest green and boxy, with opinions about modern vehicle safety standards, and those opinions were uniformly negative. The first day of summer when he turned 16, he'd picked her up in it. Fresh provisional license in his wallet and an expression of pure teenage triumph on his face.

It had terrified her then. It terrified her now.

Miles's expression shifted to something between offense and protective affection. "Hey. I *love* this truck." He patted the hood like it was a beloved pet that might need reassurance. "She's a classic. A 1996 beauty with character and history."

"She's a tetanus shot waiting to happen."

Miles wasn't listening. He'd turned that assessing gaze on her, one eyebrow raised in challenge. "And what exactly are *you* driving these days?"

Three cars down the row, her MINI Cooper sat gleaming under the parking lot lights. Chili red, chrome accents, perfectly maintained and absolutely adorable in a way that she knew—*knew*—Miles was about to mock mercilessly.

She pointed.

His laugh confirmed it. Deep, loud, absolutely infuriating. "Is that a *clown car*?"

"It is a fuel-efficient, environmentally conscious, *stylish*—"

"You drive a car for clowns." He was still laughing, the powdered sugar on his fingers catching the light as he gestured at her Cooper. "How many of you fit in there? Do you need special tiny person insurance?"

She didn't think. Didn't plan. Just reached out and snatched half the funnel cake right out of his hand—the move so quick and unexpected that Miles didn't have time to react—and then she was *running*.

"CRESSIDA—"

But she was already gone, sprinting across the parking lot with her prize held high, her crown braid finally giving up the ghost and coming loose around her shoulders, her cardigan flapping behind her like a cape.

CHAPTER FOUR

THE DRIVE DOWN MOUNTAIN View Road should have been peaceful—windows down, the warm air carrying honeysuckle and fresh-cut grass, the bright rays of sunlight gilding the ridgeline in amber and rose. Should have been.

Instead, every thirty seconds Cressida's gaze flicked to the rearview mirror, tracking the boxy silhouette of Miles's Bronco. What was left of the funnel cake sat in her passenger seat like evidence of a crime, powdered sugar cascading onto her upholstery in a way that would definitely require vacuuming later.

Worth it.

Baker Street materialized out of the afternoon haze, lined with historic homes that made preservation societies weep with joy. Gas lamp-style streetlights waited to cast pools of golden light across sidewalks buckled by ancient tree roots. At the corner where Baker Street intersected with Hawthorne Lane, Vale House Inn rose into view like something from a postcard about the idyllic South.

Three stories of Victorian grandeur painted in shades of authentic Tiffany blue-green and cream, every detail lovingly restored by Aunt Sylvia over the past two decades. The wraparound porch glowed with warm lights strung along the railings, and through the lace curtains of the front parlor, silhouettes moved—guests checking in for the weekend, probably, drawn by whatever heritage festival or antique show was happening this month.

Blackvale always had *something* happening.

The main entrance—guests only, with its brick walkway and carefully maintained flower beds—she bypassed entirely, guiding her car around the side toward the family entrance. Gravel crunched under her tires, familiar and grounding in a way that made her chest ache. Home. At least for a while.

The moment she killed the engine, she saw it.

A ladder leaned against the back of the house, extension fully deployed and reaching toward the second-story trim. At its base sat several cans of paint in neat formation—Tiffany blue-green, cream, what looked like a deep forest color for accent work. Hanging from one of the ladder's rungs, swaying slightly in the evening breeze, was a pair of paint-splattered overalls.

She got out slowly, leaving the funnel cake evidence behind, her oxfords crunching on gravel as she moved closer. The section of wall nearest the ladder had been freshly painted—new forest green meeting the older, slightly faded color. Parts of it still gleamed wet in the fading sunlight, that particular shine that said *don't touch*.

Behind her, the Bronco's engine cut off. A door opened and closed with that distinctive hollow *thunk* that only old-school vehicles produced.

When she turned, Miles was there in the driveway, hands in his pockets, that insufferably composed expression firmly in place.

But now—*now*—she understood what she'd seen before. The faint traces of green paint on his knuckles. The cream-colored specks.

"That paint on your hands," she said, her voice taking on that particular quality it got when pieces started clicking into place—sharp, certain, slightly triumphant. She gestured at the ladder, the overalls, the fresh section of wall. "My aunt has you painting her house."

Miles said nothing, but his expression shifted—caught somewhere between amusement and something harder to name.

"That's why you said she *told* you about my speeding stop." The pieces clicked together as she spoke, her voice gaining momentum. "Not called. *Told.* Because you were here. Working on the house."

"Your deductive reasoning remains impeccable," Miles said dryly.

"But why would you agree to paint my aunt's house..." She studied him—the way he wouldn't quite meet her eyes, the braced set of his shoulders. "Unless..."

He moved past her toward the Mini. For a moment she thought he was deflecting, avoiding the question entirely. But then he popped her trunk and pulled out the first of her suitcases with the easy movements of someone who'd helped her pack and unpack a thousand times before.

"You always said," he began, his voice careful and light in that way that meant he was about to say something significant and didn't want to make it *weird*, "that one day we'd end up living in the same house."

The words hung between them. Something in her chest did a complicated flip-turn-twist that she absolutely did not have time to analyze. Behind them, through the windows of Vale House Inn, guests laughed and Aunt Sylvia's voice called out something cheerful and indistinct.

"I seem to recall," she said, finding her voice somewhere underneath the surprise, "that you always said that was dependent on whether the house had an indoor pool."

Miles grinned then—a real one, not the reserved smile he'd been wearing most of the day, but the one she remembered from summers past. Mischievous and warm and just a little bit smug.

"Well," he said, hefting her suitcase as he started toward the family entrance, "your aunt's inn has a hot tub. That's basically an indoor pool if you think about it philosophically." At the door, he looked back over his shoulder. "Plus room and board in exchange for painting the house and doing odd jobs around the property seemed like a fair deal while I figure things out."

While I figure things out.

The words echoed as she grabbed her overnight bag from the backseat, her thoughts already racing ahead to questions she didn't quite know how to ask yet. Miles Stone, chess champion and perpetual planner, the boy who'd had his next five years mapped out by sophomore year of high school—what exactly was there to *figure out?*

The house seemed to exhale cool air as she stepped through the family entrance, the afternoon heat giving way to air-conditioned comfort and the bright sunlight streaming through lace curtains.

Through the door lay a mudroom—probably once a formal service entrance when Vale House had been a private residence. Hooks sagged under rain jackets and canvas totes. A boot tray showed its age near a small bench where Miles set down her suitcase with the ease of routine. Then the scent: butter, citrus, something just out of the oven that made her mouth water despite the stolen funnel cake.

Beyond the mudroom, hardwood floors gleamed under rewired old-fashioned sconces Aunt Sylvia had rescued from an estate sale. Framed photographs lined the walls—generations of Vales in Victorian severity, interspersed with recent candids of guests and local events.

The distinctive cadence of Aunt Sylvia's heels on the stairs announced her approach, purposeful and musical at once.

"—and you'll find extra towels in the armoire, sugar, just help yourself—" Aunt Sylvia's voice carried down from the second-floor landing, warm and honeyed, the kind that could make a fire-and-brimstone sermon sound like an invitation to tea. "Breakfast starts at seven-thirty, but I can have something sent up earlier if you need—oh!"

At the base of the stairs appeared a vision in coral linen—her copper bronze skin glowing against the fabric. A sculptural crown of curls, dense enough to defy gravity yet soft enough to shift with touch, framed her face in silver-streaked perfection undeterred by a full day of hosting. Costume jewelry—always layered, always intentional—caught the light: turquoise bangles, a statement necklace of amber beads, earrings that looked like tiny chandeliers. Signature red lipstick, flawless.

"Well, Lord have mercy." Aunt Sylvia's dark eyes—so like Cressida's own—went bright. "There's my girl."

Cressida barely had time to set down her overnight bag before the embrace enveloped her—cinnamon-cardamom-butter warmth, silk scarves, the fierce tenderness Sylvia Vale reserved for family. The hug was bone-crushing and wonderful, punctuated by kisses pressed to both cheeks in rapid succession, European-style but with unmistakably Southern enthusiasm.

"Honey-lamb." Sylvia pulled back just enough to cup Cressida's face in manicured hands, studying her with an intensity that saw everything. "Look at you. All grown up and beautiful and *finally here.*" Another kiss, planted firmly on Cressida's forehead. "I was starting to think Charlotte had stolen you from us for good."

"Never," Cressida managed, her voice doing something embarrassing and thick. "Just... took me a while to figure out where I needed to be."

"Mmm." Sylvia's gaze sharpened with understanding—the kind that suggested they'd be having a longer conversation later, probably over tea and whatever magnificent thing was making the house smell like heaven. She squeezed Cressida's shoulders once more before turning her attention on Miles.

"And *you*," she said, advancing on him with the same enthusiasm, "getting paint all over my nice new patio stones and then vanishing right when I needed those shutters checked."

Miles had the grace to look sheepish as Sylvia pulled him into a hug that he returned with obvious affection. "The shutters are on my list for tomorrow morning, Miss Sylvia. I promise."

"They better be, darlin'." But her tone was warm, maternal, and when she pulled back she patted his cheek with genuine fondness. "Though I suppose I can forgive the delay, seeing as how you were keeping my niece out of your dad's holding cell."

"I wasn't going to *jail*—" Cressida started.

"Mm-hmm." Sylvia's expression suggested she had *opinions* about that assessment but was graciously tabling them for now. She glanced between them, taking in Cressida's loosened braid and Miles's paint-speckled hands, the funnel cake evidence still visible through the Mini's passenger window, and something knowing flickered across her features. "Well. You two look like you've had quite the reunion. Go on upstairs and get washed up. Miles, you know where your room is. Cressida—"

"I know where mine is too," Cressida said, warmth flooding her chest at the casual assumption that of course her room on the third floor was still here, still *hers*, even after all this time away.

"Good. Twenty minutes, then right back down here." Sylvia was already turning back toward what Cressida knew was the kitchen, her scarves flowing behind her like colorful wings. She paused at the doorway, glancing back over her shoulder. "And child? I'm glad you're home."

Something warm and tight bloomed in Cressida's chest—gratitude and relief and a bone-deep sense of *rightness* she hadn't felt in months. "So am I," she managed, her voice softer than she'd intended.

Sylvia was gone, the distinctive sound of her footsteps fading down the hall, but her voice carried back clear as day: "Because I am *this close* to perfecting my entry for this year, and Henrietta Dodd *will not*—I repeat, *will* NOT—buy her win this year if it's the last thing I do. Woman thinks she can just waltz in with her *heritage recipes* and her *professional kitchen* and her PBS *special*—well, we'll just see about that—"

The monologue continued, growing fainter as Aunt Sylvia disappeared deeper into the house, something about "test batches" and "that smug look she gets" and "if she mentions her James Beard nomination *one more time*—"

Miles met her eyes.

"The Golden Spoon competition," he said, with the tone of someone confirming a natural disaster was, in fact, approaching.

"How bad?"

"Three days straight in the kitchen. Fourteen pounds of butter. The phrase 'psychological warfare' muttered at least six times." He picked up her suitcase again, gesturing toward the stairs with his free hand. "I've been instructed to taste-test everything and provide detailed feedback, which sounds great until you realize she takes notes and asks follow-up questions and has started talking about 'flavor profiles' like they're battle strategies."

"And Henrietta Dodd?"

"Showed up with what your aunt described as 'store-bought intimidation tactics disguised as a courtesy call.'" The old wood creaked familiar under their feet as they started up the stairs. "Apparently she brought samples of her entry. Sylvia spent an hour analyzing them and then declared total war."

"This is going to be a disaster," Cressida said, but she was smiling—really smiling—for the first time since she'd left Charlotte.

"Probably." Miles's mouth quirked. "But at least the food will be incredible."

She had no idea how right he was—or how wrong.

CHAPTER FIVE

THE MORNING SUN BEAT down on Blackvale's town square. The second day of the Midsummer Feast & Fair was in full swing—white tents and milling crowds packed even tighter than yesterday. The energy had shifted overnight: craft vendors called out to passersby, a bluegrass band cranked up near the gazebo, children ran wild with sticky fingers and painted faces. The air vibrated with noise and movement and the kind of chaos that only came when a small town tried to contain twice its population in a single square.

And everywhere—*everywhere*—the unmistakable scent of competition.

Cressida adjusted her grip on the covered cake carrier, careful not to jostle its precious cargo as she navigated through the crowd.

Aunt Sylvia swept ahead like a coral-clad battleship, scarves streaming, jewelry catching the light with every purposeful step. She'd been up since four am for "final preparations"—a level of kitchen activity that bordered on ritualistic. The inn had smelled like butter and lavender and something indefinably *Sylvia*: ambitious and slightly unhinged in the best possible way.

"Watch yourself, honey-lamb." Sylvia called back without turning around, somehow aware that Cressida had nearly collided with a stroller. "I did not spend three days perfecting that glaze for you to dump it on the grass five minutes before judging."

"I'm not going to—" Cressida sidestepped a poodle that had developed a sudden interest in the carrier. "I've got it. I'm good."

"Mm-hmm." Sylvia's tone suggested deep skepticism, but she'd reached the competition tent—a sprawling white pavilion with "GOLDEN SPOON COMPETITION" emblazoned across the entrance in gold script that probably violated several taste ordinances but looked appropriately dramatic.

Inside, the pavilion had been transformed into a shrine to culinary ambition. Long tables draped in white linen held dozens of entries, each with its own placard and number. The air was thick with colliding aromas: cinnamon and cardamom, caramel and citrus, chocolate and something that might have been rosemary or might have been hubris. Volunteers in matching aprons buzzed between stations, arranging entries with the solemnity of museum curators.

Sylvia made a beeline for the check-in table, where a harried-looking woman with a clipboard fielded questions from three directions at once.

"Sylvia Vale." Aunt Sylvia's voice cut through the din with the ease of someone who'd been commanding rooms since birth. "Entry number thirty-two. I believe you're expecting me."

The woman's expression shifted from stressed to something approaching relief. "Miss Sylvia! Yes, absolutely—your spot is ready, table three, right in the center—" She gestured vaguely toward the middle of the pavilion, already turning to answer someone else's question about gluten-free labeling requirements.

Cressida followed her aunt to their designated spot. When Sylvia lifted the carrier's lid with a flourish that belonged on a cooking show, Cressida had to suppress a laugh of pure delight.

The tart was *outrageous*.

It sat in its ceramic dish like edible art—a lattice-top masterpiece that managed to be both rustic and refined. The crust was golden-brown perfection, its edges crimped with mathematical precision. Through the lattice, she could see the jam filling: a deep purple-blue that caught the light like stained glass, studded with actual lavender buds suspended in the gel. The glaze elevated it from impressive to spectacular—a honey-gold wash that made the whole thing shine like it had been dipped in liquid sunlight. Tiny crystallized flowers scattered across the top like edible confetti.

It looked like something a fairy godmother would serve at a garden party in Wonderland.

"Lord have mercy," Cressida breathed. "Aunt Sylvia, this is—"

"Experimental." Sylvia adjusted one of the crystallized flowers with a fingernail. "That's what the category is, after all. Lavender-honey-blueberry jam with a hint of lemon thyme and a honey-bourbon glaze. If Henrietta Dodd thinks she can out-innovate *me*—"

"This is going to win." They'd had the test version last night for dessert—Miles had actually stopped mid-bite and stared at his fork like it had personally betrayed him by being so delicious.

"From your mouth to the judges' taste buds." Sylvia's eyes were bright with satisfaction. She fussed with the placement for another moment, angling it just so to catch the light, then stepped back with a decisive nod. "There. Perfect." She glanced at the card already positioned beside the tart, checked that it read correctly—*Entry #32: "Midsummer Night's Jam" by Sylvia R. Vale*—and smiled. "Now. I see Virginia Kemper over there, and she *still* owes me an explanation about what happened at last month's Whispering Lilies meeting."

Sylvia swept off into the crowd, leaving Cressida alone with dozens of culinary dreams and her aunt's masterpiece. She pulled out her phone—covered in pink glitter and cartoon cats—and snapped a few photos of the tart from different angles. Documentation. Not evidence that she was secretly proud of Aunt Sylvia's ridiculous, beautiful creation.

Then, because she was here and the tent was full of entries, she started walking the tables. Constitutionally incapable of *not* investigating things.

Her camera came out of her bag—a bulky DSLR she treated like a partner in crime. She photographed the entries with the same attention she'd give to a crime scene. Maybe dramatic, but in Blackvale, pastry feuds had drawn more blood than politics. People had held grudges for years over questionable judging decisions. This wasn't just baking. This was *warfare.*

Table one: elaborate cakes that looked structurally unsound but artistically magnificent. Table two: pies with lattice-work that would make a mathematician weep. She noted the entry cards, the techniques, the *ambition* baked into every entry.

Then she reached entry forty-seven.

Cressida stopped so abruptly that the woman behind her nearly walked into her back.

The tart sat on table four, two spots down from where Sylvia's entry held court. At first glance, it looked almost identical to her aunt's creation—the same lattice top, the same ceramic dish, crystallized flowers scattered across a glossy finish. But the color was wrong. Where Sylvia's jam filling was deep purple-blue, this one was lighter. More lavender than blueberry, more pink than purple.

The lattice was different too. Less precise. The edges not quite as crisp.

Like looking at a copy of a painting where the forger had gotten the composition right but missed something essential in the execution.

She raised her camera and took three shots from different angles, then leaned closer to read the entry card.

Entry #47: "Lavender-Honey Jam Tart" by Vernald D. Dowd

Cressida was adding this to her mental file labeled *"Blackvale: Where Even Baking Competitions Have Plots"* when a voice behind her said, "Why, Cressida Vale! Is that really you, sugar?"

She knew that voice. God help her, she *knew that voice.* It triggered a Pavlovian response that was half nostalgia, half dread, and entirely exhausting.

Cressida turned to find Mrs. Marianne Buckner, resplendent in a mauve pantsuit that matched her eyeshadow and holding a purse roughly the size of a small suitcase. A fixture of Aunt Sylvia's Whispering Lilies Society—part book circle, part historical preservation com-

mittee, part gossip distribution network—Mrs.
Buckner had been ancient when Cressida was
a child. Somehow she looked exactly the same
now: a cloud of white curls against dark earthy
brown skin, lipstick migrated slightly beyond
her lip line, and the expression of someone who
had Thoughts and would share them whether
you wanted her to or not.

"Mrs. Buckner," Cressida said. "How lovely to
see you."

Her face was making a Face. The kind that
said I *know exactly what's about to happen and
I am not prepared but I'm trapped by Southern
politeness and there's no escape.* She tried to
rearrange her expression into something more
neutral, but Mrs. Buckner had already launched
into conversation like a ship leaving port.

"Oh honey, I'm just so glad I ran into you! I've
been meaning to talk to someone about—well,
it's been the most *dreadful* couple of days, and
your aunt Sylvia's been so busy with the competition, I didn't want to bother her, but I don't
know what to do and—" She paused for approximately half a second to draw breath. "It's Kennard."

Kennard. The name pulled up a memory
from Cressida's childhood: an enormous tabby
cat with one torn ear and a perpetually judgmental expression, ancient even then, who'd
ruled Mrs. Buckner's Victorian house like a furry
despot.

"Kennard," she repeated, unable to keep the surprise out of her voice. "Your cat? He's still—" She caught herself before saying *alive*. "Around?"

"Oh yes, my darling boy—he'll be nineteen in November, can you believe it?" Mrs. Buckner's voice wavered. She clutched her purse tighter. "Dr. Gibbs says he's got the constitution of a cat half his age, but—" Her eyes went bright and watery. "Oh, but Cressida, he's *missing*. I let him out two nights ago—Friday evening, right around sunset—and I haven't seen him since."

A sympathetic noise. Her brain was already calculating how long this conversation would last and whether she could engineer a polite escape. But Mrs. Buckner had hit her stride.

"I've looked everywhere, sugar—*every-where*. The garden shed, the neighbor's porch, that spot under the magnolia tree—" She paused, and something shifted in her expression. The rambling quality dropped away, replaced by something more fragile.

Her voice dropped to barely above a whisper. "I've walked the neighborhood calling for him until I was hoarse. I've put out his favorite treats. I even tried that thing I read about on the Internet where you put his litter box outside so he can smell his way home, but *nothing*."

"I'm so sorry." Cressida meant it, even as her attention started to drift. "That must be really worrying—"

"And the worst part—" Mrs. Buckner leaned in, her voice dropping low—"is I'm afraid he might have wandered into the haunted forest. Everyone knows it's not safe after dark. The shadows move wrong. People see things." Her hand trembled on her purse strap. "Wraiths, Cressida. *Wraiths*."

"Mm-hmm." Cressida nodded politely while mentally filing this under "*Blackvale's Charming Local Superstitions That Are Definitely Just Fog and Overactive Imaginations*."

"I'm sure he's fine. Cats are resourceful. He probably found somewhere warm to—"

"But that's just it!" Mrs. Buckner's voice pitched higher. Heads swiveled their way. "I found his collar this morning. Near the old Blackvale cemetery gates."

Cressida paused. She looked at Mrs. Buckner more carefully—the genuine distress in her expression, the trembling hands on her purse straps.

"His collar," she repeated slowly.

"Lying there in the grass, right by the gates—you know, the old iron ones with all the scrollwork? The ones that are always locked?" Mrs. Buckner's words tumbled faster. "His collar, with his little bell still attached, like it had been—I don't know—*removed*. Not torn or chewed through, mind you. Just... *off*."

Something clicked in the back of Cressida's mind. The same instinct that had made her good at her job, the thing that made her notice patterns where others saw randomness.

Mrs. Buckner's cat was ancient, yes. Cats went missing all the time, especially elderly cats who wandered off to die in peace.

But the collar detail was odd.

"That's unusual," she said carefully. "Kennard never went that far before?"

"Never! He's strictly a three-block radius kind of cat. But the cemetery? That's got to be half a mile from my house, and Kennard hasn't walked half a mile in five years. His hips, you know."

Cressida nodded, making sympathetic noises while her brain sorted through theories. Missing cat. Collar found far from normal territory. Cemetery gates. Friday evening.

She should not be getting invested in this. Should absolutely not be treating a missing elderly cat like it was a *case*.

"—and that's why I just thought maybe you could keep an eye out, you know, since you're so good at finding things—"

"I'll definitely watch for him." Cressida seized the opening with both hands, touching Mrs. Buckner's arm gently as she stepped backward. "And I'm sure he'll turn up soon. Kennard's are survivors."

Mrs. Buckner opened her mouth—probably to launch into another tangent—but the entire tent inhaled at once.

The crowd had been drifting inward, drawn by the spectacle of the competition tables, and now the aisles between displays felt suddenly narrow as everyone shifted toward the entrance.

Conversations stuttered and died. Heads turned in unison like iron filings pulled by a magnet.

Henrietta Dodd had arrived.

She swept into the tent with a presence that couldn't be taught or bought, only earned through decades of commanding attention. Her linen dress was champagne-colored, pressed in spite of the heat, and her silver-blonde hair was arranged in a style that looked effortless but probably required an hour and a professional. A sapphire brooch—definitely real—gleamed at her throat. She moved through the crowd like a yacht cutting through water, people parting automatically.

"Oh my *stars*," someone breathed behind Cressida.

"Is that the Cartier piece?" another voice whispered. "The one from her London appearance?"

Within seconds, Henrietta was surrounded. Women from the festival committee materialized, all smiles and compliments. A man with a professional camera—press badge dangling from his neck—started snapping photos. Someone thrust a clipboard her way for an aut

ograph.Cressida watched with professional detachment. This was theater. High-quality theater, but theater nonetheless.

"Well," Mrs. Buckner murmured beside her,
voice dry as chalk, "here comes royalty."

Henrietta held court now, one elegant hand
gesturing as she spoke to the small crowd
that had formed. Her laugh carried across the
tent—warm, practiced, musical. She said something that made the festival committee members titter appreciatively. The photographer circled her like a satellite.

Then Cressida saw Susan Mitchell approaching from the opposite end of the tent.

Mrs. Mitchell cut through the crowd with
the efficiency of someone who'd been managing
Blackvale's social events since Cressida was in
elementary school. Which, given that Cressida
was thirty now, meant she'd been orchestrating
this town's public image for the better part of
two decades.

She wore a jewel-toned blazer over pressed
linen pants, her golden brown locs twisted into an elaborate updo. Everything about
her screamed *authority*—from her perfectly
matched accessories to the way she smiled with
all her teeth when annoyed.

Which she definitely was, judging by the
tension in her shoulders as she reached Henrietta.

You'd never know it from her voice.

"Henrietta!" Mrs. Mitchell's tone was warm enough to melt butter. "How wonderful that you could make it again this year. So good to see you. Love the dress."

Henrietta turned, her smile unwavering. "Susan, darling. What another lovely event you've put together. The tent looks absolutely charming."

"Oh, you're too kind." Mrs. Mitchell's smile stretched wider. "Though I have to say, everyone's been simply buzzing about your entry. I know you'll surprise us once again."

"How flattering." Henrietta's hand fluttered to her brooch. "I do hope I can live up to expectations."

They air-kissed—two cheeks, European style—while the photographer captured the moment. Both women held their poses just a beat too long, smiles frozen in place, bodies angled toward the camera with the precision of politicians at a photo op. The performance was flawless.

Beside her, Mrs. Buckner made a sound that was halfway between a cough and a laugh, one hand covering her mouth while her eyes danced with barely suppressed amusement.

"Something funny?" Cressida asked quietly.

Mrs. Buckner leaned in, her voice dropping to a conspiratorial whisper. She patted Cressida's arm, with the familiarity of someone who'd known her since pigtails. "Oh honey, those two are putting on a show that would make Broadway jealous. They *despise* each other."

Across the tent, the two women chatted animatedly about something—festival logistics, maybe, or the weather. To anyone watching, they looked like old friends catching up.

"Really," Cressida said. *Not my problem*, she reminded herself. *Just here to help Aunt Sylvia. Nothing more.*

"*Really.*" Mrs. Buckner pulled a folding fan from her enormous purse and waved it lazily in front of her face. "Just a few weeks ago—right after a festival committee meeting—I saw them going at it in the parking lot behind the community center. Voices raised, hands waving, the whole nine yards." She paused dramatically, the fan stilling for emphasis. "Susan was furious about some last-minute changes Henrietta wanted to make to the festival lineup. Something about the judging schedule, I think. Either way, Susan was *not* having it."

Cressida filed that away. "Sounds heated."

"Oh, it was." Mrs. Buckner's eyes gleamed. The fan resumed its steady rhythm. "And that's not even the worst of it. Last year—or was it the year before?—Susan actually *banned* Henrietta from a festival committee meeting for 'disruptive conduct.' Can you imagine? Henrietta Dodd, celebrity chef and town treasure, getting kicked out like a misbehaving teenager."

"What did she do?"

"Questioned Susan's authority one too many times, from what I heard. Suggested that maybe the committee should vote on decisions instead of just rubber-stamping whatever Susan wanted." Mrs. Buckner shook her head, white curls barely moving. "Susan does not appreciate having her authority questioned. She runs these festivals like she's conducting an orchestra, and heaven help anyone who plays out of tune."

Across the tent, Susan and Henrietta were still performing their friendship for the cameras. Henrietta touched Susan's arm. Susan laughed at something Henrietta said. The photographer captured it all, probably already writing the caption in his head: *Local festival organizer and celebrity chef share warm moment at Golden Spoon competition.*

The familiar tug of curiosity pulled at Cressida—the one that had gotten her into trouble more than once. She started assembling the pieces, building the narrative. *Stop it*, she told herself. She was not here to get sucked into small-town drama. No matter how interesting the players were.

Her attention was so focused on the two women that she almost missed the moment when another man approached with a camera.

He was younger than the press photographer—early thirties, maybe—with carefully styled dark hair and the kind of outfit that screamed *trying too hard*: designer jeans, untucked button-down with the sleeves rolled to show off an expensive watch, leather messenger bag slung across his chest. His camera was top-of-the-line and just came out. Cressida had been lusting after it for months.

"Mrs. Dodd?" His voice carried across the tent, bright and eager. "Jordan Quinn, from *Mountain Flavors*. Would you mind if I got a quick photo for the blog?"

Henrietta's smile flickered.

It was fast—so fast that Cressida almost missed it. A momentary tightening around her eyes, a downward twitch at the corner of her mouth, something that looked almost like annoyance or discomfort before her face smoothed back into its practiced expression. Something there, gone before she could name it.

"Of course," Henrietta said, but her voice had lost some of its warmth. She turned toward him, angling her body in a way that looked natural but was clearly designed to keep distance between them. The smile was back, wider than before.

Whatever had just passed between them—recognition, unease, something else—it mattered.

"Who's that?" Cressida asked Mrs. Buckner.

Aunt Sylvia materialized at Cressida's elbow like a scarved apparition, trailing the scent of cinnamon and intrigue.

"That," she announced with the air of someone imparting classified information, "is Jordan Quinn. He's what you call a Food Blogger and Culinary Influencer."

She enunciated each word as if Cressida couldn't have possibly heard of such a thing. Funny, considering Cressida was ninety percent certain her aunt had overheard someone else say those exact words recently and was now deploying them like she'd known all along.

"I know what a food blogger is, Aunt Sylvia."

"Well, of course you do, honey-lamb." Aunt Sylvia waved a hand dismissively. "Anyway, he visited with me yesterday afternoon to do a write-up of me for his blog. Very thorough young man. Asked all sorts of questions about my techniques and inspirations. Took about a hundred photos of my kitchen."

She paused, and Cressida recognized the look that crossed her aunt's face. It was the same look Aunt Sylvia got right before she suggested something terrible that she genuinely believed was helpful.

"You know," Aunt Sylvia said, voice taking on a carefully casual tone that fooled absolutely no one, "he's single."

Oh no.

"Aunt Sylvia—"

"And you two would have *so much* in common! He works in media, you work in media—well, you *worked* in media, but still. He's very interested in investigative journalism, he told me all about it. And he's handsome! Don't you think he's handsome? I think he's handsome."

"I really don't—"

"I could introduce you!" Aunt Sylvia's eyes lit up with the kind of enthusiasm usually reserved for discovering a secret ingredient. "Just a quick introduction, very casual. You could talk shop. Compare notes. Maybe get coffee later—"

This ranked high on Aunt Sylvia's all-time list of catastrophically bad ideas. And that was saying something, considering this was a woman who'd once tried to set Cressida up with her accountant's nephew at a funeral.

"Absolutely not."

Aunt Sylvia drew herself up, looking genuinely offended. "And why not? He's perfectly nice, very accomplished, and you're not getting any younger, Cressida Vale. I'd like at least one grand-niece or nephew to spoil before I'm too old to enjoy it."

"Talk to Roz," Cressida said, already backing away. "She's the one with the steady relationship and the ticking biological clock. I'm just here to help you change out sheets."

"Cressida—"

But Cressida was already moving. Behind her, she heard Aunt Sylvia calling her name, but she pretended not to hear. There were some battles you fought, and some battles you just *ran from.*

This was definitely a running situation.

CHAPTER SIX

CRESSIDA HAD NEARLY MADE it to the relative safety of the dessert tables—strategically positioned behind a lattice screen draped with honeysuckle—when voices stopped her cold.

Sharp. Clipped. Failing spectacularly at quiet.

Investigative instinct kicked in, before common sense could intervene. Behind one of the tent's support poles, partially obscured by a display of artfully arranged baking equipment, two figures argued.

"—absolutely cannot *believe* you forgot it, Willard. How many times did I remind you?"

Henrietta Dodd. The honey-smooth warmth from earlier had evaporated, leaving something colder in its place.

Pretending to examine a vintage rolling pin with crime-scene-level focus, Cressida edged closer. Through a gap in the display, she caught the tableau: Henrietta's perfectly coiffed head tilted in supreme disappointment, Willard's shoulders slumped in apology.

"I'm sorry, Henrietta. I thought—"

"You *thought*." The laugh that followed was brittle as spun sugar. "That's always been your problem, hasn't it? Thinking when you should be *doing*. I told you this morning, *twice*, to make sure it was in my bag. And what do I find when I go to take my pills? Nothing. How am I supposed to get through the day, you pathetic imbecile?"

"I can go back right now." Willard's voice dropped so low Cressida had to strain. "It's only fifteen minutes. I'll be back before—"

"Before what? Before you embarrass me further?" Henrietta's hand moved to her brooch. Sharp, precise adjustments. "Go. Now. But if you're not back in twenty minutes, don't bother coming back at all."

Willard didn't argue. A small, defeated nod. Then he turned away, head down, shoulders hunched. Decades of practice at making himself smaller.

Henrietta watched him go. Expression unreadable. Then she smoothed her dress, adjusted her pearls, and turned back toward the crowd with her smile firmly in place.

Three seconds. That's all the transformation took.

Public persona versus private reality. The mask versus what lived underneath.

"Spying on the suspects already?"

Her heart slammed against her ribs. She spun around—Miles, six inches behind her, hands in pockets, expression hovering between amused and exasperated.

"*Jesus Christ*, Miles." Her hand flew to her chest. "Do you *want* me to die of a heart attack? Is that your goal?"

"You'd notice me coming if you weren't so busy eavesdropping." Mild tone. Laughing eyes. "What are we investigating? Baking crimes? Unlawful use of vanilla extract?"

"I wasn't eavesdropping," Cressida said, which was technically true only if you used a very generous definition of the word. "I was *observing*. There's a difference."

"Uh-huh." Miles glanced past her toward where Henrietta had disappeared. "Observing what, exactly?"

Before Cressida could explain the fascinating dynamics of small-town social hierarchies and the performative nature of public personas, something else caught her attention.

Movement through the tent. Henrietta's trajectory took her past the competition entries; two neat rows of numbered placards. Amateur bakers had brought their best. Elaborate layer cakes. Delicate pastries. Intricate tarts that probably took hours to assemble.

At each entry, Henrietta paused. Bent slightly. Examined with the scrutiny usually reserved for museum artifacts. Pleasant expression. Detached. Mildly curious. A nod at one, a murmur at another, then moving on without comment.

Then she reached another entry.

Miles tensed beside her.

Henrietta had stopped. Her gaze fixed on an elaborate chocolate pastry—multiple layers of dark, glossy ganache alternating with what might be mousse or cream, dusted with cocoa powder and decorated with delicate chocolate curls that spiraled up like tiny sculptures.

It looked absolutely delicious.

Henrietta didn't touch it. Didn't even lean close. Something shifted in her expression: recognition, maybe. Or calculation. Her lips pressed into a thin line. Her fingers tightened on her clutch.

For a fraction of a second, her mask slipped.

Then she moved to the next entry, smile sliding back into place.

"Did you see that?" Cressida whispered.

Miles nodded slowly. "Yeah."

"What *was* that?"

"I don't know." His voice was quiet. "But whatever it was, she didn't like it."

A ripple of movement swept through the tent. Conversations paused mid-sentence. Heads turned.

The judges arrived with the weight of ceremony behind them.

Reverend Frederick Carlson led the procession—tall, broad-shouldered, his salt-and-pepper hair neatly combed, clergy collar crisp white against black fabric. His hands were clasped in that perpetual prayer position that made him look both approachable and untouchable.

Flanking him: Marisol Vega, chef and owner of *La Cazuela Azul*, a Mexican–Southern fusion restaurant on Main Street with more regional awards than Cressida could count. And Douglas Hart, a food critic from Charlotte whose reviews could make or break a restaurant's reputation.

The crowd parted. Slow as water meeting stone.

Mrs. Mitchell materialized at their side, clipboard in hand, smile wide and professional as she guided them toward the judging tables. The photographer circled. Someone adjusted the lighting. A hush fell over the tent—the kind usually reserved for courtrooms or operating theaters.

Cressida pulled out her phone. Not because Aunt Sylvia had asked her to, but because this whole scene felt *staged*. Like everyone was playing their assigned role in a script they'd all memorized years ago.

Click. Reverend Carlson examining the first entry, expression thoughtful.

Click. Marisol making notes on her scorecard.

Click. Douglas cutting into a slice of chocolate torte, face giving away nothing.

Entry to entry, they moved with methodical precision. Tasting, discussing, note-taking. A careful choreography. The crowd watched in silence, everyone holding their breath.

When the judges reached Aunt Sylvia's Midsummer Night's Jam tart, Cressida zoomed in.

Click. Reverend Carlson's eyebrows rising slightly as he took his first bite.

Click. Marisol nodding, making what looked like enthusiastic notes.

Click. Douglas going back for a second taste.

Good signs. All good signs.

Then the judges moved to Henrietta's entry.

Cressida's stomach dropped.

Henrietta's entry commanded attention. The Lemon Lavender Chiffon Cake rose in pale golden tiers, each layer impossibly light, the lavender-tinted frosting swirled across its surface. Crystallized lemon slices caught the light like stained glass. Fresh lavender sprigs crowned the top—purple against gold, garden made edible.

The judges studied it. Reverend Carlson closed his eyes after his first bite, savoring. Marisol's pen moved across her scorecard, filling lines. Douglas returned for a second taste. Then a third, letting each settle on his tongue.

Click. Click. Click.

Cressida captured it all. Already knew how this would end.

The judges bent their heads together. Mrs. Mitchell hovered at the periphery, smile fixed. Around them, the crowd pressed closer—straining, holding breath, waiting.

Reverend Carlson stepped forward. Cleared his throat.

"Ladies and gentlemen." His voice carried that sermon-calm. "The judges have reached a decision."

Silence dropped like a curtain.

"This year's competition showcased remarkable talent. Every entry demonstrated skill, creativity, and dedication to the craft of baking." His gaze swept the tent. "However, one entry stood above the rest in terms of technique, presentation, and flavor complexity."

Miles shifted. Somewhere to Cressida's left, Aunt Sylvia stopped breathing.

"The winner of this year's Golden Spoon Competition is—" Reverend Carlson smiled. "Mrs. Henrietta Dodd, for her exceptional Lemon Lavender Chiffon Cake."

Applause erupted. Cameras flashed. Henrietta's smile bloomed into something radiant as she stepped forward to accept her trophy. A literal golden spoon mounted on a wooden base, polished to mirror brightness.

Cressida turned.

Aunt Sylvia was already moving. Stalking, really. Scarves fluttering behind her like battle flags, jaw set, and eyes blazing with something equal parts rage and humiliation. The sharp intake of breath. The rigid posture. Fury radiating like heat from a furnace.

"Aunt—" Cressida started.

But Sylvia didn't stop. Didn't even look back. Just kept walking, movements sharp, furious precision, heading straight for the exit like she couldn't get out of that tent fast enough.

Cressida exchanged a glance with Miles.

"Should we—" Miles began.

"Yeah," Cressida said.

"Ladies and gentlemen!" Mrs. Mitchell's voice rang out before they could move. "The judges have concluded their formal assessments, which means we're now opening up the entries for *public sampling*. Please, come taste the wonderful creations our talented bakers have prepared. Every entry deserves to be celebrated!"

Excitement rippled through the crowd.

People surged forward—plates and forks appearing as if summoned, competitive tension dissolving into the more universal pleasure of free dessert.

Cressida paused, her hand on Miles's arm. "Wait?"

"Yeah." His tone was dry, but his eyes were already scanning the tent. "Let's hang back a minute."

Near the entrance, close enough to observe but far enough to avoid the crush, they positioned themselves. Forks diving into chocolate tortes. Fingers stealing crystallized garnishes. Enthusiastic murmurs rising as sugar hit bloodstreams.

Cressida's gaze snagged on movement across the tent.

Henrietta Dodd wove through the crowd with surgical precision, golden spoon tucked under one arm like a scepter. At each entry she stopped, accepted congratulations with gracious nods, offered compliments that somehow landed as both generous and condescending.

"Oh, Martha, your berry tart looks absolutely charming. So rustic."

"Willard, you must try Patricia's pound cake. It's quite... traditional. Willard?"

Her trajectory was clear. Deliberate.

She was working her way down the line toward...

"No," Cressida breathed.

Miles followed her gaze. "Oh, hell."

Henrietta reached Aunt Sylvia's tart with the inevitability of Greek tragedy. Her smile never wavered. She set her trophy down on the table beside the entry card.

The photographer materialized, camera raised.

"Mrs. Dodd," he said, "would you mind sampling some of the other entries? For the feature spread?"

"Of course." Her voice carried across the tent like honey over glass. "I believe in celebrating *all* the competitors. Even the ones who didn't quite make the podium."

She picked up a fork, leaned in, and cut a delicate slice of Aunt Sylvia's masterpiece.

Cressida's stomach dropped.

The tent had gone quiet again—not the reverent silence of judging, but something else. Something that felt like collective breath-holding. Like everyone knew they were about to witness something and couldn't decide if they wanted to look away or lean closer.

Henrietta lifted the fork to her lips, her expression the picture of gracious curiosity.

She took the bite.

For a fraction of a second—maybe less—her expression shifted. Surprise flickered across her face, something that might have been genuine shock or possibly appreciation. Eyebrows rising. Lips parting.

And then...

The transformation was theatrical. Masterful, even. A grimace twisted her face, so exaggerated it belonged on a Victorian stage. Her hand flew to her mouth like she'd just bitten into poison instead of prize-worthy dessert.

The sound of her fork scraping against the plate. Metallic. Deliberate. And it made Cressida flinch. The cruelty radiated from that small gesture, the performance of disgust weaponized into public humiliation.

"Oh my," Henrietta said, her voice projecting across the tent with perfect clarity.

She reached for a napkin, dabbing at her lips. "Oh my *goodness*."

The photographer's camera flashed.

Click.

Click.

Click.

"Is it—" someone in the crowd started, but trailed off.

Henrietta paused, searching for the right word. Sympathy softened her features; or something close to it. "—*ambitious*. Very ambitious. The ingredients don't quite harmonize. The lavender overwhelms the honey, and the glaze has an almost—" She let the silence hang. "*sickeningly* sweet quality. Such a shame. Sylvia clearly worked very hard."

The fork clinked against the plate as she set it down.

She smiled.

Moved on.

Murmurs rippled through the tent.

Cressida's hands had balled into fists. "*Sickeningly?*"

Miles's jaw was set. "Come on. Let's find your aunt before someone else does."

"Too late for that." Cressida let him steer her toward the exit anyway. Her phone buzzed. Aunt Sylvia. Probably already composing a verbal assault that would make Sherman's March look gentle by comparison.

Afternoon sunlight hit them as they stepped outside.

Too bright. Too cheerful.

The fairgrounds sprawled before them—carnival rides spinning against blue sky, game booths calling out prizes, funnel cakes and barbecue drifting on the breeze.

"We should walk," Miles said.

Cressida pulled out her phone. Three texts from Aunt Sylvia glowed on the screen, each more profane than the last. She silenced it. "Give her time to calm down. Or at least time to stop threatening to key someone's Mercedes."

They drifted toward the game booths, weaving between families and teenagers.

Miles paused at the ring toss, eyeing the prizes. "I should win Sylvia a stuffed bear."

"You think a stuffed bear is going to fix this?"

"No." He picked up a ring, tested its weight. "But it can't hurt."

Cressida started to point out that Aunt Sylvia's rage was the kind that required either bourbon or bloodshed to resolve—

The sound hit them.

Not a scream. More like a collective gasp rippling through the fairgrounds, followed by shouts, followed by chaos that made every nerve in Cressida's body snap to attention.

"The tent," they said simultaneously.

They ran.

By the time they shoved their way back through the crowd—*excuse me, sorry, coming through*—the Golden Spoon tent had transformed into pure pandemonium. Phones raised, voices overlapping in a cacophony of shock and morbid curiosity.

"—someone call 911—"

"—is she breathing—"

"—oh my God, is that—"

Cressida ducked under someone's arm, squeezed between two elderly women clutching each other. Broke through to the front.

And stopped.

Henrietta Dodd lay collapsed across the judges' table, face buried in what remained of her prize-winning Lemon Lavender Chiffon Cake. The golden spoon trophy had fallen beside her, its polished surface reflecting the tent's string lights. Silver-blonde hair streaked with pale frosting. One manicured hand dangling over the edge of the table, fingers slack, pearls still gleaming at her wrist.

Not moving.

Reverend Carlson knelt beside her, hand on her shoulder, face ashen. "Henrietta? Henrietta, can you hear me?"

Nothing.

Mrs. Mitchell had her phone pressed to her ear, professional composure finally cracking. "Yes, the Midsummer Feast & Festival, the competition tent. Please hurry."

Marisol stood frozen with a plate in her hands, mouth open, eyes wide with the kind of shock that suggested her brain hadn't quite processed what she was seeing.

And Willard Dodd...

Willard stood at the edge of the crowd, a paper bag from the pharmacy clutched in his hands. Utterly blank. Not shocked. Not grieving. Just empty, like someone had hollowed him out and left only the shell behind.

Miles's hand steadied her elbow.

"Is she?" someone whispered.

Reverend Carlson looked up, face grave. "Someone get the paramedics. *Now.*"

Cressida moved forward, phone already out. Her reporter's instincts kicked in; catalog everything before the scene gets contaminated.

Click. Overturned water glass beside Henrietta's hand. Click. Faint purple tinge around her lips. Click. Scattered lavender sprigs from the ruined cake. Click. Willard's blank expression.

Miles caught her arm. "Cressida—"

"I know." Quiet. Certain.

She'd seen enough death in her years as a crime reporter to recognize it.

Henrietta Dodd wasn't unconscious.

She was dead.

CHAPTER SEVEN

THE CRIME SCENE TAPE snapped in the mountain breeze like a whip crack, punctuating the surreal reality that Blackvale's Midsummer Feast & Fair had just become a murder scene.

Cressida stood at the dispersing crowd's edge, arms crossed. Deputy Jensen handled the measuring tape with military precision, the younger one marking anchor points with orange cones.

Behind them, the Golden Spoon tent loomed like a theater after curtain call. Cheerful bunting and string lights now grotesque. Through the gap in the entrance, Cressida could just make out the edge of the judges' table, the scattered dessert plates, the overturned chair.

And somewhere in there, covered by a sheet now, Henrietta Dodd's body.

The crowd thinned once reality had set in—morbid curiosity spent, appetites ruined. Those who remained clustered in small groups. Hushed voices. Phones out.

Henrietta Dodd collapsed at the baking competition.

They're saying she's dead.

Right there in the tent, face-first in her own cake.

Cressida pulled out her phone, pretending to check messages while actually reviewing the photos she'd managed to snap before the deputies arrived. The purple tinge around Henrietta's lips. The scattered lavender. Willard's blank expression.

"You're doing that thing," Miles said, voice low.

"What thing?"

"Mentally cataloging evidence while pretending you're just a concerned citizen." He watched the deputies work. "You took pictures, didn't you?"

"Maybe."

"Cressida—"

"I was documenting. It's instinct." She slipped the phone back into her purse. "Besides, you taught me to preserve the scene before it gets contaminated."

"I taught you that when you were seven and I was eight and investigating Mrs. Henderson's missing garden gnomes."

"The principle still applies."

The female deputy consulted with someone inside the tent. Cressida frowned. "Speaking of which—seriously, Miles, where is Pete? I thought he'd be the first one here."

"Pete's not with the department anymore."

Her head whipped around. "What? Since when?"

"About six months ago. He retired, moved to Florida to be closer to his grandkids." Miles nodded toward the woman securing the tape. "That's Deputy Carla Jensen. Former Army MP, joined the department two years ago. She's good—thorough, doesn't miss details."

Deputy Jensen moved with the kind of economy that came from military training, her expression professionally neutral as she directed foot traffic away from the tent.

"And the other one?"

"Deputy Luke Nash. Blackvale born and raised, knows every back road in the county. He's eager, takes detailed notes on every call." Miles's tone carried a hint of approval. "Dad's been working with him on investigative procedures."

"So we've got military precision and local knowledge." Cressida tilted her head, considering. "Could be worse."

"Could be Pete, who used to let you sweet-talk him into sharing case files over coffee."

"I never sweet-talked. I simply created mutually beneficial information exchanges."

"You brought him homemade cookies."

"The cookies were Aunt Sylvia's. That's not sweet-talking, that's strategic resource deployment." Cressida watched as Deputy Jensen conferred with her partner, their heads bent close. "Florida, though. Really?"

"Grandkids," Miles repeated, as if that explained everything.

"Florida is overrated." Cressida pulled her gaze away from the tent, turning to face Miles fully. The afternoon sun caught the angles of his face, throwing shadows that made him look older, more serious. "So what do you think happened?"

Miles was quiet for a moment, his dark eyes scanning the scene with the kind of methodical attention she'd seen him use since they were kids playing detective. "I'd say—"

"I should have known you two would find each other wherever there's trouble."

The voice cut through the moment, and Cressida went rigid. That blend of authority and barely concealed exasperation was branded into her childhood memory with the same permanence as learning to ride a bike or the taste of Aunt Sylvia's peach cobbler.

She turned.

Sheriff Danuwoa Stone stood at the edge of the crime scene tape, arms crossed, Cherokee heritage in full display in his sharp-angled face. That expression somehow managed to communicate both *I expected this* and *why do you do this to me* simultaneously. The afternoon light caught the silver threading through his short-cropped hair, and his pressed uniform bore the same quiet authority it always had.

A gust of mountain wind lifted the crime scene tape, snapping it taut before it fell slack again.

The sheriff's shadow cut across the gravel between them, long and dark in the slanting afternoon sun. Somewhere behind her, a child's laughter echoed from the fairgrounds, incongruous against the weight of the moment.

Two feet. That's how much smaller Cressida felt in that instant. Involuntary. Visceral. The way certain childhood dynamics never quite left your body. She was a woman who'd covered crime scenes and interviewed hardened criminals without flinching.

And yet.

"We have the right to be here!"

The words burst out before her brain could catch up. Defensive and sharp and *oh God why did I say that.*

Sheriff Stone's eyebrow rose fractionally. Just enough to convey *really? That's what you're going with?*

Her shoulders dropped. "Sorry," she mumbled, suddenly fascinated by the crime scene tape. Very fascinating. Incredibly important tape.

Miles shifted beside her, tension radiating off him—older, heavier tension than hers. Years of unspoken expectations and carefully maintained distance.

"Sheriff Dad," Cressida said. Humor: her panic button. "Fancy meeting you at a crime scene."

Sheriff Stone's mouth twitched. Barely. "Trouble Vale." The nickname came out smooth. "Should've known you'd be here. Where there's chaos, there's Cressida."

"That's not fair. I was here *before* the chaos. I'm practically a witness." She gestured toward the tent. "Miles and I were just—"

"That's what worries me." Sheriff Stone shifted his attention to his son, and something in his expression hardened just slightly; not anger, exactly, but something more complicated. Pride and worry and frustration all tangled together in the way only family could manage. "Miles."

"Dad." Carefully neutral. "Didn't know you were back from Asheville."

"Got back an hour ago. Heard the call on the radio."

His gaze moved past them to the tent. Jaw tightening. The string lights caught in his dark eyes like distant stars.

She watched his face. Read the micro-expressions the way she'd learned to read crime scenes. The tension around his eyes. The way his hands flexed once before settling. The way he looked at the tent like it was both evidence and tragedy.

The air between father and son thickened.

Years of history condensed into heartbeats. She'd witnessed this dynamic a thousand times growing up—two people who loved each other but couldn't speak the same language.

Sheriff Stone's gaze returned to Miles—that long, measuring look. Cataloging. Assessing. Judging.

"Still playing detective, I see."

The words carried decades of weight. *You could've joined the force. Why isn't this enough for you? I don't understand why you need to do it differently.*

Miles's shoulders squared. "Just observing, Dad."

"Observing." The sheriff repeated the word like he was testing its weight, rolling it around to see if it held up under scrutiny. His mouth pressed into a thin line. "Right."

He turned to the tent. The conversation was over.

Cressida caught the flicker across Miles's face before it smoothed to neutral. Hurt? Frustration? Some combination she couldn't name. She wanted to say something, to bridge the gap, to ease the tension hanging between them like valley fog. But some family dynamics were minefields she had no business navigating.

Boots crunched on gravel. Deputy Nash navigated around the festival-goers, still clustered at the perimeter, notebook already out. Slanted, cramped handwriting covered the page—the kind that came from being taught to conserve paper. His face had gone pale beneath his summer tan, making the freckles across his nose stand out like scattered paint flecks.

"Sheriff?" His voice strained for professional while his insides clearly churned. His Adam's apple bobbed. "I've got an ID on the victim. Henrietta Dodd, sir."

"The recent winner of the Golden Spoon," Cressida added. "Again."

Miles was already looking at her when she glanced over. His eyebrows did something she couldn't quite decipher. It was either *we're thinking the same thing, aren't we?* or *you should stand back before Deputy Nash loses it over your nice shoes.*

She stepped back just in case.

Deputy Nash continued, his gaze dropping to his notes like they might offer him courage. "Witness says she asked for a glass of water right before she started breathing funny." He looked up from his notes, and back at the tent. "I'm thinking maybe she choked on something? Food lodged in her airway?"

"That's wrong," Cressida and Miles said simultaneously.

The silence that followed felt weighted, charged. Sheriff Stone's attention shifted to them with the precision of a spotlight swinging across a stage. His jaw tightened. The look he gave them said *of course you two are already three steps ahead* and *why does it always have to be you two*. She resisted the urge to fidget with her phone case, kept her hands still through sheer force of will.

"Oh? And what makes you two experts?"

Miles stepped closer to the tent entrance. His gaze moved methodically—left to right, top to bottom, the way she'd seen him examine everything from missing bicycles to suspicious water stains. "The discoloration around her mouth. It's purple-tinged, not blue."

"Blue means oxygen deprivation—choking, suffocation," Cressida said. She gestured with one hand, fingers tracing patterns in the air. "Purple suggests something else. Chemical reaction, maybe. Something that affected the tissues directly rather than just cutting off air supply."

"Poison," Miles said quietly.

The word hung there between them like smoke.

Sheriff Stone's eyes narrowed fractionally. Recognition flickered across his face. He was seeing it too, now that they'd pointed it out.

Deputy Nash blinked, his notebook momentarily forgotten in his hand. "But she was eating—"

"She'd finished eating," Cressida's mind raced backward through the afternoon, reconstructing. "I saw her. She made some rather unladylike comments..." *about my aunt's tart.* "That was at least ten, maybe fifteen minutes before she collapsed."

Miles's hands slid into his pockets. "There were dozens of people around her. Medical professionals at the event." His gaze swept the perimeter—festival-goers in Sunday best, volunteers in matching T-shirts, EMTs by their vehicle. "If she'd choked, someone would have helped. Heimlich maneuver, back blows—basic first aid."

"She asked for water," Cressida added, the words tumbling out faster now as the pieces assembled themselves in her mind like a puzzle snapping into place. "Classic poisoning symptom. Sudden intense thirst, burning sensation, difficulty breathing as airways constrict—"

The festival-goers clustered at the perimeter weren't even pretending not to listen. A woman in a floral sundress pressed her hand to her mouth, eyes wide. Two teenage boys stood frozen with their funnel cakes, watching like they'd stumbled onto the season finale of their favorite show. An older man in a VFW cap leaned heavily on his cane, nodding along in agreement.

Deputy Nash stared at them both like they'd just performed some kind of magic trick, his notebook hanging forgotten in his hand.

"Well," the sheriff said slowly. His voice went dangerously quiet—the kind that made Cressida's spine straighten involuntarily. Thunder rolling in before the storm hit. "Aren't you two just a regular Holmes and Watson."

Pleasure flickered through her chest. Pride. *Maybe he's impressed?* The corner of her mouth twitched upward before she could stop it.

Miles looked over at her. Something in his expression made her freeze mid-thought. "It's not a compliment," he said quietly. "Make your face stop making that look."

Oh. Right. Of course it wasn't a compliment. Her expression dropped immediately.

Sheriff Stone sighed—long and heavy. His radio crackled to life on his shoulder, and he lifted it without breaking eye contact. "Marnie, get the ambulance rolling. And call the state lab in Asheville—tell them we need a team down here. Suspicious death, possible poisoning." He waited for the affirmative crackle. "Stay out of this, you two. I'm only going to give you this one warning. You're adults now. Act like it."

His gaze moved between them, lingering on each face long enough to drive the point home.

"This is an official investigation into a suspicious death, not some game you can play at solving."

Suspicious death. Unexplained circumstances.

Murder?

It settled into her chest, heavy and real and impossibly complicated.

Sheriff Stone's attention shifted to his deputy. "Deputy Nash, get their statements and send them home."

Miles's jaw tightened. The muscle jumped in his cheek. But he didn't argue. Didn't protest. Just stood there with his hands still in his pockets, his expression carefully neutral in that way that meant he was feeling everything but showing nothing.

A figure approached the perimeter—older, African American, distinguished by a salt-and-pepper beard. He wore khakis and a polo shirt, and moved with the careful deliberation of someone accustomed to being watched, to being *important*. Dr. Norman Wade. She recognized him vaguely from town—one of the local doctors. Had a practice somewhere off Main Street.

"Sheriff Stone." His voice carried professional courtesy laced with concern. "I was at the fair when it happened. Thought I should take a look before they move her." A pause. His gaze shifted past the sheriff to the tent. "If you don't mind."

Sheriff Stone lifted the tape. "Appreciate it, Doc."

Dr. Wade ducked under and disappeared into the tent with the measured stride of someone who'd seen death before.

The silence stretched. Deputy Nash shifted his weight, boots scraping gravel. Miles remained perfectly still beside her, attention fixed on the tent entrance.

Three minutes.

When Dr. Wade emerged, his dark skin had gone ashen. His hands trembled as he pulled off the examination gloves.

"Sheriff." Low. Urgent. He moved toward Sheriff Stone. Those at the perimeter shifted closer. "This wasn't natural causes. Clear signs of toxins—chemical poisoning. Ingested, most likely. The discoloration around the mouth—" He shook his head. "Need a postmortem to confirm."

He paused.

"I'd say this is murder."

The crowd spiraled—not loudly, but with that particular quality of panic that came from dozens of people processing terrible information at once. Murmurs rose and swelled. *Murder? Here? Poison? Oh my God.* Someone's phone went up, camera pointed at the tent. Then another. Then five more.

Vindication and horror warred in Cressida's chest. Her eyebrows rose. Her mouth parted. An expression that probably looked insufferably smug even though ice water had just dumped through her veins.

Sheriff Stone turned. His gaze landed on her with the precision of a targeting system.

He saw exactly what her face was doing.

Miles's hand closed around her arm. "Come on." His voice stayed quiet, but firm. Already pulling her backward—away from the crime scene tape, his father's stare, the escalating chaos.

"But we—"

"*Now*, Cressi." No room for argument. His fingers tightened. He was already moving, guiding her through the cluster of gawking festival-goers.

She let him pull her away. Couldn't resist one last glance back.

Sheriff Stone had already turned back to Dr. Wade, gesturing for Deputy Jensen. Damage control mode. The tent glowed behind him like a lantern left burning over a grave. Somewhere inside it lay Henrietta Dodd—celebrity chef, social queen, Aunt Sylvia's nemesis—murdered at the annual Midsummer Feast & Fair in front of half the town.

Despite Miles's warning grip on her arm, and blatantly ignoring Sheriff Stone's explicit order to stay out of it, Cressida's mind raced ahead. Assembling timelines. Suspect lists. Questions that needed answering.

One thought crystallized:

This is murder.

Chapter Eight

THE KITCHEN AT VALE House smelled like heaven drowning in butter—warm, decadent, almost obscene in its richness. Outside, clouds gathered over the mountains, turning the morning light soft and gray.

Cressida wedged herself into the corner of the breakfast alcove, a cozy nook carved into the bay window overlooking Aunt Sylvia's herb garden. Her coffee cup sat empty. Two days since Henrietta Dodd collapsed face-first into her prize-winning cake. The whole town held its breath, waiting for the storm to break.

Miles sat across from her, his back to the window. The charcoal henley made his features even more striking in the soft light—the strong jaw, dark eyes, and bronze skin inherited from his Cherokee father. His phone lay face-down beside a half-empty coffee cup, ignored for once. He reached for another biscuit, movements easy and unhurried. As if there wasn't a murder investigation happening right under their noses.

The inn's other guests had cleared out by eight—a retired couple from Wilmington heading to the Biltmore Estate, a pair of antique dealers off to estate sales in Asheville, and a Californian travel blogger chasing whatever picturesque angle she could find for her next Instagram post. The sudden quiet felt both blessing and curse. No need to maintain the cheerful innkeeper façade, but nothing to distract from the weight of unanswered questions either.

Thunder rumbled somewhere distant, barely audible.

Aunt Sylvia moved between stove and table like a woman possessed, her floral apron dusted with flour, silver-streaked curls pinned back with what looked like actual cake decorating tools. When Sylvia Vale stress-cooked, she went *big*. This morning's spread proved she'd been up since dawn channeling anxiety into carbohydrates. Worry transformed into biscuits and gravy, fear kneaded into dough.

The old pine table groaned under a full Southern breakfast: buttermilk biscuits stacked in a cloth-lined basket, fluffy scrambled eggs with chives, thick-cut bacon on her grandmother's china platter, hash browns crisped to golden perfection, sawmill gravy in a porcelain boat.

Blueberry muffins cooled by the window. Cinnamon and cardamom hung in the air like incense.

For twenty minutes, Cressida had been picking at her plate. Fork moving food around more than eating it. *What are we missing?*

The *Blackvale Chronicle* lay spread across the table in front of her—a slim publication that usually covered zoning disputes and high school sports with equal gravitas. This morning's front page featured a grainy photo of the competition tent cordoned off with crime scene tape, and a headline that managed to be both dramatic and uninformative: **LOCAL CELEBRITY CHEF DIES AT FESTIVAL: INVESTIGATION ONGOING**.

She'd read the article twice, then threw the paper down with enough force to make the silverware jump.

"Two days." Her voice came sharp with frustration. "Two *full* days, and still nothing new on Mrs. Dodd's death." She gestured at the paper like it had personally offended her. "Just the same 'authorities are investigating' and 'pending toxicology results' nonsense. Dr. Wade said it was poison. *Poison.* And we're just supposed to sit here eating biscuits like—"

"Speaking of," Miles interrupted. "Pass the biscuits?"

She shot him a look sharp enough to chip a plate.

He met her gaze with that patient amusement that made her want to throw things—affectionately, but still. "Tests and postmortems take time, Cressi. Chain of evidence, lab processing—" The biscuit split open in his hands, releasing a curl of steam. "You know my dad. He keeps things close to the chest."

"This is full-on lockdown," Cressida muttered, stabbing her eggs. "I tried calling Deputy Nash yesterday and he practically hung up on me. Said the sheriff gave 'explicit instructions' not to discuss the case with civilians." She did air quotes with one hand. "Like we didn't hand him the poison theory on a silver platter."

Aunt Sylvia appeared beside the table with fresh bacon. "Dan Stone is good at keeping secrets." Her voice carried that knowing quality that came from almost seven decades of reading people. "But he's *terrible* at keeping a poker face." A smile. "I'm up three-to-one, thanks to last Friday's game."

Miles paused mid-reach for the gravy. "You took three hands off my father in one night?"

"Four hands, sugar. But he won one back on a lucky draw." Sylvia patted his shoulder as she passed, heading back toward the stove. "Man's got a tell the size of Texas when he's bluffing. Left eyebrow twitches."

A pause.

"Just like his son's does."

Miles's hand rose automatically to his eyebrow. Dropped when he caught Cressida grinning at him.

"Don't," he warned.

"I didn't say anything."

"Your face said it for you."

She reached for a piece of bacon. The crunch punctuated her next words. "So." Her voice carried that carefully casual tone—the one that meant she'd been sitting on information, waiting. "I was talking to Mrs. Hampton yesterday."

"When were you talking to Mrs. Hampton?" Miles's tone suggested he already knew the answer wouldn't be something simple like *we ran into each other at the market.*

"She came by to drop off flower cuttings for Aunt Sylvia." The bacon waved like a conductor's baton. "And while we were chatting—very casually, very naturally—she mentioned something interesting about Mrs. Dodd."

Miles set down his coffee cup. His dark eyes sharpened. "What kind of something?"

"Apparently Henrietta had been seeing an allergy specialist in Charlotte. Her food allergy had gotten worse." Cressida leaned forward, elbows on the table. "Mrs. Hampton knows because she filled a prescription a few weeks ago—Willard picked it up when Henrietta's regular prescription ran out and he didn't want to drive all the way to Charlotte."

A sound from the stove—surprise or recognition. Aunt Sylvia turned, wooden spoon in hand, her expression caught between curiosity and something darker. "Henrietta had a food allergy?" She shook her head slowly, curls bouncing. "I didn't know that. She never mentioned it during all the years I've known her."

"Did Mrs. Hampton say what kind?" Miles asked, his investigator instincts clearly engaged now contrary to his earlier reluctance.

Cressida shook her head. "She wouldn't say. Patient confidentiality and all that. But she made it clear it was serious enough that Henrietta needed regular medication for it."

"That's significant." Sylvia returned to the table with a large stack of pancakes. The plate landed with a decisive *thunk*. "If Henrietta had a severe food allergy and someone knew about it..." She let the implication hang.

Cressida shot Miles a look—eyebrows raised, mouth quirked in that expression that said *see? this matters*. "In Blackvale, sometimes the smallest details are worth more than obvious motives. You know that."

The kitchen fell quiet except for the soft ticking of the grandmother clock in the corner and the distant sound of a cardinal singing in the garden.

Miles held her gaze. Something shifted behind his dark eyes—recognition, maybe. Resignation.

"You're not wrong." He reached for the pancakes. "I just don't want you jumping to conclusions before you have actual evidence."

"I'm not jumping." Even though they both knew she absolutely was. "I'm *considering possibilities*. There's a difference."

"The difference being that 'considering possibilities' usually ends with you climbing through someone's window at two in the morning."

"That was *one time*, and I got us the evidence we needed on the Hartley case—"

"And nearly gave Mrs. Hartley a heart attack when she found you in her study—"

"She was *fine*, Miles. Dramatic, but fine."

Aunt Sylvia watched them volley back and forth, absently refilling coffee cups and adjusting the placement of serving dishes. The pleased expression of someone watching her favorite show.

"You two sound married," she observed. Far too innocent.

They both turned to stare at her.

"We do not—"

"That's not—" Miles said at the same time.

Sylvia smiled serenely. Returned to the stove, humming something that might have been "Chapel of Love."

Cressida cleared her throat. She focused on the newspaper, on the grainy photo of the crime scene tape, on the *questions* spinning through her mind like a carousel that wouldn't stop.

Miles's ears had gone slightly red, and Cressida determinedly tried not to notice.

"So we've got Susan Mitchell with a public grudge over competition rules," she said. Her fingers drummed against the table. "We've got Aunt Sylvia's very public rivalry—"

"I did not kill Henrietta Dodd," Sylvia interjected calmly, not turning from the stove.

"I know that, obviously. I'm just saying from an outside perspective—"

A sharp knock echoed from the front of the house. Three deliberate raps that carried the weight of official business rather than friendly visiting.

The kind of knock that made people stop mid-sentence.

Sylvia's expression shifted, something moving behind her eyes—not quite concern, but close. She patted down her apron and smoothed her silver-streaked curls. "Well," she said, her voice carrying that particular lilt that meant she already suspected who was calling. "Let me see who's come visiting at breakfast time."

Cressida pulled out her phone, her thumbs moving across the screen. *Just making notes,* she told herself. Though the energy coiling in her chest said otherwise.

Easier to pretend this was casual documentation than to admit she was already obsessing.

Miles leaned forward. His dark eyes fixed on her with laser focus. "We're not getting involved. My dad was clear."

Cressida met his gaze with perfect innocence, her phone still glowing in her hand. "I'm just making notes. Very casual notes. And maybe engaging in a little small talk if the opportunity arises—"

"You don't do small talk without a reason for it." Miles's mouth quirked upwards. "You're constitutionally incapable of asking about someone's day without an ulterior motive."

"That's not true—"

"Yesterday you asked Mrs. Shong about her garden and somehow ended up with a detailed timeline of everyone who'd been in the community center during that argument."

"She volunteered that information—"

"Because you steered the conversation there like a sheep dog with a flock." He reached across the table, his hand hovering near hers but not quite touching. "You heard my dad, Cressi. *Let them handle it.* Besides—" His tone shifted, gentling. "Aren't you supposed to be looking for freelance photography jobs? I thought that was the whole point of coming back here. Taking time to figure out what you actually want to do."

The words landed with more weight than he'd probably intended.

Cressida's thumb stilled on her phone screen. Her jaw tightened in that way it did when someone hit too close to an uncomfortable truth. She could feel the deflection rising in her throat—something sharp, something that would redirect the conversation away from her own avoidance.

But the sound of voices from the front of the house shattered the moment.

Sheriff Dan Stone's distinctive baritone, measured and authoritative. And beneath it, another voice—Deputy Jensen's steady alto, professional and careful.

Miles's gaze snapped toward the doorway. Cressida was already moving, phone sliding back into her pocket as she rose from her chair.

They moved through the house in tandem, following the voices to the drawing room—that formal space Sylvia kept for "company" with its antique settee and carefully curated collection of framed photographs spanning seven decades.

Sheriff Dan Stone stood near the fireplace, his weathered face carved into the same impassive expression Miles sometimes wore when he was working a problem. Beside him, Deputy Carla Jensen had her notebook out, pen poised, her military posture somehow both respectful and alert. And Aunt Sylvia stood between them and the door, arms crossed over her apron, chin lifted in that angle that meant she was ready for a fight.

"What's going on?" Cressida asked.

Sylvia turned. Irritation and something darker—hurt, maybe, or betrayal—moved across her face. "Dan seems to think I had something to do with Henrietta's death," she said, her Southern accent thickening with emotion. Each word dripped with wounded dignity and barely suppressed fury.

"Ma'am, that's not what the sheriff said at all," Deputy Jensen interjected smoothly, her tone professionally diplomatic. She shot a glance at Dan Stone that might have been apologetic or merely procedural—hard to tell with Jensen. "We're just conducting interviews with everyone who had access to—"

"You're absolutely right, *sugar*," Sylvia interrupted. Sweet as honey and twice as sticky. She tilted her head, silver curls catching the light, her smile sharp enough to cut glass. "He only asked for me to explain how my tart contained something I have never even heard of."

She paused.

"My mistake."

Miles stepped forward. "Dad?"

Sheriff Dan Stone's jaw worked. His weathered face carved into lines of exhaustion. Regret. He exhaled slowly through his nose—that particular sound that meant he was about to deliver news no one wanted to hear.

"Initial reports show signs of a chemical agent," he said, his baritone dropping into the careful neutrality of official business. "Porpheyne." He paused, his dark eyes flickering to Sylvia before settling back on Miles. "Trace elements of the same compound were found in Ms. Vale's tart."

The words hit like ice water.

Cressida's mind—always so quick to leap ahead, to find the pattern, to *solve*—seized on the impossibility of it. Porpheyne. Chemical. The words kept echoing, each repetition tightening the knot behind her ribs.

"Maybe it's natural—" she started, sharper than she'd intended.

"It's synthetic," Deputy Jensen said. Professional but not unkind. She shifted her weight, her posture softening just enough to acknowledge the discomfort. "not found outside controlled environments. We also have several witnesses who made statements about Mrs. Dodd's comments on said tart after tasting it." She paused. Something flickered across her face—the grace to look uncomfortable, maybe. "Ma'am, everyone in town knows about the ongoing dispute between you and Mrs. Dodd."

Cressida's hands clenched. Nails biting into her palms. The restless energy that usually drove her forward now coiled tight in her chest, dangerous and sharp.

"This is ridiculous," she said, her voice rising overriding her best efforts to keep it level. She gestured emphatically, her hands cutting through the air. "If *everyone* knows about their feud, then anyone could have spiked Aunt Sylvia's tart to frame her. You're looking at the most *obvious* suspect when you should be asking who *benefits* from making it look obvious."

Sheriff Dan's expression didn't change—that impassive mask he wore when duty demanded distance—but Cressida caught the muscle that jumped in his jaw. The way his fingers flexed at his sides.

"I'm sorry, Ms. Vale," he said, his voice gentling just a fraction. Enough that she could hear the man beneath the badge. "I need you to come down to the station and answer a few more questions." He reached into his jacket, slow and deliberate, and withdrew a folded document. "We also have a warrant to search the premises. Deputy Nash will conduct that search now."

Miles moved before Cressida could process it—a fluid step forward that put him between his father and Sylvia, his hands raised in a gesture that was part plea, part protest.

"There has to be some kind of mistake," he said, and there was something raw in his voice that made Cressida's throat tight. "Dad, you *know* Sylvia. You've known her since before I was born. She would never hurt anyone."

Something flickered in his father's eyes—regret, maybe. Exhaustion. The particular kind of pain that came from doing the right thing when it cost you something personal. The morning light caught the silver at his temples, the deep lines around his mouth that spoke of too many hard calls at ungodly hours.

"I hope," he said quietly, "that the questioning will prove exactly that."

Sylvia smoothed her apron with hands that barely trembled—just the faintest quiver at the fingertips. She lifted her chin with that defiant angle Cressida had seen a thousand times before, the one that meant she was hurt but damned if she'd show it.

"Don't you worry, honey-lambs," she said, her voice carrying that honeyed Southern lilt. But it lacked its usual confidence. The words came out steady enough, but her eyes gave her away. "I'll be back before the biscuits go cold."

She moved toward the door with measured grace, her hand briefly touching Cressida's shoulder as she passed.

Deputy Nash appeared in the doorway as Sylvia reached it, his boyish features twisted into genuine discomfort. His uniform looked too crisp for the moment. His posture too rigid. Like he was trying to disappear into professionalism and failing.

He clutched the warrant in one hand, the paper crinkling slightly in his nervous grip. "Ma'am," he mumbled as Sylvia passed, his voice barely above a whisper. "I'm... I'm sorry."

Sylvia paused, her hand on the doorframe. She offered Nash a smile that didn't reach her eyes. "You're just doing your job, sugar." No bite. No edge. Just weariness wrapped in grace.

Cressida and Miles followed them onto the porch. Their footsteps echoed on worn boards. The morning had shifted—clouds rolling in from the mountains, casting shadows across the garden where cardinals still sang their oblivious songs. The air tasted like rain and copper.

Sheriff Dan guided Sylvia toward the patrol car with careful courtesy. Deputy Jensen followed, notebook tucked under her arm. Deputy Nash lingered on the porch, shoulders hunched, before heading back inside to begin the search with the kind of reluctance that made his every movement apologetic.

The patrol car pulled away. Its engine purred through the morning quiet, taking Aunt Sylvia down the winding drive toward town.

Cressida's hands trembled. Not with fear—with that burning energy that came when everything in her screamed *wrong, this is wrong, fix it.*

She opened her mouth. "We're—"

Her voice was tight. She didn't look at Miles. If she looked at him she might lose the careful control she was clinging to.

His hand found hers before she could finish. Warm. Solid. Steady. His fingers laced through hers, grounding her, pulling her back from the edge of that spiraling panic that threatened to drown out logic.

It wasn't comfort she felt in his grip.

It was permission—to fight back.

"I know," Miles said quietly.

CHAPTER NINE

THE PATROL CAR'S TAILLIGHTS vanished around the bend, swallowed by morning mist. Cressida stood on the porch, hands curled into fists, nails biting crescents into her palms. That restless energy—always there, always coiled beneath her skin—was building now. Hot. Tight. Demanding *action*, not this helpless watching while Aunt Sylvia was carted off like a common criminal.

Miles's hand was still warm in hers, his fingers steady and grounding. She couldn't stop Sylvia's arrest, but she could do this. She squeezed once—hard enough to hurt, maybe—before letting go and turning back toward the house. "Come on. Deputy Nash is probably already tearing through the kitchen looking for evidence that doesn't exist."

They found him exactly where she'd predicted: standing in the middle of Aunt Sylvia's beloved kitchen, turning in a slow circle like a man who'd been dropped into foreign territory without a map. The breakfast spread still covered the table—biscuits going cold, gravy congealing, the coffee pot half-empty. Deputy Nash held a pair of latex gloves in one hand and wore a slightly desperate expression on his boyish face.

Cressida stopped in the doorframe, arms crossed. "Deputy Nash," she said, her voice carrying just enough edge to make him jump. "What exactly are you looking for?"

Nash turned, shoulders hunching like he'd been caught doing something he shouldn't. Morning light from the window caught the nervous sweat on his forehead, the bob of his Adam's apple when he swallowed. "I, uh—" He gestured vaguely at the cabinets, the counters, the pantry door standing slightly ajar. "Sheriff Stone said to search for... anything that might be relevant to the case."

"Anything." Cressida let the word hang there like smoke. She pushed off the doorframe and moved into the kitchen with fluid grace. "That's real specific."

Nash had the decency to look embarrassed. He ran a hand through his short hair—regulation cut, probably got it trimmed every two weeks on the dot—and shifted his weight. "I don't actually know," he admitted, his voice dropping to something closer to confession. "But Sheriff Stone always says..." He paused, seeming to search for the exact words. "You'll know it when you see it."

Miles made a sound that might have been amusement or exasperation—hard to tell with him sometimes. He moved to stand beside her and she felt some of that coiled tension ease. Just a fraction.

Nash's gaze drifted to the breakfast table, lingering on the spread with the kind of longing that spoke of skipped meals and early shifts. "It all smells so good," he said, almost to himself. His face flushed—a deep red creeping up from his collar—and he shook his head quickly. "But I don't think that's proper procedure. Eating at the scene, I mean."

Cressida seized the opening.

Charm wasn't deception; it was survival. No one guarded secrets around someone who seemed safe.

She moved to the coffee pot, pouring a fresh cup with deliberate ease. "You can't solve a murder on an empty stomach." Her voice warmed to something almost maternal. She set the cup at an empty chair and gestured to the biscuits with a smile. "The biscuits are fresh. Take a load off." She paused, head tilting with calculated innocence. "There's nothing wrong with us just talking, is there?"

Nash hesitated, his gaze flickering between the food and the doorway like he expected Sheriff Stone to materialize with a lecture about protocol. Then his shoulders sagged and he pulled out the chair with a grateful sigh that spoke volumes about long shifts and skipped breakfasts.

"I suppose a few minutes won't hurt." Nash reached for a biscuit and broke it open. Steam rising in lazy spirals. He slathered it with butter that melted instantly into golden pools. His first bite was cautious, professional. The second was pure appreciation with his eyes closing briefly.

"Between you and me," he said, leaning forward slightly, his voice dropping to something conspiratorial, "this whole thing's got everyone at the station on edge."

Cressida settled across from him, arranging herself with deliberate casualness—shoulders relaxed, hands wrapped around the warm mug, her expression open and sympathetic. Behind her, Miles remained standing, leaning against the counter with his arms crossed. His calm wasn't passive; it was the stillness before he struck, watchful and ready. Giving her space to work.

"I imagine so." She let genuine empathy color the words. The silence stretched just long enough to feel companionable rather than interrogative. "Must be hard investigating someone everyone in town knows."

Nash's expression turned troubled as he reached for his coffee. "You have no idea. Half the folks at the Piggly Wiggly this morning were asking me if it's true Sylvia Vale poisoned Henrietta Dodd. The other half were ready to storm the station if we didn't focus on someone else immediately." Frustration bled through his professional veneer. "It's like the whole town's split down the middle. My own mama called me this morning asking if I'd lost my mind."

She mirrored his posture; a subtle psychological trick she'd learned years ago. *Make them feel heard. Make them feel understood.* "That sounds exhausting." And she meant it. The weight of community pressure was real, carved into the lines around his young face.

"Did the lab say how much of that porpheyne stuff was in Aunt Sylvia's tart?"

Nash set down his cup with a soft *clink*, his brow furrowing. Something flickered across his face that looked like confusion wrapped in concern—the expression of a man trying to solve a puzzle that refused to make sense. "Trace amounts, they said. Not enough to kill anyone on its own, which is the weird part." His gaze went distant like he was replaying conversations, re-examining evidence in his mind. "The medical examiner thinks Mrs. Dodd had a much larger dose in her system—way more than what was in the tart. Like, significantly more."

The kitchen air sharpened—cold prickling down her arms despite the warmth from the stove.

Someone else poisoned her. Aunt Sylvia's tart was just... what? A red herring? A frame job?

She kept her expression carefully neutral—interested but not too interested—even as her fingers itched to grab her phone and start making notes, mapping timelines, listing suspects.

Miles reached across the table and pushed one of Aunt Sylvia's mason jars of homemade jam toward Nash. The glass caught the morning light—blackberry preserves so dark they looked almost purple. "Surely my dad's not just looking at Ms. Vale?" His voice carried that particular blend of casual curiosity and calculated prodding. "We all know how Mrs. Dodd was."

Nash unscrewed the jar lid with a soft *pop* and spooned preserves onto the split biscuit. He took a bite. For a heartbeat his entire body went still—eyes closing, a look of pure bliss crossing his features.

"My mom wishes her biscuits could taste like this," he said, his voice soft with reverence. He opened his eyes with a rueful smile. "Now, no one can touch her smothered pork chops...but these biscuits...perfection."

Cressida set down her coffee with a gentle *clink*. "But there are other suspects, right?" Her silver hoop earrings caught light. "Mrs. Dodd had a way of making enemies."

Nash reached for his coffee, his gaze drifting to the window where morning clouds were thickening. The furrow between his brows deepened. "We've been told about her argument with

Susan Mitchell." His voice dropped—like he was remembering that he probably shouldn't be having this conversation at all. "Apparently someone overheard Mrs. Dodd say to a friend—"

His mouth closed with an almost audible click.

"Say what?" Cressida's fingers tightened around her mug.

Nash shifted, suddenly fascinated by the contents of his cup. "Sheriff Stone always says not to—"

"We won't tell." The words tumbled out. She glanced at Miles, then back to Nash. "This is my aunt we're talking about. Everyone in this kitchen knows she didn't do it."

She paused.

"Please."

Nash's jaw worked as he fought some internal battle between duty and compassion. His shoulders sagged. "Ms. Vale has always been nice to me," he mumbled, almost to himself. "And my mom did say..." He trailed off, then cleared his throat. "Mrs. Dodd allegedly told a friend—'If Freddy slips up, I'll be ready to remind him.'"

Her pulse quickened. *Freddy? Frederick Carlson. The reverend.*

"That's an odd thing to say." The words came out gentle, conversational. "Go on."

Nash ran a hand through his short hair. "There was something also with her recent protégé, Ayita Craig. They were heard arguing the day before the competition at Mrs. Dodd's annual Midsummer luncheon." He shook his head. "Afterwards, witnesses overheard her muttering about leaving Blackvale for good."

New suspect added. Ayita Craig. Protégé. Argument. Leaving town.

"Which is bad." Nash glanced toward the doorway, then back to his coffee. "Since no one's seen her since the competition." He met Cressida's gaze with genuine concern. "After I'm finished here, I'm supposed to pay a visit to her dad's butcher shop downtown."

He straightened. Set down his cup.

"Speaking of which, I should start working."

A sharp knock split the quiet. Cressida's head snapped toward the sound, pulse spiking. *Who now? Sheriff Stone back to haul us in too?*

Miles caught her eye and tilted his head toward the door.

She frowned. Pointed at herself, then Nash, then her chair. *I'm staying.*

He shook his head. Jabbed his finger toward the hallway.

She pointed back at him, mouthing *you go.*

Nash rummaged through his forensics case, oblivious.

Miles crossed to the table, his hand closing around her elbow. He physically lifted her from the chair. She stumbled up with a hiss of indignation as he steered her bodily toward the doorway, his grip unyielding.

She shot him a look that could have curdled milk. His expression remained maddeningly calm, though something flickered in his eyes—amusement, maybe.

"I'll get it," she said through gritted teeth, her voice determinedly cheerful for Nash's benefit.

CHAPTER TEN

CRESSIDA PULLED OPEN THE heavy oak door. Its hinges creaked.

Susan Mitchell stood on the porch, framed by morning light that had grown pale and thin, filtered through clouds that had thickened over the mountains while Cressida was inside. Susan wore a linen suit the color of champagne—impeccably tailored, not a wrinkle in sight despite the humidity that was already making Cressida's own blouse cling to her spine. Her locs were swept up in an intricate twist secured with what looked like actual antique tortoiseshell combs, and her makeup was camera-ready: precisely lined lips in coral, subtle gold at her temples, not a single element out of place.

Her expression didn't match the polish. Concern perched there like a poorly fitted mask.

The kind of concern that came with an agenda attached.

"Mrs. Mitchell," Cressida said, keeping her voice warm. "This is unexpected."

"Cressida, honey." Susan's smile was immediate. All teeth. She shifted the leather tote bag on her shoulder—expensive. Probably Italian. "I hope I'm not intruding. I just wanted to stop by and see how Sylvia was holding up." A pause, her voice dropping. "The gossip machine kicked in before sundown yesterday. Everyone's saying she 'finally snapped.'"

The words landed with the weight of accusation dressed up as sympathy. Cressida felt her jaw tighten, felt that surge of protective fury rise hot and sharp in her chest, but she forced her expression into something neutral—pleasant, even. *Play it cool. Find out what she knows.*

"That's kind of you." Cressida stepped back, pulling the door wider. Her voice stayed warm, gracious. "Please, come in. Aunt Sylvia's out, but I'd love to hear what people are saying." She gestured toward the sitting room. "Coffee? Tea?"

Susan's heels clicked across the threshold—sharp reports against hardwood. "No, dear, I've cut out caffeine." Already moving toward the sitting room like she owned it, her gaze cataloging everything: the antique side tables cluttered with Sylvia's collected treasures, the floral wallpaper that hadn't been updated since the eighties, the framed photographs of family gatherings that lined the walls in mismatched frames.

Cressida positioned herself near the doorway where she could see both Susan settling into the velvet armchair and the sliver of kitchen down the hall. Miles's silhouette moved past the doorframe—deliberate, unhurried.

Susan smoothed her linen skirt. The morning light from the window caught the gold threads in the fabric, made them shimmer like something precious. Her eyes darted toward the kitchen doorway—quick, assessing, curious—and Cressida caught the flicker of calculation behind the worried façade.

"So, what are people saying?" Cressida asked.

Susan waved a manicured hand—dusty rose nails, perfect half-moons. "Oh, the usual nonsense. You know Blackvale." She leaned forward, bringing with her a waft of expensive perfume, cloying—peony and white musk. "But between you and me, honey, tensions were running *very* high at that competition. Henrietta had a way of pushing people to their limits."

Her smile tightened. Something bitter flickered beneath the polish.

"Lord knows she pushed *me* past mine more than once."

Cressida let the silence stretch. A beat. Then two. The kind of pause that made people fill the void with words they hadn't planned to say.

"You were there, weren't you?" she said finally. "When she collapsed?"

Something crossed Susan's face—too fast to name. Her fingers found the chunky gold bracelet at her wrist, turning it in restless circles. "I'd been called away. So much going on all at once. Vendors needing direction, the sound system acting up, someone knocked over an entire display of preserves near the craft tent."

Frustration bled through the polished veneer.

"When I heard the commotion and got back to the tent, Henrietta was already..."

She trailed off. Shuddered. One hand rose to her throat.

"It was horrific," Susan whispered. "Just horrific."

"Did you notice anything unusual before that? Anyone acting strange?"

Susan's eyes brightened. She'd been waiting to share this, holding onto information like a card she was dying to play. Her spine went rigid. "Well, I don't want to speak out of turn"—the kind of preamble that always precedes someone speaking *exactly* out of turn—"but Sylvia *did* storm out after Henrietta's win. Everyone saw it."

She paused, gaze locking onto Cressida's face.

"And then there's Reverend Carlson."
Freddy.

"The reverend?" Cressida echoed.

"He gave Henrietta the highest score. Every single year, without fail." Susan leaned back, crossing her legs with elegant precision. Her smile said I *know something you don't*. "Some people might find that... curious. Given their history."

"Their history?" Cressida prompted.

Before Susan could answer, Miles appeared in the doorway.

"Kitchen. Now."

His voice was level. Too level.

Cressida stood immediately, her body moving before her conscious mind had fully processed the command.

Susan rose too, following without invitation like she'd been waiting for exactly this kind of development. Gossip didn't gather itself. "Is everything all right?" she asked, concern layered thick over what sounded an awful lot like anticipation.

The kitchen felt smaller with all four of them crowded inside—Cressida and Miles, Susan hovering near the doorway, and Deputy Nash standing by the counter with his back to them, latex gloves stretched tight across his hands. The morning light slanting through the window caught dust motes in the air, made them dance like tiny spirits in the sudden stillness.

Nash turned slowly, deliberately, and Cressida's gaze locked onto what he held.

A small evidence bag, clear plastic catching the light. Inside, a brown glass bottle—small, maybe four inches tall, with a screw-top cap and a printed label that was perfectly, horrifyingly legible even from across the room.

Porpheyne. Caution: Toxic if Ingested.

The air went still. Not quiet—stillness was different, heavier, like the moment before lightning strikes when every molecule freezes in anticipation. Cressida's mouth went dry. The world narrowed to that label, the bold black letters against white. She couldn't look away from it, couldn't unsee.

Her heartbeat kicked hard against her ribs—once, twice, a frantic rhythm that felt too loud. The edges of her vision blurred slightly.

Behind her, Susan gasped—a sharp, theatrical sound that cut through the silence like breaking glass. "Oh my God," she breathed, her voice rising with horror. "It's true. Sylvia actually killed her."

CHAPTER ELEVEN

MILES SHIFTED IN THE passenger seat, one hand braced against the doorframe, the other gripping the handle above the window like it was the only thing tethering him to reality. He shot her a look—part exasperation, part genuine concern for his own mortality.

"My whole left side has gone numb," he said. "Where are we going?"

She didn't answer immediately. Cressida's gaze was locked on the road ahead, tracking the traffic light at the intersection—still yellow, but fading fast. She calculated the distance, speed, and margin for error. Her foot pressed harder on the accelerator, and the Mini's engine gave an eager growl as they surged forward.

The Mini shot through just as the light flicked red. Tires squealed on the turn. A horn blared behind them, angry and indignant, but she was already straightening the wheel.

"I told you," she said.

Miles exhaled slowly through his nose—years of practiced patience wearing dangerously thin. "Your driving hasn't gotten better since you were sixteen." He braced himself against the door. "And no, you *haven't* told me. After Deputy Nash found those receipts, you grabbed my arm, grabbed your keys, and next thing I know we're going ten over in your clown car."

"It's not a clown car. It's fuel-efficient and adorable." Another turn—not quite as sharp, but still enough to make him grip tighter. "We're heading to the library to research Porpheyne." Her hands wrapped tighter around the steering wheel. "This is *exactly* why I told Aunt Sylvia to install security cameras. We'd have video evidence of whoever planted that stuff. But no—she says it'll 'disrupt the house's charm.'"

Miles was quiet for a beat, gaze fixed on the road ahead. When he spoke, his voice was careful, measured—someone stepping onto ice they knew was too thin. "Security cameras wouldn't have helped if your aunt was the one who planted it."

Her head snapped toward him, look sharp enough to cut glass. "She didn't. And you know it."

She wasn't angry at Miles. Not really. Anger was just easier to steer than fear.

He held up both hands in surrender, expression staying serious. "I'm just saying what the evidence suggests. Deputy Nash found receipts, Cressi. Dated two months ago. Online supplier. Porpheyne. Your aunt's credit card information."

"You can buy credit card info on the dark web." The words tumbled out fast, each one sharp-edged with defensive certainty. "I did a whole series on it back in Charlotte—identity theft, fraudulent purchases, the works." Her grip tightened on the wheel. "*Anyone* could have planted that stuff. It was just sitting in the drawer with the cooking utensils, Miles. Not with the baking ingredients. And do you honestly think my aunt is stupid enough to leave evidence lying around if she—"

The words died. Her jaw locked tight, tendons standing out in her neck.

If she actually did it.

"She didn't." Quieter now, like she was trying to convince herself as much as him. The sharp edge had gone, replaced by something rawer. "Someone's framing her, Miles. And we're going to prove it."

Silence stretched between them. Out of the corner of her eye, she caught the shift in his expression—concern melting into something closer to resignation. The same look he'd worn when she was eight and had decided Mr. Morten's prize-winning pig hadn't run away but had been *stolen*, and she'd dragged him through half of Blackvale's backyards until they found it napping in a toolshed three houses down.

He'd followed her then, too.

Something settled in her chest at that—not relief exactly, but a kind of grounding. He didn't argue. Didn't try to slow her down or reason her into caution. He just steadied himself against the next turn and followed, same as always. That quiet, unshakable loyalty that had been there since they were kids, still holding firm even when her theories sounded half-crazy and her driving bordered on reckless.

The Mini's engine hummed as they rounded another curve. Blue Ridge peaks rose like sentinels in the distance, their slopes thick with fog that clung to the valleys below. Morning light filtered through clouds that promised rain before nightfall. Somewhere ahead, the Blackvale Public Library waited.

She pressed harder on the accelerator.

Porpheyne. Receipts. Dark web. Framing. The pieces were there. She just had to find the pattern.

They didn't talk for the rest of the drive. The silence between them wasn't awkward—it was the taut, humming kind that lived between problems and their solutions.

The Blackvale Public Library sat on the corner of Maple and Third like a brick-and-ivy fortress against time itself. 1920s Carnegie architecture, all Gothic arches and leaded glass windows that caught the thin morning light.

The building had survived the Depression, two world wars, and countless budget cuts through sheer stubborn presence; much like Ms. Elsie Patterson herself, who'd ruled its stacks for the better part of four decades.

Cressida pushed through the heavy oak doors, the familiar scent hitting her immediately: old paper and citrus-scented cleaner, coffee from the staff room, and something indefinably comforting that she could only describe as *organized knowledge*. The lobby was quiet this early on a Monday morning, just the distant hum of the heating system and the soft tick of the antique clock above the circulation desk.

Ms. Elsie sat behind the desk, silver-gray hair swept back in soft waves, reading glasses perched on her nose as she typed with the precise two-finger method she'd been using since the library got its first terminals in 1989. When she looked up, her expression shifted—recognition, sympathy, determination—all in a heartbeat.

"Cressida Vale." Her voice carried that particular blend of warmth and authority that only longtime librarians and elementary school teachers could master. She rose, smoothing the front of her forest green dress, small embroidered acorns marching down the button line. "And Miles Stone. I heard you two were back in town."

Her gaze lingered on Cressida's face a beat longer than casual. The weight of it settled like a stone. The unspoken acknowledgment of *everything*. That look adults got when they knew something terrible had happened and were trying to decide whether to address it head-on or pretend normalcy for your sake.

"I already heard about your aunt." Ms. Elsie's voice dropped, direct. "About Sylvia being taken in. About what they found in her kitchen." She shook her head, lips pressing thin. "Small towns, honey. News travels faster than good sense."

Heat flared behind Cressida's ribs—that familiar surge of defensive anger sparking hot. Before she could launch into the explanation she'd been rehearsing since they left the house, Ms. Elsie held up one hand.

"I'll reserve the little study room for you." She gestured toward the back where the reference section sprawled in ordered rows. "Second door on the left, past the periodicals. It's quiet back there, and the door locks from the inside."

Her expression softened, something almost maternal flickering across her features.

"And I thought you two might still like goldfish crackers? I know it's been a while, but some things don't change."

Miles made a sound that was half laugh, half exhale—surprise cutting through the tension that had been riding his shoulders since they left Vale House. His mouth curved into a grin.

"Do you still keep them in that ceramic jar shaped like a fish?" Genuine delight threaded through his voice, the kind that came from touching something long-forgotten and finding it still warm.

Ms. Elsie's smile widened, crinkling the corners of her eyes. "Where else would I keep them? That jar's been on my desk since 1987. It's practically a landmark."

Cressida's shoes squeaked faintly against the worn hardwood as she headed toward the reference section. The familiar electric hum of *momentum* built in her chest—pieces starting to shift, patterns beginning to resolve from chaos.

"We need everything you've got on porpheyne," she said over her shoulder, not slowing her pace. "Toxicology, agricultural use, purchase restrictions, chemical composition—anything in the system." She paused at the entrance to the reference section. "And Ms. Elsie? This stays between us."

Ms. Elsie nodded once, sharp and certain. Already she was moving toward her computer terminal with the quiet intent of someone who'd kept plenty of Blackvale's secrets over the years. Two-fingered but practiced, her hands moved across the keyboard—decades of database searches and oddball requests.

"I'll pull what we have in the system and check our inter-library loan database." She didn't look up from the screen. "Give me ten minutes."

Her hand hovered over the keyboard. When she looked up, her gaze locked onto Cressida's with an intensity that made the younger woman stop mid-step.

"Your aunt didn't do this, sugar." Quiet, absolute certainty—the kind that came from knowing someone through decades of library card renewals and book club meetings and quiet conversations over the circulation desk. "I've known Sylvia Vale for forty years. That woman would poison you with her *words* long before she'd ever use actual poison."

A small smile. A single nod. Cressida turned back toward the study room before the sudden sting behind her eyes could become anything more than that.

The little study room was exactly as she remembered: cramped and windowless, with a rectangular table scarred by generations of students' nervous pencil-tapping and a single overhead light that buzzed faintly when you first turned it on. Reference materials lined the walls—thick volumes on local history, agricultural records, outdated medical journals with cracked spines.

Miles closed the door. The sound of the library's main floor—distant hum of heating, Ms. Elsie's typing, the tick of that antique clock—faded into muffled background noise. The room felt insulated, separate, like they'd stepped into a pocket of stillness carved out of the chaos swirling around them.

Cressida dropped into one of the chairs and pulled out her phone, opening a new note file. Fragments of thoughts, questions, connections that were half-formed but insistent.

Porpheyne—receipts—dark web—framing—who had access—

Miles settled into the chair beside her, close enough that their shoulders almost touched, and pulled out his own phone. He started pulling up supplementary searches—toxicology databases, chemical supply regulations, anything that might give them context.

For a few minutes they worked in companionable silence—the soft tap of screens, Cressida's occasional muttered half-sentences as she worked through theories aloud.

"If someone used Aunt Sylvia's credit card info," she murmured, not really talking to Miles so much as thinking *at* him, "they'd need to know enough about her shopping habits to make the purchase look legitimate. Which means either someone close to her, or someone with access to her financial records—"

A knock interrupted her train of thought.

Ms. Elsie appeared a moment later, arms laden with a stack of reference books and print-outs that looked heavy enough to qualify as a workout, and balanced on top—a bright orange ceramic fish with its mouth open in a permanent smile, filled to the brim with goldfish crackers.

The books landed on the table with a muted *thump*. "Start with the industrial chemistry section," she said, tapping the spine of a weathered volume bound in dark green cloth. "Porpheyne's mostly forgotten now, but back in the fifties and sixties, it was used in textile dyes. There's a chapter on obsolete chemical compounds that should have what you need."

"Thank you," Cressida said, and meant it with an intensity that made Ms. Elsie pause, her hand still resting on the book's spine.

"You find whoever did this, honey." Quiet, resolute. "Blackvale takes care of its own."

She left then, pulling the door closed behind her with a click that felt final, protective—like she was sealing them into a space where the work could be done without interruption.

The green volume was already in Cressida's hands. She flipped it open, scanning the table of contents with the kind of focus that made everything else—the buzzing light, the cramped room, even Miles's presence beside her—fade into peripheral awareness. Her finger traced down the chapter listings until she found it: *Chapter 7: Obsolete Industrial Compounds and Their Modern Implications.*

The marked page opened to dense paragraphs of chemical formulas and outdated safety warnings, the kind of technical jargon that would have made most people's eyes glaze over but that she absorbed like puzzle pieces clicking into place.

Miles settled beside her properly now, his shoulder pressing against hers as he leaned in to read over her arm. The ceramic fish sat between them. He ate goldfish crackers one at a time, absently, the way he always did when he was worried but didn't want to say so.

"Here." Cressida's finger landed on a paragraph halfway down the page, her voice sharp with discovery—that particular edge that meant she'd found something *important*.

She read aloud, tracing the words: "'Porpheyne—a laboratory synthesis originally developed for textile dye applications—was largely discontinued by 1968 due to toxicity concerns and the development of safer alternatives. When combined with certain organic plant oils the compound causes temporary cyanosis-like discoloration and rapid respiratory distress in predisposed individuals. Symptoms typically manifest within minutes of ingestion and may include dizziness, shortness of breath, and—'" Her frown deepened. "'—slate-gray discoloration around the mouth and extremities, particularly the fin gertips.'"

She looked up, meeting Miles's gaze.

"Slate-gray. Not purple."

Miles had gone very still beside her, his hand frozen halfway to the fish jar. He worked through the logic the way he always did—methodically, carefully, following each thread to its conclusion before moving to the next.

"So either Henrietta's symptoms don't match porpheyne exposure, or something else was mixed with it."

CHAPTER TWELVE

CRESSIDA TAPPED HER STYLUS against the table, the rhythmic *click-click-click* punctuating the silence that had settled between them like dust motes in the overhead light. She stared at the paragraph about porpheyne, brow furrowed.

"Purple lips." She spoke the words aloud, testing their weight. "Lavender cake. What if it wasn't *just* porpheyne?" Her gaze snapped to Miles. "Certain oils can act as catalysts. What if, chemically— the lavender oil acted as a catalyst? Changed the gray discoloration to purple?"

Miles started typing notes on his phone, his expression thoughtful. "Possible. We'd need the medical examiner's report, though. See what else was in her system."

Cressida nodded, already scribbling fragments into her phone: *lavender = catalyst? check ME report. lavender oil + porpheyne = purple?*

A soft knock interrupted her train of thought. Ms. Elsie reappeared, arms laden with glossy cookbooks—spines barely creased, covers still bearing that showroom sheen. She arranged them beside the reference volumes with a knowing look.

"Thought you might want these too. Henrietta's entire collection. Including the prepub copy of her latest—*The Southern Table Reimagined*." Something sad flickered across her features. "She was supposed to do a book talk here next month. Was going to demonstrate that lavender cake."

The prepub copy was in Cressida's hands immediately. Elegant script against artfully arranged herbs and edible flowers, all soft focus and Instagram-ready. She flipped it open. Glossy food photography that looked more like museum installations than actual cooking: geometric microgreens, dramatic reduction sauces, sculptural desserts that seemed to defy gravity.

In the margins, she found handwritten annotations in neat, precise script—notes about plating, reminders about timing, occasional suggestions for ingredient substitutions. Henrietta's handwriting, presumably, though Cressida had nothing to compare it to.

Miles took an older volume from the stack—*Heritage: A Southern Kitchen Legacy*, published nearly two decades ago—and scanned the index with methodical precision.

"Something's off," Cressida flipped between the glossy pages of Henrietta's latest and a dog-eared volume from fifteen years prior. Her finger traced ingredient lists that should have felt familiar but didn't—recipes from entirely different culinary universes.

"Look at this." She angled the pre-pub copy toward Miles, tapping the page. "Her earlier books were all classic Southern desserts—pound cakes, pecan pies, fruit cobblers. Traditional stuff." The spread before her showed a recipe for "Miso Caramel Tarts with Black Sesame Tuile," staring back with aggressive sophistication. "But this new one? Miso caramel tarts. Lavender-black pepper shortbread. Cardamom-rose panna cotta with beetroot reduction."

She looked up. "This isn't evolution. This is revolution."

Miles pulled another book from the stack—*Secrets of the Southern Table*, published eight years ago—and opened it beside the new one. The visual comparison made the disconnect impossible to miss.

"You're right." His finger moved between the two books. "Experimental. Almost..." He paused. "Aggressively modern. Like she's trying to prove something to someone who doesn't believe she can do it."

With each turn of the page, her unease sharpened. Cooking show marathons, magazine features, that whole "heritage cooking" empire built on nostalgia and grandmother's wisdom—none of it matched what lay before her.

"And they're all savory-sweet combinations." Her voice took on that edge that meant her detective brain had kicked into high gear. "Things that *sound* sophisticated but..." She stopped on a recipe for olive oil cake with preserved lemon and thyme honey. "These don't even sound like her voice. Henrietta Dodd built her entire brand on 'heritage cooking' and 'grandmother's wisdom.' This is food truck fusion meets James Beard Award pretension."

She shifted in her chair, rolling one shoulder back. Miles was still bent over the comparison, but something in his posture had gone rigid.

"Two completely different chefs wrote these books. The voice, the approach, even the *philosophy* behind the recipes—nothing matches."

She set the prepub copy down. Possibilities raced—ghostwriters, evolving tastes, desperate rebranding attempts to stay relevant in a changing culinary landscape—but none quite fit. None explained the *completeness* of the transformation.

"I don't know what this means." Frustration threaded through her voice. Pieces that should connect but wouldn't lock into place. "But a celebrity chef doesn't just abandon the entire foundation of her career without a reason. Especially not someone like Henrietta, who built an empire on being *authentically Southern*."

Her stylus drummed against the table—*tap-tap-tap*—matching the rhythm of her racing thoughts. "Either Henrietta was trying to reinvent herself and hiding it from her core audience, or someone else was writing these recipes."

The implications sharpened.

"And if someone else had access to her cookbook drafts..."

"Then maybe they had access to more than just recipes," Miles finished quietly.

Miles pulled out his phone. His fingers moved with focused intensity across the screen—public records, business filings, the digital paper trail most people assumed was invisible.

Cressida watched. Her own fingers drummed against the table. The overhead light buzzed. Beyond the study room door, the quiet movements of library patrons, the distant tick of that antique clock.

After a few minutes, Miles went very still.

"What?"

He turned the screen toward her. "Willard Dodd. Three separate articles in regional business journals over the past five years. Irregularities at Blackvale Savings & Loan—missing funds, misallocated accounts, clerical errors that somehow resolved themselves before audits." He scrolled down, highlighting passages. "Every incident attributed to 'simple mistakes' or 'outdated software.' No formal investigations. No charges."

Everything swept under the rug.

The articles filled Cressida's vision—dates, amounts, carefully worded euphemisms her mind cataloged and cross-referenced against everything else they'd learned. "That's a cover-up if I ever heard of one." She leaned closer. "Who reported the irregularities?"

"Anonymous tips, mostly. A few from junior staff who no longer work there—transferred to other branches or left entirely within months of filing reports." Miles pocketed his phone, jaw tight. "If Willard was embezzling—even small amounts over time—Henrietta would've noticed it eventually. She controlled everything in that house, including the finances."

"So either she knew and was protecting him," Cressida said slowly, working through the logic like solving an equation, "or she found out and he needed to silence her." She paused. "Before she destroyed his reputation and career."

Miles leaned back, his expression shifting. "Slow down. We're building a theory, not a conviction. Let's confirm the embezzlement before we crucify the man."

Cressida's jaw tightened. She stood abruptly, gathering her things with decisive movements—phone into purse, cookbooks snapping shut. "Fine. But we need to talk to Willard. And Ayita Craig. If Henrietta's protégé disappeared right after the competition, she might know something. Or seen something."

Miles was already on his feet. "Agreed. Let's start with Willard—he's easier to find." He met her gaze. "But we approach this carefully, Cressi. If he killed his wife, confronting him directly could be dangerous."

"Carefully," Cressida agreed, though the gleam in her eyes suggested her definition of *careful* might differ significantly from his. Adrenaline hummed through her veins, that electric pull of a case coming together. "But we're not letting a potential murderer walk free just because he wears expensive suits."

The overhead lighting cast long shadows across neatly alphabetized shelves. Cressida's mind was already mapping the route to the Dodd residence—down Main, left at the courthouse, up into the hills.

She was halfway to the door when Ms. Elsie's voice called out.

"Oh, before you go—" The librarian's tone carried that particular quality of someone remembering something significant. "That food blogger was in here a few weeks back. The one writing about local cuisine?"

Cressida stopped mid-stride.

The air in the library suddenly felt heavier, as if the temperature had dropped. As if all those watching portraits on the walls had leaned in to listen.

"What food blogger?"

"Jordan Quinn." Ms. Elsie adjusted her reading glasses, peering over the tortoiseshell frames. "Runs that website—*Mountain Flavors*, I think? He was asking all sorts of questions about Henrietta and Willard. Wanted to see old newspaper archives, town records, anything about the Dodd family history."

She paused, something thoughtful crossing her features as she recalled the encounter.

"Said he really takes his research seriously. Even checked out some of Henrietta's older cookbooks for reference."

Miles and Cressida exchanged a look. His eyebrows lifted fractionally; her eyes narrowed with calculation.

"When exactly was this?" Miles took a step closer.

"Three weeks ago, maybe?" Ms. Elsie tilted her head, silver-streaked hair catching the light. "Right around the time competition registration opened." Her tongue made a soft tsk-tsk-tsk against the roof of her mouth as she sorted through memory. "Nice young man. Very thorough. Asked about the Whispering Lilies Society too, and Reverend Carlson's judging history."

"Did he say why?" Cressida moved back toward the desk.

"Said he was planning a feature piece on Blackvale's culinary traditions. Wanted to get the full story." Ms. Elsie's smile turned knowing. The overhead fluorescents hummed. Somewhere deeper in the library, that antique clock continued its steady tick-tick-tick. "You two might want to have a word with him."

Her smile faltered.

"Though if he was digging into Henrietta's past, and she ended up dead three weeks later..."

The silence settled heavy between them.

"Jordan Quinn." Cressida met Miles's gaze—grim determination, no question. "We need to talk to him."

Miles nodded, already pulling out his phone. His thumbs moved across the screen, searching—website, social media, contact information, anything that might lead them to Jordan Quinn before the trail went cold.

"Thank you, Ms. Elsie," Cressida said. "You've been a lifesaver."

"Happy to help, sugar." Ms. Elsie adjusted her glasses, returning her attention to the stack of books waiting to be reshelved. But the worried crease between her brows remained, her fingers lingering on the desk's edge. "Just... be careful. If someone killed Henrietta to keep secrets buried, they won't take kindly to you digging them back up."

"Careful," Cressida echoed. "That's our middle name."

Miles made a soft sound—disagreement or amusement, impossible to tell—but didn't look up from his phone as they made their way toward the exit. Their footsteps echoed through the quiet library.

The clock kept ticking. Marking the hours they had left to solve this before someone else got hurt, before evidence disappeared, before Aunt Sylvia went down for someone else's crime.

CHAPTER
THIRTEEN

THE MINI'S ENGINE HUMMED beneath them, a familiar sound that should have been comforting but felt all wrong—Cressida wedged into the passenger seat, *her* passenger seat, while Miles drove with infuriating competence along the winding mountain road out of Blackvale proper.

She shifted against the leather. Arms crossed tight. Fingers drumming an irritated rhythm against her elbows. The overcast sky pressed down through the windshield, gray with the promise of rain, but she felt only the prickle of displaced autonomy crawling up her spine.

"I can drive my own car." Third time since they'd left the library parking lot, her voice carrying that particular pitch that meant she was approximately two minutes from staging a full rebellion. Being a passenger ranked just below being wrong on her list of personal hells. "I've been driving this car for seven years. I know every quirk, every—"

"Uh-huh." Miles kept his eyes on the road, navigating a hairpin turn with smooth precision that only amplified her annoyance. Hands steady on the wheel, relaxed but attentive. He didn't even glance her direction. "Jordan Quinn. Food blogger. *Mountain Flavors.*" Like he was reading off a grocery list, methodical and focused, completely ignoring her simmering frustration. "If he was digging into Henrietta's background three weeks before she died, that's not coincidence. That's investigation. But why is she dead and not him?"

Arms uncrossed just long enough for an emphatic gesture at the dashboard, at him, at the general injustice of the situation. "I'm *saying*—I can multitask. I can drive *and* think about Jordan Quinn. I do it all the time. It's called being a functional adult."

"You were up until 3 a.m." Miles continued in that same even tone, downshifting smoothly as the road began its climb toward High Glen Estate. Pine trees pressed close on either side like cathedral walls. "You've had—" A pause, finally glancing at her with one eyebrow slightly raised. "approximately four cups of coffee and half a plate of bacon today. When you're running on fumes and adrenaline, you get..." He trailed off diplomatically. Returned his attention to the road.

"Get *what*?"

She knew exactly what he meant. She'd seen her own driving when overtired and over-caffeinated—aggressive lane changes, muttered curses at stop signs, that one time she'd forgotten she was driving and tried to walk away from her parked car with the engine still running.

Miles just shook his head slightly, the corner of his mouth twitching with suppressed amusement. "Enthusiastic."

"That's a diplomatic way of saying reckless."

"I didn't say that."

"You were *thinking* it."

He made a noncommittal sound, his focus shifting back to the investigation as he navigated another curve. "Quinn asking about the Whispering Lilies Society and Reverend Carlson's judging history? That's not a puff piece. He was building a profile."

Cressida exhaled sharply, slumping against the seat. Fine. *Fine*. This was bigger than her wounded pride.

She pulled out her phone, opening her notes app with sharp taps. The screen glowed against her lap.

"Okay." Her voice shifted—investigative now, that mental gear-change perfected over years of detective work. "Jordan Quinn. Food blogger. Digging into Henrietta's past." Memory surfaced sharp and sudden. "I saw him at the competition."

Miles's gaze flicked toward her. She caught the tension in his jaw, the shift in his grip on the wheel. "You did?"

"Right before judging started. He approached Henrietta while she was talking to Mrs. Mitchell." The scene reconstructed itself with methodical precision: Jordan with his camera raised, that practiced smile, angling for the perfect shot. "Asked for a photo. Said something about featuring her on his site."

"Innocent enough," Miles offered, though his tone suggested otherwise.

"Should have been." Her gaze fixed on the passing trees, mind still in that tent. "But her face did a *thing*."

"A thing."

"A *face*." She gestured to illustrate what words couldn't capture. "Her smile flickered—so fast I almost missed it. Her eyes tightened. The corner of her mouth twitched down."

She searched for the precise emotional register. "Annoyance. Or discomfort. Maybe recognition she didn't want to show."

Cressida snapped her fingers, the sound sharp in the small space. "Then her expression smoothed back into that practiced charm she wore for cameras. All gracious Southern hospitality. But for a second? It was gone."

Miles was quiet for a moment. The Mini climbed steadily upward, the road narrowing as they left the valley floor behind, and somewhere overhead a hawk circled lazy spirals against the overcast sky.

"If I was a betting man—" he began slowly.

"And we know you're not." Cressida interrupted with a slight smile, some of her earlier irritation melting into familiar affection. "Your eyebrows give you away every single time."

Miles ignored her completely, though she caught the tiny uptick at the corner of his mouth. "—I'd bet that Henrietta knew him. Knew *of* him, at minimum. And wasn't happy about him being in that crowd."

He paused.

"Question is why."

The pieces were there—scattered across the table like puzzle fragments—but the picture wasn't clear yet. Not quite. "We could ask Mr. Dodd," she suggested. "My hunch? Jordan being a food blogger means he probably got a copy of Henrietta's most recent cookbook. Maybe he noticed the same things we did—the shift in style, the sudden departure from her signature approach."

She trailed off, letting Miles fill in the rest.

"He starts poking around," Miles finished, his jaw tight. "Asking questions. Looking for explanations. And if Henrietta had something to hide—something about those recipes, about where they came from or who actually wrote them—"

"Then Jordan Quinn becomes a problem." The words came quiet. "A threat. Someone who could expose whatever she was trying to keep buried."

She frowned.

"But as you said, why isn't he the one in the morgue?"

They rounded another bend and suddenly the trees fell away. High Glen Estate sprawled across the hillside like something from a Gothic novel—three stories of weathered brick and white columns, its windows catching the afternoon sun and throwing it back in fractured brilliance. Formal gardens terraced down the slope in geometric precision, boxwood hedges and roses and that immaculate lawn maintained with obsessive care.

The Mini's tires crunched against gravel. Cressida's investigator brain clicked into gear—cataloging, assessing, preparing.

Miles put the car in park. She glanced at him, equal parts determined and giddy. Despite the stakes—despite everything—she was *excited.* Investigating with her partner again. Solving puzzles that mattered.

Even if the cost might be higher than she'd ever wanted.

"Ready?" Miles asked.

Cressida reached for the door handle. "Let's go talk to the grieving widower."

The smell hit Cressida first—cut grass and roses, that particular perfume of wealth and careful maintenance. Grief always had a scent, she thought, and here it was botanical, ordered, relentlessly cultivated.

The young woman who answered couldn't have been more than twenty-two. Auburn hair pulled into a severe bun. Crisp black uniform, white apron, sensible shoes. But her eyes—red-rimmed, swollen. The kind of crying that came in waves throughout the day.

"May I help you?" Her voice was hoarse. Fingers twisted in her apron—uncertainty about protocol when the lady of the house was dead and the world had tilted sideways.

Miles stepped forward, hands visible. Making himself smaller, less imposing. "Good afternoon. I'm Miles Stone, and this is Cressida Vale. We're very sorry for your loss." A pause. "We were hoping to speak with Mr. Dodd, if he's available. We understand this is a difficult time."

The maid hesitated, her gaze moving between them. Cressida softened her expression, dialing down her usual brightness. Grief required a quieter energy. She let Miles carry the request.

The young woman nodded and stepped back. "He's in the garden." Her voice caught. "Follow me, please."

The foyer was everything Cressida expected and nothing she was prepared for emotionally. Marble floors. A chandelier that probably cost more than her car. Walls papered in silk damask the color of old money. A grand staircase curved upward, its bannister polished to mirror brightness.

And everywhere—*everywhere*—flowers. Arrangements in crystal vases, bouquets propped against walls, sympathy cards tucked among white lilies and roses that filled the air with funeral sweetness.

The portraits made Cressida slow her steps.

The hallway stretched long and dim, lined on both sides with family photographs in ornate frames. Henrietta at various stages of her life, always perfectly coiffed, always commanding attention. Accepting awards. With politicians and minor celebrities. Cutting ribbons at grand openings.

And in the background of many shots, barely visible, stood Willard—smaller somehow, perpetually positioned just outside the spotlight's reach.

The maid led them deeper into the house, her shoes soft against hardwood that had probably been here since the estate was built a century ago. They passed a sitting room—folders spread across an antique desk, tissues wadded in a wastebasket, the ghost of perfume lingering like memory itself.

Then: french doors. Glass panes offering a view of terraced gardens cascading down the hillside. The maid pushed them open and stepped aside with a small gesture that said *there.*

"Mr. Dodd is among the roses," she murmured. Her voice trembled. Her eyes filled fresh with tears before she turned quickly away, retreating back into the shadowed house.

The garden was immaculate in that way that spoke of obsessive care. Boxwood hedges formed perfect squares around flower beds bursting with late-season blooms—peonies and irises, ornamental grasses gone golden. A stone path wound between them.

At its far end, where the roses grew in careful rows, they found him.

Willard Dodd moved like an automaton. His pruning shears opened and closed with mechanical precision. *Snip. Snip. Snip.* Each deadheaded bloom fell into a wicker basket at his feet, the pile growing steadily as he moved from plant to plant without pause, without seeming to register the world beyond this small circle of botanical order.

He wore the same kind of outfit Cressida had seen him in at the competition—pressed khakis, a cardigan despite the warmth, wire-rimmed spectacles catching the sun.

His thinning hair was combed neatly. His wedding ring glinted gold against soil-stained fingers. Everything about him suggested a man going through motions because motions were all that remained.

Cressida hung back, letting Miles take the lead. Gentleness. Patience. Qualities Miles possessed naturally and she had to work for.

She clasped her hands. Forced stillness into her body. Her mind raced anyway.

Miles approached slowly, gravel crunching under his feet. No surprise. No ambush. Just respectful presence. "Mr. Dodd?"

The pruning shears paused mid-snip.

Willard turned, blinking as though surfacing from deep water. His gaze unfocused for a long moment before settling on them. Recognition. Or resignation. "Yes?"

"I'm Miles Stone, and this is Cressida Vale." Miles gestured toward her, voice low and steady. "We're so very sorry for your loss. Henrietta was... she was a remarkable woman. Her presence in this community won't soon be forgotten."

Something flickered across Willard's face—grief, certainly, but underneath it something else Cressida couldn't quite name. He set the pruning shears in his basket. Wiped his hands on a small towel tucked into his belt. Removed his spectacles and cleaned them with the same methodical attention he'd given the roses.

"Thank you," he said quietly, replacing the glasses. His watery eyes held exhaustion and something that looked almost like relief. "Forgive me, I'm...I find the garden helps. Gives the hands something to do when the mind won't settle."

Cressida stepped forward. "We understand completely. And we apologize for intruding during such a painful time. We were hoping...if you felt up to it...we might ask a few questions. About Henrietta. About who she was, and..." She let the sentence trail off, leaving space for him to fill.

Willard's gaze shifted to her. Recognition dawned. "You're here about her death."

Not a question. A statement of fact delivered without inflection.

"We're trying to understand what happened," Miles said. "The circumstances were unusual. And we know Henrietta had...a presence in Blackvale. A history. People who admired her. People who perhaps didn't."

A ghost of something—amusement? bitterness?—touched Willard's mouth before fading back into grief's mask. "Henrietta made an impression wherever she went. Not always a favorable one, but always memorable."

He gestured toward a wrought-iron bench nearby, shaded by a climbing rose trellis heavy with blooms. "Would you like to sit?"

They settled onto the bench—Miles and Cressida on one side, Willard perched on the edge as though ready to flee back to his roses at any moment.

The afternoon sun peeked through scattered clouds, dappling everything in patterns of light and shadow.

Somewhere a mourning dove called its lonely three-note song.

"What was she like?" Cressida leaned forward, voice soft. Even villains—especially villains—were whole people, complex and contradictory and worthy of understanding. "Not the public persona. The person you knew."

Willard's gaze traveled somewhere distant. When he spoke, his voice carried decades. "Driven. Brilliant. Uncompromising." He paused. "She knew what she wanted and went after it with everything she had. No halfway with Henrietta. No second place."

"That must have been..." Miles trailed off.

"Difficult?" A wry twist touched Willard's mouth. "At times. But I understood who I married. She never pretended to be anything else." He cleared his throat. "I managed the practical matters—staff, estate, logistics. She managed everything else. It worked."

The careful neutrality. The practiced justification. A marriage described in terms of function rather than feeling. Cressida filed it away. "Did she have enemies? People who might have wished her harm?"

His hands tightened on his knees before relaxing. "Enemies is strong. Henrietta had...rivals. Competitors who resented her success. Susan Mitchell, for one—at odds over festival politics for years. Susan wanted changes to judging, more community involvement. Henrietta thought it would dilute standards." He shook his head. "There was a food blogger, too. Young man named Jordan Quinn. Coming around, asking questions, wanting to feature her on his website. Henrietta found it intrusive. Said he asked too much about her recipes, her process. Proprietary information."

Cressida's pulse quickened. Her expression stayed neutral. "Jordan Quinn. Did she seem worried about him? Or just annoyed?"

"Both, perhaps." Willard removed his glasses, held them to the light as though inspecting for smudges only he could see. "She mentioned him several times in the weeks before...before. Said he was persistent. Pushy. Didn't understand boundaries." The spectacles slid back into place. "There were the usual competitors, too. People who envied her wins, her reputation. Baking turns pride into something combustible."

Miles leaned back, posture open. "We understand there was tension between Henrietta and Sylvia Vale as well."

The air shifted.

Subtle but definite. A temperature drop Cressida felt in her bones. Willard's gaze cut to her—sharp and assessing despite the grief clouding everything else. His voice quieter when he spoke. More careful. "Everyone knew about their... disagreements. Years of competition. Philosophical differences about baking, about tradition versus innovation. Public knowledge. Painful to watch at times."

He paused. Cressida braced herself.

"Your aunt left the tent in quite a state after the judging, Miss Vale." His voice was careful. Measured. "I saw her go. Everyone did. The look on her face when Henrietta won..."

He trailed off. Gathered resolve.

"But I wouldn't dare think Sylvia capable of murder. Anger, yes. Humiliation, certainly. But taking a life?" A pause. "That's a different thing entirely. A different kind of person."

The words should have comforted. A vote of confidence from the victim's own husband. But the way he said it—the careful construction, the slight emphasis on *wouldn't dare think* rather than *don't believe*—left room for doubt. For possibility. For the terrible space between what people said and what they meant.

Cressida held his gaze. Steady voice despite the defensive fire rising in her chest. "Aunt Sylvia is many things, Mr. Dodd. Passionate. Proud. Stubborn as the day is long. But she's not a killer."

"Of course not." Too quick. His agreement came too quick. "I'm sure the authorities will sort everything out properly. Justice will be served, I've no doubt."

It was the certainty in his voice that unsettled her the most.

CHAPTER
FOURTEEN

THE GARDEN FELT SUDDENLY smaller, the hedges
pressing in despite the manicured sprawl. Cressida shifted her weight, feeling the restlessness
building in her chest—that familiar itch when
pieces didn't quite fit and politeness stood between her and answers. She clasped her hands
tighter, then released them, fingers drumming
once against her thigh before she caught herself.

"Mr. Dodd." Her voice gentle, with steel underneath. "I couldn't help but notice something
at the competition. You weren't there when
Henrietta collapsed."

Willard's gaze flickered to her. Something
cautious slid behind his glasses.

"You came back afterward with a pharmacy
bag. I saw you at the edge of the crowd, holding

it." She let the observation hang. Not quite an accusation. Not quite innocent curiosity. "Where were you when your wife collapsed?"

Miles shot her a look—*careful*. But didn't interrupt.

Willard's hands twitched. Fingers curling and uncurling as though searching for the pruning shears he'd set aside.

"I..." He blinked. Confusion crossed his features like clouds over sun. "I was at the pharmacy. I'd forgotten—" He stopped, forehead creasing. "Henrietta's allergy medicine. She mentioned it that morning and I...I volunteered to go pick it up."

The word *volunteered* landed with peculiar weight.

Her mind flashed back to the tent before the competition—Henrietta's voice sharp as cut glass, the talking-down she'd given Willard, the way she'd *ordered* him to fetch it like a trained dog.

Volunteered. Right.

"Unfortunately," Willard continued, voice thin, "that meant I missed the competition entirely. I was at Blackvale Pharmacy when..." His voice cracked. He cleared his throat hard. "When it happened."

She said nothing.

The silence screamed.

A convenient alibi—sent away before the poisoning, returning after the damage was done.

If he'd already planted something in her cake or her water, leaving the scene would be brilliant. Calculated.

Miles's attention sharpened beside her. The shift in his posture meant he'd caught the same thread. But instead of pulling it, he pivoted—smooth as silk, redirecting before the moment could crack open entirely.

"Mr. Dodd," Miles said, his tone shifting to something warmer, more conversational, "I understand you work at Blackvale Savings and Loan. Assistant branch manager, correct?"

Willard seemed almost grateful for the change of subject, straightening slightly. "Yes. Twenty-eight years now."

"That's impressive dedication." Miles leaned forward, elbows on his knees, the picture of casual interest. "I imagine you handled a lot of the financial matters for Henrietta as well—her business ventures, that sort of thing?"

"I did." Willard's voice steadied fractionally. "Henrietta was brilliant with recipes and presentation, but numbers weren't her forte. I managed the accounts, the taxes, the investments."

"Were there any troubles recently?" Miles asked carefully. "Financial difficulties? Business disputes that might have caused stress?"

The question was gentle, almost offhand, but Cressida saw the way it hit. Willard's composure simply *crumbled*. He pressed one hand to his face, fingers splayed across his forehead, and his shoulders began to shake.

"I don't—" His voice broke completely, dissolved into something raw and animal. "I don't know how I'm going to go on without her."

The sobs came hard and sudden, racking through him like a storm breaking. They filled the garden, spilling over the roses and the boxwood hedges, and Cressida felt the uncomfortable weight of witnessing something private, something too real for the careful choreography of their investigation.

Something in Cressida's gut twisted, sharp and sudden—like an internal alarm she didn't yet know how to interpret.

She caught Miles's eye, held it, and gave him a pointed look—one eyebrow raised, gaze cutting deliberately toward Willard, then back. *Do something.*

Miles shook his head fractionally, a silent *no* that said he was no better equipped for this than she was.

Cressida practically shoved him forward with the force of her glare, gesturing again with more insistence. *You're the empathy expert. Handle it.*

Miles sighed—barely audible—and shifted closer to Willard, one hand resting gently on the man's shoulder. "I'm so sorry," he murmured. "Take all the time you need."

Cressida rose. "I'm going to find the ladies' room." Already stepping back from the bench. "Take your time."

She left them there—Miles murmuring comfort, Willard's sobs subsiding into ragged breathing—and slipped through the French doors into High Glen Estate's cool interior.

The house was silent. Distant sounds of the maid upstairs. Cressida moved quickly through hallways lined with oil paintings and antique furniture.

She found the kitchen.

Massive. A chef's dream: granite counter-tops stretching in pristine expanse, commercial-grade appliances gleaming like surgical instruments, a pantry that looked more like a small grocery store than home storage.

Cressida pulled out her phone. *Click.* Immaculate counters, not a crumb out of place. *Click.* Six-burner Wolf range, double ovens, Sub-Zero refrigerator. *Click.* The pantry with its labeled glass jars in perfect alphabetical order.

Precise. Controlled. Exactly as Henrietta would have demanded.

Her gaze swept the counter. A recipe card. A bottle out of place. Evidence of competition prep. Her fingers itched to open drawers, search cabinets. She forced herself to stick to what was visible—what could be explained as idle curiosity if someone walked in.

On the far counter, near the window over-looking the garden: a collection of prescription bottles lined up like soldiers.

She leaned closer, zooming in with her phone camera.

Henrietta Dodd. Fexofenadine. Take one tablet daily for allergies.

Dated three months ago.

The bottle was nearly full.

So why had Willard rushed out to refill it the morning of the competition?

The kitchen felt suddenly oppressive. Too perfect. Too controlled.

Too much like a stage set for something terrible.

She moved to the fridge and it opened with a sigh. Cressida pulled it wider, phone already raised, camera app open.

Click.

The interior was... ordinary. Shockingly, mundanely ordinary.

No towering cakes wrapped in plastic. No elaborate confections waiting to be pho-tographed for the next cookbook spread. In-stead: milk, eggs, withered lettuce, condiments lined up like tired soldiers, and what looked like leftover takeout in mismatched Tupperware.

Cressida zoomed in on a sad-looking con-tainer of congealed orange sauce. *This* was what a celebrity chef kept in her fridge? This was the woman who'd just published her fifth cookbook, who'd built an empire on the promise of home-made perfection?

She lined up another shot.

A voice cut through the kitchen's silence like a hot knife through cold buttercream.

"Can I help you with something, Miss?"

Her heart kicked against her ribs. She spun, phone still clutched in one hand, the refrigerator door hanging open behind her like evidence of guilt.

Another maid stood in the door-way—mid-thirties maybe, with warm brown skin and dark hair pulled back in a neat bun. She wore a simple gray dress and an apron, hands folded at her waist, expression caught somewhere between polite inquiry and suspicion.

Her brain scrambled for purchase, then found it. She let her face bloom into a bright, slightly sheepish smile—the kind that said *caught me* without admitting to anything serious. "Oh my goodness, I'm so sorry." She gestured vaguely toward the open fridge, laughing softly. "This is going to sound ridiculous, but I've always wondered what a professional baker kept in her fridge. I imagined it chock-full of desserts and elaborate confections, you know? Like opening a treasure chest."

Laying it on too thick, but sometimes saccharine disarmed faster than logic.

The maid studied her for a long moment—taking in the 1940s style blouse, the phone with its ridiculous pink glitter case, the earnest curiosity that she'd learned to weaponize over years of investigative work.

Slowly, her posture softened. The wariness bled out.

"You're Ms. Sylvia's niece," she said, not quite a question.

"Great-niece, technically." She closed the fridge gently, as though that might erase the last thirty seconds. "Cressida Vale."

"Summer Patton." The woman's smile was small but genuine now, warming at the edges. "My family goes to church with Ms. Sylvia. She always makes the best meatloaf for the potlucks—brings it in this big glass dish with the flowers on the side. Nobody could touch hers."

Cressida felt something loosen in her chest. *Of course* Aunt Sylvia's meatloaf had a reputation. *Of course* it did.

"She still makes it," Cressida said warmly. "I had some the other night. Nearly cried into my plate."

Summer laughed—soft and brief, but real. "Sounds about right." She moved further into the kitchen, her demeanor shifting from suspicious to something closer to conspiratorial. "I've only been working for the Dodds a few months. Started right when Mrs. Dodd was writing her new cookbook."

"That must have been exciting. Being here while she worked on it."

Summer glanced toward the hallway, as though checking for eavesdroppers, then leaned in slightly. Her voice dropped, not quite a whisper but close. "Hand on Bible, Miss Vale—I never saw Mrs. Dodd in this kitchen the entire time I worked here."

She blinked. Then frowned. "What do you mean?"

"I mean she didn't cook here. Not once." Summer's tone was matter-of-fact, no judgment, just observation. "Mr. Dodd would come in sometimes. He'd wait until Mrs. Dodd went to sleep, then tell me I could finish for the night. Said he'd take care of things."

Cressida's fingers itched to pull out her phone again, to take notes, to record this, but she forced herself to stay still, to listen like this was just polite conversation. "That does sound odd."

"I'd hear him in here late at night," Summer continued, her expression faintly annoyed at the memory. "Moving things around, running water. I was irritated, honestly. Knew I'd have to clean up whatever mess he made the next morning."

"And did you?" Cressida asked carefully. "Have to clean up?"

Summer shook her head slowly, confusion flickering across her face. "That's the thing. When I'd come in the next day, the whole place was spotless. Cleaner than I'd left it."

"Do you know what he made?"

"No clue. Probably stuff he knew she wouldn't approve of him eating. She was like that." Summer's voice was quiet now, thoughtful. "But I'd ought to start packing, I suppose. Right before you and the sheriff's son came, Mr. Dodd told me my services were no longer needed."

Fired? Right after his wife died. Interesting.

Before Cressida could respond, footsteps echoed from the hallway—two sets, one heavier than the other. Miles appeared first, followed by Willard Dodd, whose face had gone stone-cold, all traces of grief wiped clean.

Willard's gaze swept the kitchen—Summer standing near the counter, Cressida by the refrigerator—and his jaw tightened. "What's going on here?"

Summer opened her mouth, hesitated, glanced at Cressida with something like panic.

Cressida stepped forward smoothly, smile bright and apologetic. "My fault entirely, Mr. Dodd. I got turned around coming back from powdering my nose. Summer was kind enough to help me find my way."

Willard's eyes—cold, flat, nothing like the grieving widower from the garden—locked onto hers. The temperature in the room seemed to drop ten degrees.

"I think," he said, "it's time you both left. I have arrangements to take care of concerning my late wife."

It wasn't a suggestion.

Miles moved toward Cressida, his hand brushing her elbow—a silent *don't push it*. She nodded once, still smiling, still playing the role of apologetic visitor.

"Of course," she said gently. "We're so sorry for your loss, Mr. Dodd. Thank you for your time."

Willard didn't respond. He simply stood there, arms crossed, watching them with the kind of stillness that felt like a threat.

Cressida and Miles moved toward the hallway, Summer stepping aside to let them pass. As they reached the doorway, Cressida glanced back once—catching Summer's eye, offering a small, reassuring nod.

Then they were out, moving through the shadowed halls of High Glen Estate, the weight of Willard Dodd's gaze pressing against their backs until they finally stepped out into the golden afternoon light.

The door closed behind them with a soft, final click.

Cressida exhaled slowly, her hands shaking just slightly as she pulled out her phone. Miles was already beside her, his voice low and urgent.

"What did she tell you?"

"Everything," she said quietly. "She told me everything."

CHAPTER FIFTEEN

THE MINI COOPER'S ENGINE ticked as it cooled. Miles had parallel-parked with precision—front tire kissing the curb, rear end tucked behind a faded blue pickup. The parking meter's red EXPIRED flag jutted between them and Main Street.

Cressida stepped onto the sidewalk and took a deep breath. The air carried fried dough and caramelized sugar, too cheerful for what they'd left behind at High Glen Estate.

Beyond the parked cars, the Midsummer Feast and Fair sprawled across the fairgrounds. Brightly colored tents fluttered. The Ferris wheel turned lazy circles. Children shrieked near the ring toss booth. A brass band played something jaunty and off-key from the gazebo.

Hands on her hips, Cressida stared. Something between disbelief and bitter amusement pulled at her mouth.

Of course they're still going. Someone died yesterday, and here we are—cotton candy and all.

It was so perfectly, absurdly Blackvale that she almost laughed.

Miles locked the car with a soft *beep* and came to stand beside her. He followed her gaze toward the fairgrounds, taking in the cheerful chaos with his usual quiet assessment.

"What are you thinking?"

The breeze tugged at her collar. "The show must go on, apparently—even when someone's just been murdered at it."

Miles exhaled through his nose—not quite a laugh, but close. "That's small towns for you." He gestured toward the fair. "Tragedy gets compartmentalized so life can continue. People need normal. Otherwise, everything falls apart."

"Or," Cressida said, turning to face him, "they're all just really good at pretending nothing happened."

"Maybe both," Miles conceded.

They started walking. Their footsteps found an easy rhythm along Main Street's cracked sidewalk—patched in places, lined with lampposts trailing last week's event banners. A few tourists peered into shop windows, clutching paper bags from the bakery.

Cressida turned over the pieces they'd collected. "Henrietta wasn't the genius behind the latest cookbook. If what Summer said was true."

Miles glanced at her, one eyebrow lifting. "You're thinking the protégé? Ayita?"

"It's obvious." Cressida's hands moved as she spoke, painting invisible diagrams. "Henrietta didn't cook in her own kitchen. Summer never saw her touch a spatula. But Ayita? What if she's the one with the skills, the talent, the *work*—and what if she wasn't happy about Henrietta taking all the credit?"

Miles went quiet. Thoughtful. Then he shook his head. "She's just a kid, Cressida."

Cressida stopped. She turned to face him fully, tilting her head back to meet his eyes—tall, steady, impossibly patient Miles—and gave him a look that was equal parts affection and exasperation.

So tall. So naive.

"Kids," she said slowly, "can be just as dangerous as adults. Sometimes more so, because they don't know how to hide it yet."

Miles opened his mouth to respond—

"Hot on the trail of a suspect?"

The voice came from behind them, warm and teasing, with a lilt that suggested the speaker was smiling even before they turned around.

Cressida spun, her heart doing a quick, startled jump in her chest.

Standing on the sidewalk behind them, arms crossed loosely over a flowing linen blouse, was Dr. Maeve "Mae" Stone.

Miles's mom.

Or, as Cressida had privately called her since childhood: *Big Red.*

Mae's copper curls blazed in the afternoon sun, framing a freckled face full of laugh lines. Her blue eyes—faded denim, sharp as glass—flicked between them with the kind of knowing warmth that made you feel both seen and slightly guilty.

She smelled of sugared tangelo and something freshly baked.

"Hi, Mom," Miles said.

Mae's smile widened. "Hi yourself, honey." She turned to Cressida, expression softening. "Cressida Vale. Look at you, all grown up and stirring up trouble just like when you were six."

Cressida grinned. She'd missed Big Red. "Hi, Dr. Stone."

"Mae, darling. We've been over this." Mae stepped closer, her long skirt flaring, and squeezed Cressida's hand briefly. Warm. Grounding. "Now, what's this I hear about you two poking around Henrietta Dodd's estate?"

Miles's jaw tightened. "Word travels fast."

"Always does in Blackvale." Her tone was gentle, but her eyes were sharp—therapist sharp, the kind that saw through deflection. "So? What did you find?"

"Mom, what are you doing here? Shouldn't you be at work?"

Mae adjusted the basket on her arm—wicker, lined with checkered cloth. The scent of blueberries and brown sugar wafted out. "I'm bringing your father some muffins—," she said, as if delivering baked goods during a murder investigation was perfectly normal.

She turned to Cressida, warmth sharpening into steel. "And to demand he let Sylvia go. My money's on Susan Mitchell. Her or Reverend Carlson."

Cressida's eyebrows shot up.

"You're the third person to mention Reverend Carlson," Cressida said slowly.

Mae's smile turned knowing, the kind that said *exactly*. "Well, there you go." She shifted the basket to her other arm. "Now, you two promise me when this is over, you'll come for dinner. Proper dinner, not just pizza and ice cream."

Miles opened his mouth to respond, but Mae was already moving, her skirt swishing as she stepped toward the crosswalk. She paused, glancing back over her shoulder. "If you need me, I'll be at the station until your father comes to his senses. I'll make sure your aunt gets home, sugarplum."

She started across the street, basket swinging at her side, her copper curls catching the afternoon light like wildfire.

"Thanks, Bi—uh—Mae!" Cressida called after her.

Mae stopped mid-stride, turning back with a grin that said she'd heard the slip and found it endearing. "Oh, and if you're looking for Ayita?" She pointed vaguely east. "She's at her father's butcher shop on Maple Street. Right next to the hardware store. Poor girl works harder than anyone I know."

Miles lifted a hand in acknowledgment. "Thanks, Mom."

Mae nodded once, then disappeared into the sheriff's office, the glass door swinging shut behind her.

Cressida watched her go, a small smile tugging at the corner of her mouth. Then she turned to Miles, one eyebrow raised. "Big Red always was a force of nature."

Miles exhaled through his nose—half laugh, half resignation. "She just deputized herself again."

Through the glass, Mae's silhouette was visible, already deep in conversation with someone inside. *Probably already working her magic*, Cressida thought. *Getting Aunt Sylvia released before Sheriff Stone even realizes he's been outmaneuvered.*

"So." She turned back to Miles. "Maple Street. Butcher shop. Ready to meet the protégé?"

His jaw set in that quiet, determined way he had when a plan was forming. "Let's go."

The bell above the door chimed—brass, old, the kind that announced every customer with cheerful authority—as Cressida and Miles stepped into Craig's Butcher Shop.

The smell hit first. Not unpleasant, but *specific*: sawdust and cold meat, the sharp metallic tang of blood scrubbed away daily, the kind of clean that came from industrial refrigeration and relentless hygiene. The air was cool, almost uncomfortably so, and carried with it the faint mineral scent of ice machines working overtime.

The shop was small but immaculate. White tile gleamed under fluorescent lights. Along the left wall, a glass counter displayed cuts of beef, pork, and chicken arranged with the precision of someone who cared. Behind it, stainless steel hooks hung from overhead rails—empty now, but stained with memory. A chalkboard menu on the back wall listed daily specials in neat, looping handwriting: *Bone-In Ribeye - $18/lb. Ground Chuck - $6/lb. Fresh Sausage Links - Thursday Only.*

Behind the counter stood Ayita Craig, arranging cuts of beef with methodical precision.

She looked up as the bell chimed. Her hands paused mid-motion over a tray of marbled steaks. Professional courtesy shifted to wary recognition in a heartbeat.

Young—maybe twenty-two, though exhaustion aged her. Short and wiry, all sharp angles and restless energy, like someone wound too tight for too long. Her dark hair was cut in a choppy bob with turquoise streaks. Nose ring. Eyebrow piercing. Multiple studs climbing her left ear. A small crescent moon tattoo peeked from behind her right ear.

A stained white apron over black skinny jeans and a faded band t-shirt. Worn sneakers, scuffed at the toes. Her hands were red from the cold—raw-looking, chapped. Something dark (blood? grease?) smudged her left forearm.

"Help you?" Clipped. Cautious. Not rude, exactly, but not welcoming either.

Miles stepped forward, mouth opening to introduce them.

Cressida touched his arm—just a light press against his sleeve—and moved ahead.

The hurt was visible in Ayita's posture. Barely contained beneath professional courtesy. The way her hands had stilled over the beef, fingers tense, bracing.

This needs a softer touch. Not police questions. Not even unofficial ones.

Cressida let her expression soften, her smile warm but not intrusive. She gestured vaguely around the shop. "This place is *gorgeous*. I mean it. You don't see shops like this anymore—everything's so corporate now. But this? This feels *real*."

Ayita blinked. The wariness flickered. "Oh. Uh. Thanks." Her hands relaxed incrementally. "My dad's been running it for thirty years. He's... big on keeping things traditional."

"Thirty years." Cressida leaned slightly against the counter, careful not to invade Ayita's space. "That's impressive. I bet you've been helping out since you were a kid, huh?"

Ayita's expression shifted—softening, just a fraction. "Since I could reach the counter." Her voice lost some of its edge. "Started wrapping packages when I was, like, eight. Dad taught me how to cut meat when I was twelve." She glanced down at the steaks in front of her, her mouth twitching into something that might have been a smile. "He used to say if I was gonna work here, I had to know the whole process. No shortcuts."

"Smart man," Cressida said. "And clearly you learned well. These cuts look *perfect*."

Ayita's shoulders dropped another inch. She set the tray down and wiped her hands on her apron, leaving faint red streaks on the white fabric. "Yeah, well. He's a perfectionist. Comes with the territory, I guess."

Cressida let the silence settle for a beat. Then she tilted her head slightly. "So you've been doing this your whole life. That must've been... a lot, growing up."

A shrug. Ayita looked down at the counter. "It's not so bad. Keeps me busy." Her voice was quieter now. "Dad's good at what he does. And people here... they know quality when they see it."

"I bet." Cressida paused, then added, almost offhandedly, "I heard you're pretty talented yourself. With baking."

Ayita's head snapped up. Her eyes narrowed just slightly. The wariness was back—sharper, more personal. "Who told you that?"

Cressida kept her tone light, conversational. "Word gets around. Small town, you know how it is."

"Yeah." Ayita crossed her arms over her chest, fingers digging into her elbows. "I know exactly how it is."

Cressida glanced at the meat display, then let her voice soften. "I'm sorry about Henrietta. Losing a mentor—that's never easy."

Ayita's face shuttered. Her arms tightened across her chest like a shield. "*Mentor.*" The word came out bitter, sharp enough to draw blood. She exhaled hard through her nose, gaze drifting past Cressida. "Yeah. Sure. That's one word for it."

Cressida waited. Patient. Open but not pressing. Miles hovered near the door—a concerned shadow giving the girl space.

The fluorescent lights hummed. Sawdust and meat pressed in from all sides. Ayita's fingers dug deeper into her elbows, knuckles pale. Her jaw trembled once before she forced it still.

Then it spilled out.

"I wrote every single recipe in her latest cookbook." Low. Trembling with fury. "Every. Single. One."

Cressida's eyebrows lifted. Her mouth twitched. The vindication radiated off her like heat—*I knew it. Called it.*

Behind her, Miles cleared his throat. *Cressi. Your face.*

She softened her features, leaned in incrementally. Listening. Not gloating. Not mentally high-fiving herself. Just present. Compassionate.

Professional, she reminded herself. *This is a real person's pain, not a puzzle piece.*

Ayita met her gaze, raw anger bleeding through exhaustion. "I worked with her for two years. *Two years.* Learning techniques, sharing my own stuff—modern twists on Southern classics, fusion approaches that honored tradition while pushing boundaries." Her voice cracked. She pressed on, words tumbling faster. "She was so *effusive* about it. Told me I was talented, told me I had a future, promised me co-authorship, promised exposure, promised a way out of Blackvale and butcher paper and this—" She gestured sharply at the shop, hand shaking. "She even drew up a contract. I still have the signed copy."

Cressida sighed softly and nodded. She knew where this was heading.

"But when the prepub of *The Southern Table Reimagined* was delivered," Ayita continued, her voice cracking again, "my name appeared exactly *once*. A single line in the afterword thanking me for 'invaluable assistance during the recipe testing phase.'" She laughed, but it was hollow, brittle. "Like I was some... some unpaid intern who fetched ingredients."

Her eyes were bright now, not quite tears but close. She blinked hard, her jaw tightening. "I remember opening the box. Seeing the cover. My heart was pounding. I thought—finally. Proof that I'm more than just the butcher's daughter who smells like meat and never got out." She swallowed hard. "And then I flipped through it. Page after page. My recipes. My ideas. My *work*—all with her name in bold print at the top."

Cressida's nails dug into her palms. The hope. The betrayal. The crushing weight—all of it written in every tense line of Ayita's face.

"What did you do?"

"I confronted her." Flat. Final. "Three weeks before the festival. Showed up at High Glen Estate with the contract in hand, demanded answers."

Miles shifted near the door. "Didn't go well?"

Ayita's mouth twisted. "She was cold. Dismissive. Said my contributions were 'developmental' and that the recipes had been 'significantly refined' before publication." Her voice dropped into a mocking imitation—clipped, imperious. "She suggested I should be *grateful* for the mention I received. Said making a fuss would only damage my own reputation."

She paused. Her jaw worked. Cressida watched emotions flicker across her face—anger, hurt, bitterness competing for dominance. Something had cracked in her that day. A fracture that ran deep.

Ayita reached for the tray of steaks. Sharp. Aggressive. She repositioned cuts that didn't need repositioning, fingers pressing into marbled flesh. The metal tray scraped.

A laugh—bitter as burnt sugar. "My reputation. In *Blackvale*." She grabbed another steak, slapped it down. Wet thud. "Like I had anything to lose."

The girl who'd dared to hope. Who'd believed in promises. Who'd trusted someone who saw her as disposable.

"So I decided to prove myself." Steadier now, but still edged with bitterness. "Entered the Golden Spoon competition with a dark chocolate and smoked bacon tart with salted caramel ganache. Took me weeks to perfect every layer, every balance of sweet and savory, every texture." She shook her head. "But I didn't win. Didn't even place. Despite *knowing* my entry was technically superior to half the finalists."

She looked past Cressida. Eyes unfocused. "So yeah. I lost my mentor. And my future. And any shred of proof that I'm worth something beyond this town."

The fluorescent lights buzzed. Refrigeration units hummed. Somewhere in the back, a door creaked.

Cressida held Ayita's gaze, quiet fury in her expression. That must have been the entry Henrietta had recognized. The one that caused her mask to slip for that brief moment.

"That's not fair," she said softly. "None of that is fair."

Ayita's shoulders sagged. "No," she agreed, barely above a whisper. "It's not."

CHAPTER SIXTEEN

AYITA'S JAW TIGHTENED, THE muscles working beneath her skin like she was chewing on something bitter. Her gaze flicked toward the back of the shop—quick, guilty—before she leaned in.

"Henrietta always had her thumb on the judges. Every year. Every competition."

"What do you mean by that?" Cressida asked, elbows resting on the counter.

Ayita hesitated, fingers curling against the edge of the meat tray. The fluorescent lights hummed overhead like a hive too full of wings. Finally, she spoke, voice barely above a whisper.

"Last summer, I was at High Glen Estate dropping off a test batch of biscuits. Henrietta wanted to see if my buttermilk technique would work for her autumn menu." She paused, expression darkening. "I got there early—she wasn't expecting me yet. I walked into the kitchen, and she was sitting at that big marble island, writing something on cream-colored stationery. Fancy stuff, with her initials embossed at the top."

The sharp spark of recognition—that electric moment when a witness offers up something real, something that *matters*—shot through Cressida's chest. This girl had seen something. Something *concrete*.

She liked Ayita for it—liked her precision, her willingness to speak up despite the risk. Liked that she wasn't hedging or softening the edges.

Let her tell it her way.

"She was muttering to herself," Ayita continued, voice gaining momentum. "I couldn't hear all of it, but I caught bits—'overdue favors' and 'time to collect.' Something like that." A shake of her head. "I didn't think much of it at the time. Figured she was writing a reminder to herself or something."

Her fingers drummed against the counter, a nervous rhythm. "Later that same day, at the Blackvale Summer Social, I saw her again. I was working the buffet table—Dad's catering business does events all over town. Henrietta was at the reception, holding court like she always did." Her mouth twisted. "And then I saw her slip that same folded note to Reverend Carlson during the dessert course."

Cressida's eyebrows lifted. "The reverend?"

"Yeah." Ayita nodded, expression tight. "She handed it to him like it was nothing—just a casual exchange. But I watched him read it." Her voice dropped. "He went *pale*. Like someone had opened a vein. Then he nodded, all stiff and formal, and walked away without saying a word. Didn't even finish his dessert."

Cold air pressed in from the refrigeration units. Sawdust and raw meat thickened in Cressida's throat.

"Two weeks later," Ayita continued, voice barely above a whisper now, "Reverend Carlson was announced as one of the Golden Spoon judges. Everyone was surprised—he'd stepped down after last year, said he was too busy with church duties. But suddenly, there he was. Back on the panel."

The pieces were starting to fit. Cressida straightened from the counter. "Where were you during the competition?"

Ayita's expression didn't change. Gaze steady. "Here. My dad had a catering order for the Whitmore wedding reception—forty pounds of brisket, custom cuts for their barbecue station. I was in the back all morning, breaking down beef and trimming fat." She shrugged, nodding toward the back. "You can ask him. Or check the order forms. I didn't leave until after noon."

The girl met her eyes directly. Unflinching.

"I didn't need to kill her," Ayita said.

Then, without another word, she turned and disappeared into the back room.

"Should we follow her?" Cressida whispered to Miles.

Miles' expression remained deadpan. "Following people who are good with sharp implements into back rooms is generally not advisable."

Fair point. Cressida's mouth twitched—half smile, half exasperation.

The fluorescent lights buzzed. The shop felt suddenly too quiet, as if the walls themselves were holding their breath.

A moment later, Ayita returned. A manila folder clutched in her hand. She placed it on the counter with deliberate care, fingers lingering on the edge for just a second before pulling them back.

"Here," she said.

The folder opened carefully under her fingers. Inside: copies of a contract, signatures at the bottom—Henrietta's elaborate flourish beside Ayita's smaller, neater script.

Beneath that: email correspondence printed and highlighted in yellow. Recipe drafts with timestamps. And a formal complaint filed with Henrietta's Publisher's Ethics Board, complete with case number and filing date.

Four days before the Midsummer Feast.

Breach of contract. Intellectual property theft. Career sabotage. Every accusation backed by evidence—emails, drafts, signed agreements. The faint smell of toner mixed with the shop's ever-present scent of cold meat and sawdust.

Ayita tapped the date stamp. "I'm doing this the right way. Let the board investigate. Let the truth come out through proper channels."

Her chin lifted. "Despite what my dad wants for me, I'm not spending my life behind a butcher's counter." Steady now. Resolute. "I'm a pastry chef. That's who I am."

Steel in that voice—not the brittle, performative anger from earlier, but something forged in the heat of betrayal and tempered by stubborn will. Yet beneath it, something else flickered. Her gaze drifted toward the back room. Her mouth thinned. What exactly did her father know about all of this? What conversations had happened back there, surrounded by hanging carcasses?

This girl—this young woman—had chosen legal recourse over revenge. Had documented her exploitation with the precision of someone who knew the world wouldn't believe her without proof. Had filed a complaint with an ethics board instead of showing up at High Glen Estate with a rolling pin and rage.

Miles stepped forward, extending his hand across the counter. Warmer now. "Thank you for your time, Miss Craig. And good luck with the ethics board."

"Your tart should have placed," Cressida added.

Ayita's expression softened, the hard edges smoothing just enough to reveal something vulnerable beneath. A ghost of a smile flickered across her mouth—brief, barely there, but real. "I know," she said simply.

The words weren't arrogant. Certain. The quiet certainty of someone who'd stopped needing external validation because she'd finally claimed her own.

Miles paused near the door as they turned to leave, glancing back. "We should probably take something. For appearances."

The tension in Cressida's shoulders eased for the first time since they'd walked in. "A roast, please. Whatever you recommend."

Ayita nodded, moving toward the refrigerated case with practiced efficiency. She pulled out a beautiful three-pound chuck roast, inspecting the marbling with the same critical eye Cressida imagined she brought to laminating pastry dough. Brown butcher paper. Folded corners. Tape. Label. Done.

She slid the package across the counter. "That'll be twenty-two fifty."

"Thank you again," Cressida said as Miles paid. And she meant it.

Ayita nodded once, her expression unreadable now, shuttered again. Professional. The mask back in place.

The bell above the door chimed softly as they stepped back out into the afternoon sun of Maple Street.

Miles carried the roast. Cressida carried the weight of new information—cream stationery, a pale face, a folded note.

The air outside was warm, thick with asphalt and honeysuckle. A truck rumbled past, heading toward the highway. Somewhere down the block, a dog barked.

The world continued, oblivious and ordinary, while Cressida's mind spun through the pieces they'd just collected.

She pulled out her phone, the glittery pink case catching the sunlight as she unlocked the screen. Her thumbs flew across the keyboard, typing notes in rapid bursts.

Reverend Carlson — coerced back onto judging panel. Henrietta had leverage. Note exchange at Summer Social. Ayita witnessed. Timeline: summer → competition → death. Connection to other suspects? Check church records? Willard's involvement?

Miles waited patiently beside her, shifting the roast to his other hand. He'd learned that lesson years ago—back when they were kids and she would spend twenty minutes staring at a footprint in the dirt, muttering theories to herself until the answer clicked into place.

She looked up, her dark eyes bright. "We need to talk to the good reverend."

Miles nodded slowly, thoughtful. "Agreed. But carefully." His gaze drifted past her shoulder toward the white spire rising above the oak trees two blocks over, visible through the gap between storefronts. The steeple gleamed in the afternoon sun, its cross casting a long shadow across the valley. "Church politics in a town like this are more dangerous than actual politics."

"I know." She slipped her phone back into her pocket. "But if Henrietta had leverage over one of the judges, and that judge happens to be a pillar of the community..." She trailed off, letting the implication hang in the warm air between them.

Miles shifted the roast to his other hand again, adjusting his grip. "What are you thinking?"

Their steps fell into a steady rhythm as they walked back toward the Mini. "I'm thinking we have a young chef who was systematically exploited, a husband who might have finally snapped, a reverend who owed favors he couldn't refuse, and a victim who collected secrets like other people collect antique spoons."

She glanced back at him over her shoulder, her expression bright with that familiar spark—the one that meant she was three steps ahead and loving every minute of it. "And I'm thinking Blackvale has more skeletons than Aunt Sylvia has skeleton keys."

Miles caught up to her in two long strides. "That's a lot of skeletons."

"Exactly," Cressida said, and there it was again—that gleam in her eyes, unstoppable.

The back door of Vale Inn House swung inward with a familiar creak—a sound Cressida had known since she was six. The hinges needed oil. And had needed oil for twenty years. But Aunt Sylvia called it "character," which meant she couldn't be bothered to fix things that still worked. Today, though, the creak felt louder. As if the house were announcing them.

The kitchen's warmth wrapped around them, though something felt different. Rain whispered against the tall windows above the farmhouse sink. Cinnamon and lemon polish lingered in the air. Copper pots hung from the ceiling rack, their surfaces catching storm-gray light and throwing it back in muted flashes. Thunder rumbled.

Miles moved toward the refrigerator, the butcher paper-wrapped roast cradled in his hands. "I'll put this in the fridge."

"I'll leave a note for Aunt Sylvia and then we can go talk to Reverend—"

"Oh no you won't, Cressida Edythe Vale!"

The voice sliced through the kitchen—sharp, authoritative, exasperated in that particular way reserved for younger siblings caught mid-scheme.

Her hand froze halfway to the notepad. Eyes wide. Breath catching. "Mom?"

Miles snorted. Actually snorted. "Close enough." He slid the roast onto the middle shelf and closed the refrigerator door with a soft click.

Turning slowly, bracing herself, Cressida found her older sister standing in the doorway. Rosalind Vale had her hands planted on her hips, navy blazer perfectly tailored, emphasizing sharp posture. Her chestnut hair was swept into a sleek updo—effortless and expensive, not a strand out of place despite the humid afternoon. Those dark brown eyes—so much like Cressida's own, but cooler—fixed on her with the kind of look that made city council members reconsider their arguments mid-speech.

A draft slipped through the room as Roz stepped fully into the kitchen. Cold. Unexpected. The copper pots swayed on their hooks.

Shadows pooled in corners where storm light couldn't reach, and Vale House—with all its centuries of creaking boards and whispering walls—felt unsettled by her sister's rigid order.

Cressida lifted her chin, trying for defiance but landing somewhere closer to petulant. "You really are starting to sound too close to Mom," she said, crossing her arms. "You should work on that."

Roz's frown deepened. "You're not funny."

"I wasn't trying to be funny." Cressida's eyes narrowed. "Why are you home and not at work, anyway? Doing... whatever it is you do."

"I'm the Executive Administrative Officer at City Hall." Ice crept into Roz's voice. "And I *was* doing that when Mayor Whitfield called about Mr. Dodd's formal complaint. Apparently, two nosy parkers have been harassing the bereaved spouse of a recent murder victim."

A quick glance at Miles—his expression carefully neutral, exit strategies clearly calculating behind those calm eyes. Then back to her sister with an innocent smile that wouldn't fool a toddler, let alone Rosalind Vale. "We weren't harassing anyone. We were offering condolences. Which is what compassionate neighbors do. And Mr. Dodd seemed perfectly willing to talk to us."

"That's not what he told the mayor, who called the city manager, who found *me*. Now I'm here to make sure my baby sister doesn't turn a tragic death into a public relations nightmare for the entire town."

Her hands dropped to her sides. "Well, did anyone deign to mention that Sheriff Dad took Aunt Sylvia to *jail* this morning?"

Miles leaned back against the counter, arms crossed, watching the sisters with resigned patience—someone who'd witnessed this particular dynamic play out a hundred times before. "My dad took her in for questioning. And my mom was there with muffins to break her out of jail within hours."

"They're on their way back here even as we speak." Finality settled into Roz's tone like a gavel strike. "So you are *not* going anywhere."

"But Roz—"

"Not until tomorrow." Her sister's voice cut clean through the protest. "Tonight, we're having a family dinner to discuss this in an *orderly* fashion." She turned to Miles. "That trim in the Blue Room isn't going to paint itself."

Miles straightened. "Yes, ma'am."

Cressida's head whipped toward him, her eyes wide with betrayal. *Seriously?*

Roz's gaze swung back to her sister. "Cressida, Mr. and Mrs. Horne just checked out of the Riverside Room. And Aunt Sylvia has another couple checking in tomorrow—we'll work on getting that room ready."

Cressida opened her mouth to protest, the words forming on her tongue—half argument, half plea—but Roz's expression stopped her cold. It was *the* look. The same one their mother had perfected years ago: calm, immovable, and absolutely final. The look that said I *have already won this argument, and you are wasting both our time by continuing it.*

Cressida exhaled through her nose, her shoulders dropping in reluctant defeat. "Fine," she said, her voice tight. "But tomorrow we're talking to Reverend Carlson, and I'm not taking no for an answer—not from you, not from Aunt Sylvia, not from anyone."

A flash of lightning split the sky outside the kitchen windows—sudden, jagged, and brilliant—followed a heartbeat later by a low rumble of thunder that rolled through the valley like a warning.

The storm was coming. And so, tomorrow, was she.

CHAPTER
SEVENTEEN

THE STORM HAD SWEPT through Blackvale overnight—loud, messy, leaving everything damp with regret. Morning air hung thick with wet earth and crushed honeysuckle. Drizzle fell in thin curtains across Cressida's windshield as she navigated winding streets toward Reverend Carlson's neighborhood.

Slick roads glistened black beneath overcast skies. Puddles pooled in uneven asphalt, reflecting storefront signs and traffic lights in wavering patterns. She kept the radio low—Louis Armstrong crackled through the speakers—while rehearsing questions and calculating angles of approach.

Rounding onto Main Street, she passed the pharmacy with its faded green awning, then the antique shop that never seemed open despite its posted hours. The sidewalks were mostly empty. A handful of early risers clutched coffee cups and newspapers, hurrying beneath umbrellas toward whatever Tuesday morning obligations awaited.

And then she saw him.

Jordan Quinn stepped through the glass door of *The Daily Grind*—tucked between the used bookstore and the old hardware store. Dark curly hair damp from rain. Leather jacket zipped halfway over a gray hoodie. Phone in one hand, thumb typing, oblivious to the world.

Her foot hit the brake before her brain caught up. The Mini lurched to a stop mid-turn, tires squealing faintly against wet pavement. She cranked the wheel hard right, cutting across the lane to pull into an empty spot along the curb.

Behind her, a massive Ford—Confederate flag sticker peeling off the bumper—blared its horn. Long, angry, entirely justified. The driver leaned on it for three full seconds, face red behind the windshield, mouth forming words she couldn't hear but could easily imagine.

She ignored him completely.

Opportunity didn't honk twice. Her hand was already on the door handle, pulse jumping. Jordan Quinn. Right there. She could ask him about the competition, about Henrietta, about whatever the hell he'd been doing at the fairgrounds that day.

The door swung open. She stepped onto the sidewalk, sidestepping a puddle. Rain had lightened to fine mist settling on her hair and shoulders. She reached up to smooth a stray lock back as she started toward the coffee shop entrance.

"Miss Vale."

The voice stopped her cold—calm, measured, and entirely too close.

Cressida turned slowly, her hand still halfway to her hair.

Deputy Carla Jensen stood barely three feet away. To-go cup of coffee cradled in one hand. Uniform crisp, posture military-straight, expression unreadable behind mirrored aviators that threw Cressida's own startled face back at her in miniature.

"Deputy Jensen." Cressida forced her voice into something approaching casual. "Good morning."

Jensen didn't return the greeting. A slow, deliberate sip of her coffee. Steam curled up past the edge of her sunglasses. "What you just did was an illegal maneuver."

Cressida's stomach dropped. Her face stayed perfectly composed—bright, innocent, faintly confused. "I'm sorry?"

"No turn signal." Jensen ticked off the violations on her fingers with the precision of someone who'd written this particular ticket a hundred times before. "Cutting across traffic without checking your mirrors. Reckless operation of a motor vehicle." A pause. Head tilting slightly.

An exhale through her nose. Deputy Jensen wasn't Deputy Nash—she couldn't be charmed or deflected with Southern pleasantries and vague assurances. Sharp. Methodical. Entirely too good at her job. But she also wasn't hauling Cressida down to the station, which meant there was still room to maneuver.

"I was experiencing car trouble." The words came quickly, one hand gesturing vaguely at her car while her brain scrambled for something more convincing. "The steering felt off, so I thought it safest to pull over immediately rather than risk—"

"Miss Vale." Jensen interrupted, one hand raised—still holding the coffee cup—and the gesture was so calm, so final, that the words died on Cressida's tongue before they could take shape.

Another slow sip of coffee. The faint quirk at the corner of her mouth was unmistakable now. "What are you really doing here?"

Cressida bit the inside of her cheek, weighing her options. Then she sighed—a soft, defeated little sound—and let her shoulders drop in what she hoped looked like reluctant honesty. "Okay. Fine." She glanced toward the coffee shop, then back at Jensen. "I saw Jordan Quinn through the window, and I thought—" She paused, biting her lower lip as if embarrassed. "Look, you know how it is once you hit thirty. Aunt Sylvia's been on me about settling down, and Jordan's... well, he's charming, he's educated, he's got that whole foodie influencer thing going on." She waved one hand in a vague, self-deprecating gesture. "I thought maybe I'd chat him up over some coffee. Appease her and, you know, see if there's anything there."

Jensen stared at her through mirrored aviators, giving nothing away. Then she lowered the coffee cup, crossed her arms. The movement slow. Deliberate. "Sheriff Stone's told me all about you and Miles." Her tone dry as dust. "Sniffing out trouble. Sticky situations." A pause. "Mrs. Hartley's near heart attack being one of them."

Cressida's eyes widened. "That was *one* time!"

"Mm-hmm." Jensen's expression didn't change. Just that faint quirk at the corner of her mouth, deepening slightly. She took another sip of coffee, then turned. Started walking back toward her patrol car—parked two cars down, engine still running.

Relief washed over Cressida in a cool, dizzying wave. She'd dodged a bullet. Barely. Now she could—

"Be careful, Miss Vale."

Jensen's voice carried back over her shoulder. Calm. Clear. She paused with one hand on the patrol car door, aviators catching the dull gray light. "We all want to see justice done." A beat of silence, heavy with implication. "Oh, and if I was you, I'd maybe ask Jordan about his whereabouts during the judging."

Then she was gone. Sliding into the driver's seat. Door closing with a soft click. Pulling away from the curb with smooth, unhurried precision.

Deputy Jensen's words hung in the air like a challenge wrapped in a warning.

Rain misted against Cressida's face. *Ask Jordan about his whereabouts during the judging.* Not *before.* Not *after. During.*

Deputy Jensen had noticed something. Something that placed Jordan Quinn somewhere he shouldn't have been—or absent from somewhere he should have been—right when Henrietta Dodd collapsed across that judges' table. Face buried in Lemon Lavender Chiffon. Death already darkening her lips.

If the official investigation had stumbled across something interesting, Cressida Vale had never been the type to let someone else solve the puzzle first.

The coffee shop wrapped around her like a hug she didn't quite deserve.

Warm cinnamon and roasted beans mingled in the air, underlaid by something sweeter—vanilla, maybe, or burnt sugar from the pastry case near the register. The low hum of conversation rose and fell like tide water, punctuated by the hiss and gurgle of the espresso machine behind the counter. Acoustic guitar drifted from overhead speakers, some indie track Cressida half-recognized but couldn't name.

She spotted Jordan immediately.

He stood at the counter with his back to her, leather jacket slung over one arm, phone in his other hand. His thumb scrolled with the casual absorption of someone who was never truly off the clock—someone whose entire life existed in carefully curated squares and optimized engagement metrics.

Cressida slipped into line behind him, close enough to catch the faint scent of expensive cologne. Something woody and sharp with a hint of citrus and... ambition. Or calculation.

Jordan glanced back over his shoulder and Cressida offered a smile that was all Southern politeness and zero threat. Bright. Innocent. The kind of smile that said *I'm just standing here minding my own business, how about you?*

He returned it with a perfunctory nod, then turned back to the counter as the barista—a girl with pink hair and a sleeve of floral tattoos—smiled at him expectantly.

"Oat milk latte, extra shot, please," Jordan said, his voice smooth and practiced.

The barista nodded and scribbled on a cup. Jordan stepped aside.

Cressida hesitated. Her stomach was still uncomfortably full of Aunt Sylvia's grits and sausage and biscuits that could double as weapons. The pastry case gleamed with temptation—croissants, cinnamon rolls, blueberry muffins—but the thought of adding anything else made her wince.

"Just a coffee. Cream and sugar," she said. "Small."

The barista reached for a cup, and Cressida moved to the pickup counter where Jordan scrolled through his phone, his expression blank and faintly bored.

She counted to three. Then spoke, her voice pitched just loud enough to sound spontaneous.

"You're Jordan, right? The food blogger?"

He looked up.

For a split second his expression was completely blank—pleasant but empty, like a mask waiting to be assigned a role. Then he blinked, and the mask shifted into something that approximated curiosity.

"I'm sorry," he said, tilting his head slightly, "do I know you?"

"We haven't met," Cressida said, waving one hand. "My aunt Sylvia Vale mentioned you. Said you were in town covering the festival."

The transformation was immediate.

His eyes lit up—genuinely lit up, like someone had flipped a switch—and his posture shifted forward, shoulders opening, smile widening into something that was *almost* genuine except for the calculating gleam beneath it. Someone who'd just spotted an opportunity and was already running the angles.

"Sylvia Vale!" Jordan's voice warmed instantly. "I've heard so much about her—her reputation precedes her. She's a legend in the baking community."

"She'd love to hear that," Cressida said mildly, watching him lean in, his body language screaming *tell me more.*

"So you're her niece? That's amazing." He turned fully toward her, phone forgotten. "I'd love to hear more about her process. Does she use family recipes? Does she experiment much, or is she more traditional?"

The questions came rapid-fire, carefully casual but transparently hungry. Cressida clocked it immediately: he was pumping her, but he was *terrible* at it. His eagerness showed through like a slip peeking from under a dress.

She tilted her head as if considering. "A little of both, I think. She's very private about her recipes."

"Oat milk latte, extra shot!" the barista called out followed by: "Small coffee, cream and sugar!"

Cressida wrapped her fingers around the cup, letting the heat seep into her palms. The coffee smelled dark and bitter—salvation in ceramic form.

Jordan gestured toward a table by the window. "You want to sit? I've got a few minutes before my next appointment."

They settled into their chairs—Jordan claiming the seat facing the window, his back to the wall. A defensive posture, or maybe just the habit of someone always performing, always aware of his angles. She took the opposite chair and watched him arrange himself: phone placed face-down on the table within easy reach, jacket draped over the back of his chair with calculated carelessness, latte positioned precisely in the center of a napkin he'd smoothed flat with one palm.

Everything about him was *just* so. Curated. Deliberate.

"So." His smile was warm and open and practiced. "How long has Sylvia been competing?"

She took a slow sip of her coffee and let the pause stretch just long enough to feel deliberate. "Oh, you know. Years. She's been baking since before I was born."

"That's amazing." He leaned forward slightly, elbows on the table. "What's her relationship like with the other bakers? Does she collaborate much, or is she more of a solo artist?"

"She keeps to herself mostly." Her tone stayed light and vague. "But she's friendly with everyone, of course. It's a small town."

Another non-answer. Another deflection. His smile tightened at the corners—just a fraction—before he recovered.

"Of course." The little wooden stick made slow circles through his latte foam, disrupting the heart shape into abstract swirls. "Small towns have such interesting dynamics. Everyone knows everyone, right? Must make things complicated sometimes."

"Sometimes." Cressida pivoted, tilting her head. "What about you? First time in Blackvale?"

"Yeah, first time." He nodded, his expression brightening as if relieved to be on safer ground. "But I've heard so much about it. The food scene here is really underrated. People don't realize how much history is baked into these small Southern towns."

"*Baked into.*" Her smile widened slightly. "I see what you did there."

He grinned, pleased with himself. The silence stretched. Five seconds. His grin faltered. He shifted in his seat, reaching for his latte.

"So what drew you here specifically?" Light. Curious. "Just the festival?"

"Partly." Then—as if he couldn't help himself, as if the words were being pulled out by some invisible hook—"But honestly, the Dodd story is fascinating. Henrietta's built this whole empire on tradition and elegance, but there's so much complexity beneath the surface, you know? The way she and her husband navigate their... dynamic. The financial pressures of maintaining that lifestyle. It's all very *Grey Gardens*, if you think about it."

Cressida's coffee cup paused halfway to her lips.

The café noise receded—espresso machine hiss fading to white noise, conversations blurring into static.

"Financial pressures?"

"Well, you know." He waved one hand in a gesture meant to look casual but practiced. "Maintaining an estate like High Glen isn't cheap, and with Willard's position at the bank. It's not exactly high-income, right? Plus Henrietta's brand relies on this image of effortless refinement, but the overhead for that..." He trailed off, seemed to catch himself. His hand dropped back to the table. "I mean, that's all speculation, obviously. Just things you pick up when you're researching."

Another sip. A buying motion while her mind dissected every word: *How does a food blogger visiting for the first time know about Willard's salary? The overhead costs of High Glen? What kind of "research" involves digging into a small-town couple's finances?*

"You do thorough research," she observed, her tone mild.

"I like to be prepared," he said, and pivoted—smooth as silk, practiced as a dance step. "I've worked with some incredible people over the years. Dominique Ansel in New York, Christina Tosi, even had a consultation with Thomas Keller once. You learn to look beyond the surface when you're in those kitchens."

The name-dropping was shameless. Each one delivered with the kind of casual confidence meant to impress, his left hand gesturing in broad strokes as if painting his credentials in the air. Maybe it would have impressed someone else—someone who wasn't trained to listen for what people *didn't* say as much as what they did.

The way he talked about working *with* these people rather than *for* them. His thumb rubbed against the side of his cup—once, twice—a small tell. Consultations could mean anything. Could mean nothing.

"Blackvale must be quite different from New York."

"Oh, completely." His shoulders dropped half an inch as he took a sip of his latte. "But there's something about these small towns—they have their own rhythm. Like that little antique shop on Maple, or the way everyone knows each other at the farmer's market by the old courthouse."

Her fingers tightened around her coffee cup. Jordan had just revealed he knew Blackvale's layout far better than any first-time visitor should.

There *was* an antique shop on Maple—Thornton's, with its dusty windows full of skeleton keys and tarnished silver. There *was* a farmer's market every Saturday morning in the parking lot beside the old courthouse, where Mrs. Wolfe sold honey and Mr. Baptiste sold vegetables from his garden.

The silence stretched. Deliberate. *Heavy.* She took another sip of her coffee, watching him over the rim. His expression shifted—jaw tightening, a flicker of uncertainty crossing his face before he caught himself.

"You've really done your homework."

His upper lip tensed. The corners of his mouth pulled back ever so slightly. Then he recovered.

He blinked. Once. Twice. The mental replay was happening in real time: their entire conversation, the sudden realization that she'd given him *nothing*. Not Sylvia's process, not her recipes, not her relationships with other bakers. While he'd been talking freely about things he shouldn't know: financial details, household dynamics, the specific geography of a town he claimed to be visiting for the first time.

His phone buzzed against the table—sharp, insistent. They both glanced down. Relief flooded his features as he reached for it.

"Oh man," he said, already standing, already gathering his jacket. "I'm sorry, I've got to run. But this was great. Really great." He slung the jacket over one arm and flashed her another smile—too bright now, the edges forced. "Tell your aunt I'd love to feature her sometime."

"I'll be sure to mention it," Cressida said. Her smile never wavered.

And then he was gone. Leather jacket, expensive cologne, barely contained urgency—weaving between tables toward the door, phone already pressed to his ear before he cleared the threshold.

Cressida finished her coffee in two long swallows. Still too hot. Burning all the way down. She pushed back from the table, heels clicking against tile as she headed for the door, already pulling on her coat.

Deputy Jensen had been right to point her in this direction. And Cressida Vale had never been the type to ignore a lead—especially one that smelled this strongly of secrets and lies wrapped in expensive cologne and practiced charm.

CHAPTER EIGHTEEN

THE RAIN HAD STOPPED while she was inside, leaving the pavement slick and gleaming, puddles reflecting the gray sky overhead. She stepped outside and drew a slow breath—cool air, clarifying.

Her mind was already racing ahead down the path Jordan Quinn had accidentally revealed. She pulled her phone from her coat pocket, turned toward her car—

And stopped.

Someone was leaning against her driver's side door.

Miles Stone stood with his arms crossed, one boot heel propped against her rear tire. Patient amusement and long-suffering tolerance warred across his features—the particular expressions that came from over two decades of friendship. He looked unbothered by the damp: worn jeans, dark charcoal shirt under a water-resistant jacket, black hair mussed from wind.

"You know," he said, his Southern drawl soft and deliberate, "when Deputy Jensen called to tell me you'd nearly caused a traffic incident downtown, I assumed she was exaggerating."

Cressida stopped mid-stride. One hand rose automatically to shield her eyes from the sudden break in clouds, pale sunlight muscling through.

"She called you?"

"She thought I'd want to know my childhood friend was engaging in reckless driving and suspicious behavior." A slight tilt of his head. Dark eyes catching light with that familiar sharpness—the way he used to study crime scene photos in his father's study before the sheriff caught them. "Was she wrong?"

"Technically I was *investigating*." Cressida gestured back toward the coffee shop with her free hand. "And I got some very interesting information from our friendly food blogger."

The shift was immediate. Miles pushed off from her car in one fluid motion, amused becoming attentive in the space of a breath. His full focus locked onto her; the same look he'd had at seven years old when they'd been investigating the great pet-napping mystery in Aunt Sylvia's backyard, and she'd announced she'd found actual evidence.

"How interesting?"

"Interesting enough that I think Jordan Quinn isn't who he says he is." She met his gaze squarely. "He knows too much about this town for someone visiting for the first time."

Miles was already moving closer, boots soft against wet pavement.

"Tell me everything."

Cressida reached for her car door handle, keys already in hand. Miles's hand shot out—gentle but firm—and intercepted her wrist.

"No way." His voice stayed mild, but absolute. "I'm not getting in that clown car again. Not after you nearly took out a mailbox yesterday."

"That mailbox was *in my blind spot*—"

"The mailbox was stationary, Cressi." He released her and gestured toward his truck, parked three spaces down. "We're taking mine."

For once, Cressida didn't argue. Partly because Miles was right about her somewhat creative approach to parking and traffic laws. Mostly because riding passenger would give her time to dig into Jordan Quinn while Miles drove.

She pocketed her keys and fell into step beside him, already pulling up her phone's browser.

"Fine, but you're buying coffee later."

"Deal."

He unlocked the truck. They climbed in—Cressida into the passenger seat that smelled like coffee and old leather and something woodsy she'd never been able to identify. Miles settled behind the wheel, started the engine. Let it warm up while he turned to face her.

"So. Jordan Quinn."

"First things first." Cressida twisted in her seat to face him properly. "How did it go with your dad?"

A muscle jumped in his jaw—there and gone so fast she might have missed it if she hadn't been watching. He put the truck in gear and pulled out of the parking space with the kind of careful precision that was the exact opposite of her driving style.

"Just as you'd expect." His tone stayed carefully neutral. His knuckles flexed against the steering wheel—just once, a brief tension that came and went. "When I told him Sylvia had hired us to consult based on his questioning, he was less than thrilled."

Aunt Sylvia hadn't exactly asked. She'd declared it over dinner last night, spooning mashed potatoes onto Cressida's plate.

"Define less than thrilled."

"He said he'd asked a handful of questions and she'd spent most of the day talking to Aunt Marnie." Miles glanced at her, one eyebrow raised. "And then he warned us off. Again."

Aunt Marnie Clark, the elderly dispatcher who'd been at the sheriff's office longer than anyone in recent memory could remember.

Everyone called her Aunt Marnie, related or not, and she had a habit of knowing things before they became official facts. Cressida made a mental note to pay her a visit.

"Okay but did he give you anything?" Cressida asked, already typing Jordan Quinn's name into her search bar. "Anything useful?"

Miles turned onto Main Street, his hands steady on the wheel. "He let me look at the coroner's report. Nothing we didn't already know, except—" He paused, checking his mirrors before continuing. "Deputy Nash was wrong. Or rather, the initial report was wrong. Mrs. Dodd didn't have a large dose of porpheyne in her system. The amount was enough to make her sick but shouldn't have been fatal. That quickly."

Cressida's fingers stilled on her phone screen. "What?"

"I suggested he have them test for organic plant oils in her system. Aunt Marnie said she'd let me know as soon as the results come back from Asheville."

"What about Mr. Dodd's finances?" she asked. "And the irregularities at Blackvale Savings and Loan?"

Miles's jaw tightened. Frustration—not anger—flickered across his features before settling into something harder. "He wouldn't tell me anything about their finances. Active investigation. Needed to stay out of it." A pause. "He's got a call into the state investigators about the irregularities."

At a stop sign, the truck went still. Tick of the turn signal. Rain started up again, soft against the windshield. When Miles spoke again, his voice had that careful neutrality he always used when talking about his father. The tone that suggested whole conversations happening beneath the surface.

"When I left, he was heading to the Savings and Loan."

"So we're officially warned off." Cressida didn't look up from her phone. "Which means we're on the right track."

"Or it means my father is trying to keep us from interfering in a legitimate investigation."

"Same thing." She went back to her phone, cheerful. Jordan Quinn's Instagram loaded slowly—too slowly. Her thumb tapped against the edge of her glittery phone case. "Besides, we're not interfering. We're consulting. There's a difference."

"Tell that to Sheriff Dad."

"I will, next time I see him."

Her screen finally loaded. She started scrolling through Jordan Quinn's feed—polished food photography, carefully curated aesthetic shots, captions that sounded just a little too practiced.

"Miles, look at this."

At a red light, she angled her phone toward him. Jordan's Instagram was immaculate: artfully arranged plates, behind-the-scenes shots at trendy restaurants, selfies with people who might be famous chefs or might just be people with good lighting. Something about it felt *off*. Too perfect. Too rehearsed.

Miles leaned closer. "Forty thousand followers, but look at the engagement. Maybe two hundred likes per post, handful of comments. That's not organic growth."

"Bought followers." Cressida nodded. "And the posts about working with Ansel and Tosi—they're vague. No specific dates, no real details. Just name-dropping."

Green light. Miles accelerated smoothly.

"So either he's padding his résumé or he's using food blogging as a cover for something else."

"That's what I'm thinking." Cressida kept scrolling, thumb moving faster. "If he's not really a food blogger, what's he doing in Blackvale? And how does he know so much about the Dodds' finances?"

Miles went quiet. Eyes on the road, mind somewhere else—working through possibilities, weighing probabilities. "We need to know who's paying him," he said finally. "If he's here for a reason beyond the festival, someone hired him."

"I'll have my old editor at the Charlotte paper run his credentials." Cressida was composing a text. "She owes me a favor. And I can check with some of my contacts in the culinary world—see if anyone's actually worked with him."

"Good." Miles turned onto Oleander Road, heading toward the church where Reverend Carlson would presumably be preparing for evening services. "Meanwhile, let's see what the good reverend has to say about Henrietta Dodd and her charitable donations."

Cressida finished her text and looked up.

The tree-lined street stretched ahead—neat houses, carefully maintained lawns. Everything in Blackvale looked so *normal* on the surface. So polished and proper and Southern-genteel. But underneath, in the shadows between the magnolia trees and behind the lace curtains, secrets festered like rot in floorboards.

She was going to dig every single one of them up, no matter how deep they'd been buried.

The parking lot behind Blackvale First Baptist Church was nearly empty when Miles pulled into a space near the main entrance—just a handful of cars scattered across cracked asphalt that probably hadn't been repaved since Cressida was in high school. She was already reaching for the door handle when movement caught her eye near the church's side entrance.

A figure in a pastel pink suit hurried toward the building, enormous handbag clutched in one hand, the other waving at someone inside. That walk—quick, purposeful, bouncing with urgency—Cressida knew it instantly.

"Oh no." She slumped lower in her seat. "Oh no no no."

Miles followed her gaze, sympathy mixing with amusement. "Mrs. Buckner?"

"Mrs. Buckner." The woman stopped mid-stride, head swiveling toward the truck like a hunting dog catching a scent. "And she's spotted us."

"Maybe if we just sit very still—"

Too late. Mrs. Buckner changed direction, pink patent leather heels carrying her across the parking lot, one hand raised in an enthusiastic wave visible from space. Her smile could power the sanctuary lights.

"Well *bless my soul!*" Her voice carried with the projection of decades making herself heard over library patrons and book club debates. "Cressida Vale and Miles Stone! Together! In one vehicle!"

Cressida shot Miles a look that clearly said *this is your hometown*. He opened his door with resigned grace—resistance was futile. She followed suit, plastering on what she hoped was a friendly smile.

Mrs. Buckner reached them before they'd fully exited, her perfume—floral and slightly powdery—arriving a beat ahead. The pink suit was accessorized with a cat-shaped brooch (of course), matching lipstick that had migrated beyond her lip line again, and chandelier earrings.

"I *knew* I recognized that truck." Her dark eyes danced between them. "What brings you two young people to the church on a Tuesday afternoon? Please tell me you're here for book club! We're discussing *The Secret Garden* this week—well, officially, but Dianne always lets us veer into more exciting territory." She leaned in. "Last month we spent forty-five minutes debating whether the butler did it in that Agatha Christie novel she 'accidentally' brought."

Cressida opened her mouth to politely decline, but Mrs. Buckner was already barreling forward, her attention suddenly shifting to Miles with laser focus.

"Now Cressida, sweetheart, have you heard *anything* about my Kennard?" Mrs. Buckner's voice dropped—an attempt at discretion that still carried halfway across the parking lot. "I've put up flyers, called the shelter, even asked Deputy Nash to keep an eye out. But you know how cats are. One minute they're there, the next—" She snapped her fingers. "Gone."

Kennard. The elderly tabby with the torn ear and the disposition of a Civil War general. Cressida had completely forgotten about Mrs. Buckner's missing cat. Which made her a terrible person. But also: *murder investigation.*

"We're keeping an eye out," she said, mustering what she hoped passed for concern. "I'm sure he'll turn up. Kennard's a survivor."

Mrs. Buckner's expression crumpled before rallying. "He's eighteen years old and has only one good eye. But you're right, sugar. He fought off raccoons. Outlasted two husbands. If anyone can survive whatever shenanigans he's gotten himself into, it's my Kennard."

Miles cleared his throat. "Mrs. Buckner, we'd love to catch up, but we're actually here to speak with Reverend Carlson. We have an appointment—"

"An appointment?" Her eyebrows climbed. "On a Tuesday afternoon? How official." A pause, wheels visibly turning behind those dark eyes. "Well, book club starts soon. Reverend Carlson won't mind if you're a few minutes late. Besides—" She linked her arm through Cressida's with surprising strength. "—Mrs. Carlson always serves the most *wonderful* casseroles. Her taste in books is questionable, but that woman can make a broccoli cheese casserole that'll make you weep. You two look like you could use some feeding."

"Mrs. Buckner, we really should—" Miles tried.

Too late. The older woman was already steering Cressida toward the church entrance with the kind of gentle-but-inexorable force usually reserved for moving furniture.

"Nonsense! The reverend is probably in his office doing paperwork anyway. You can catch him after book club—he always comes down to help Dianne clean up." A glance back at Miles. "Come on now, honey. Don't make me drag you."

And *somehow*—before Cressida could formulate a polite but firm refusal—they were being ushered through the church's side entrance.

The hallway smelled like old hymnals and lemon furniture polish.

One of the church's small meeting rooms materialized around them.

The same room where she'd attended Sunday school as a child, counting down the minutes until she could escape to find Miles and whatever mystery they'd concocted that week. The walls: still that same pale yellow. The cross: still hung above the doorway. The round table in the center: still slightly too small for the mismatched chairs surrounding it.

Mrs. Buckner deposited them cheerfully with a group of elderly women, pressed cups of lukewarm tea into their hands, then bustled off. The women—names she couldn't quite remember but faces vaguely familiar from childhood church services—immediately resumed their gossip session.

She glanced at Miles and had to suppress a laugh.

He looked *comically* out of place—broad shoulders hunched slightly to fit between Mrs. Galloway (or was it Mrs. Patterson?) and another woman in a lavender cardigan, his large hands wrapped around a delicate teacup that looked like it might shatter if he breathed too hard. His expression was carefully neutral, but she could see the muscle ticking in his jaw—that tell-tale sign that he was absolutely, definitely not amused by this turn of events.

His eyes met hers across the table, and the look he gave her was pure *this is your fault somehow.*

She bit her lip to keep from laughing and took a sip of her tea, which tasted like it had been brewed sometime last week and forgotten about.

"—completely unnatural, if you ask me," the woman in lavender was saying, leaning forward with the kind of enthusiasm that suggested she'd been waiting for an audience. "Poisoned at a baking competition of all places! It's like something out of one of those murder mysteries Dianne pretends she doesn't read."

"I heard it was the husband," Mrs. Galloway (definitely Galloway, Cressida decided) said, her voice dropping to a stage whisper. "Willard Dodd finally snapped after all those years of her treating him like hired help. You know she made him sleep in the guest room?"

"Well, I heard it was someone from *out of town*," Lavender Cardigan countered. "One of those food bloggers or journalists. You know how competitive those people are. Probably couldn't stand that Henrietta won *again*."

"Or maybe it was—"

The door swung open, cutting off whatever wild theory was about to be proposed. Dianne Carlson swept in carrying a glass dish that steamed gently, her blonde hair styled in smooth, elegant waves that framed her face, her coral lipstick freshly applied. She set the casserole down on the table with practiced grace, her smile warm and welcoming—until her gaze landed on Cressida.

"Oh!" Dianne's smile flickered, just for a second, before recovering. "Cressida Vale. What a lovely surprise." Her tone suggested it was anything but. "I didn't realize you were joining us today. Though I suppose with you stirring things up all over town, it was only a matter of time before you found your way back to the church."

"Mrs. Buckner was very persuasive," Cressida said, setting down her teacup before she accidentally crushed it. She'd caught the edge in Dianne's voice. "But actually, Mrs. Carlson, I was hoping to speak with Reverend Carlson. If he has a moment?"

Something flashed across Dianne's face—concern or calculation, there and gone. Her gaze flicked to the doorway. "Alone?"

Mrs. Buckner materialized in the doorway. "Obviously not alone, Dianne! She's with her beau, Miles Stone here." She beamed. "It's about time these two started talking wedding bells, don't you think?"

The room erupted. Cressida choked on her tea.

"Oh *absolutely*," Lavender Cardigan said, patting Miles's arm hard enough to leave a mark. "Pop out babies when you're young, dear. Have the energy. My daughter waited until thirty-five and now she can barely keep up with the twins."

"A spring wedding would be *perfect*," Mrs. Galloway added. "It's been so long since we've had a good spring wedding in Blackvale. I do so look good in pink."

Words failed Cressida entirely. Miles went very still across from her.

This was how she died: not poisoned, not shot—socially executed by church ladies over tea.

"What the hel—"

But before she could finish—before she could explain that they were *not* engaged, *not* planning a wedding, and definitely *not* having this conversation—Reverend Carlson appeared in the doorway.

His hazel eyes swept the room with prac- ticed calm, taking in the scene—the eager faces,

Cressida's mortified expression, Miles's barely contained panic—and something like understanding flickered across his features.

Miles was on his feet before the reverend could speak, his hand shooting out to grasp Cressida's wrist in a grip that was gentle but absolutely firm. "Reverend Carlson," he said, his voice impressively steady despite the chaos. "We need to speak with you. In private. Please."

And then he was moving, pulling a still-stunned Cressida toward the door with the kind of polite urgency that somehow managed to be both respectful and desperate. The last thing she saw before they escaped into the hallway was Mrs. Buckner's delighted smile and Dianne Carlson's calculating expression as she watched them go.

As the door clicked shut behind them, Cressida exhaled hard. The air smelled like fruit scented cleaner—and underneath it, something sour, something secret.

CHAPTER
NINETEEN

REVEREND CARLSON'S PRIVATE OFFICE was a study in contrasts—warm wood paneling that absorbed the afternoon light filtering through stained glass windows, bookshelves crammed with theological texts and dog-eared paperbacks, a mahogany desk that had probably been inherited from some previous pastor. An uncomfortable-looking leather couch sagged against the far wall, like it wanted to apologize for existing. The air smelled of old paper, furniture polish, and something faintly medicinal—maybe the mentholated cough drops Cressida remembered him keeping in a glass jar on his desk.

The reverend settled into his chair with practiced ease, gesturing for them to take the seats across from him. Before either could speak, he folded his hands on the desk and smiled that distinctive pastoral smile—the one that suggested he was about to dispense wisdom whether you wanted it or not.

"Now, I know Mrs. Buckner got a bit carried away with the wedding talk," he began, his tone warm and reassuring in that way that had probably comforted countless parishioners over the decades, "but if you *are* considering taking that step, I'd be honored to offer some counsel. Marriage is a sacred bond, and in these modern times, young couples often rush into things without proper preparation—"

"We're not engaged," Cressida said flatly, cutting through the sermon before it could gain momentum. "We're not getting married. We're not even dating."

Miles shifted beside her. She could feel the tension radiating off him like heat. "We're here about Henrietta Dodd's murder, Reverend."

The change in Carlson's expression was subtle but unmistakable—the pastoral warmth flickering like a candle in a draft. "I see. Well, that's certainly a tragedy. Poor Henrietta. She was a pillar of this community—"

Cressida leaned forward.

If she wanted honesty, she'd have to buy it with shock.

Beating around the bush was a luxury they couldn't afford. "Were you having an affair with her?"

The silence that followed was so absolute she could hear the tick of the clock on the wall behind her. Miles went very still beside her—the kind of stillness that meant she'd just lobbed a grenade into polite conversation and he was calculating the fallout.

Reverend Carlson's face went through a series of expressions in rapid succession: shock, offense, and finally something that looked uncomfortably like fear.

"I beg your pardon?"

"You heard me." Her heart was hammering, but she kept her voice level. "Were you having an affair with Henrietta Dodd?"

"Cressida—" Miles started, but she held up a hand.

"The way Mrs. Carlson reacted when I asked to speak with you alone." Cressida kept her eyes locked on his face. "She's always been *protective* when women are around you. Made me wonder about a wandering eye."

She let that sit between them.

"We're in a place of God, Reverend. You always said lying was bad."

Miles cleared his throat. "This is a murder investigation. If you didn't kill Mrs. Dodd, it's best to come clean so the authorities can focus on the real killer."

Carlson's hands tightened. Tendons stood out like cords.

He didn't speak—just stared at them with hazel eyes that suddenly looked older, wearier. The carefully maintained façade cracking under pressure.

"I wasn't having an affair with Henrietta." His voice was rough. "We had a fling when we were young. Before Dianne, before—" He rubbed a hand over his face. "It ended decades ago. *Decades.*"

A puzzle piece sliding into place. "Then what did she have on you? What made you give her the Golden Spoon year after year?"

The reverend's jaw worked. She watched him weigh his options—truth or continued deception, confession or evasion.

"We have a witness," Miles said quietly, "who saw her pass you a blackmail note."

Something in Carlson collapsed. Spiritually.

The weight he'd been carrying finally became too much. He hung his head, shoulders sagging, and for a moment he looked every one of his sixty-seven years.

He reached into his desk drawer—one of the lower ones, locked with a small key from his pocket—and pulled out a stack of cream-colored stationery. All bearing the same elegant, looping handwriting.

He set them on the desk between them with the careful precision of someone handling evidence at his own trial.

"She never let me forget. Not for forty years."

Cressida studied the stack of cream-colored stationery. Each page a testament to years of systematic exploitation. The elegant handwriting—Henrietta's handwriting, the same as in the cookbook margins—mocked them from beyond the grave.

Carlson's voice came out rough. "I once had a wandering eye. As Miss Vale so crudely put it." He looked up, meeting Cressida's gaze with what seemed like genuine desperation. "But those days are behind me. I swear to you, they're behind me. Henrietta somehow knew about each one of my mistakes. And she used that knowledge."

Miles leaned forward slightly, taking one of the letters. "What kind of knowledge, Reverend?"

The silence drew long and thin, fragile as glass.

Carlson's hands trembled as he pressed them flat against the desk, as if trying to ground himself through touch alone.

"Over the years, I strayed from my marriage vows more than once." Each word seemed to cost him. "Henrietta somehow discovered each affair—names, dates, even hotel receipts. She threatened to expose me to the congregation unless I ensured she won the Golden Spoon every year. Said she'd destroy everything I'd built. My reputation, my ministry, my marriage."

His voice cracked. "She'd have done it too. Henrietta never made empty threats."

Something cold settled in Cressida's stomach. The woman had been methodical in her cruelty, surgical in her exploitation.

"Did you kill her?" Cressida asked point-blank, watching his face for the telltale flickers that would betray deception. "Or did your wife?"

Carlson's head snapped up, genuine alarm flooding his features. "Dianne knows nothing about any of this. *Nothing*." His voice took on a desperate edge. "She'd have no reason to want to harm Henrietta. And I was giving a blessing at the children's pie-eating contest in a different tent when Henrietta collapsed. I had to rush over there right after the judging concluded. There are dozens of witnesses."

Miles pulled out his phone, making a note. "Have you ever heard of porpheyne, Reverend?"

Confusion flickered across Carlson's face. "No. What is it?"

"Where were you in the days leading up to the competition?" Cressida asked. Her aunt was fastidious about keeping her kitchen clean. If the chemical had been in her house for more than a few days, she'd have noticed it.

"I was leading a three-day church retreat—Tuesday through Thursday. No cellphones or internet-capable devices allowed. It's meant to be a digital detox, a chance for spiritual reflection." He gestured vaguely toward the window. "We were in Asheville, at the mountain retreat center. Dozens of parishioners can confirm my presence."

Miles gestured toward the letters on the desk. "You need to take these to my father. Tell him everything."

Carlson's face went ashen.

"If they haven't already found out about the blackmail, they will soon," Miles continued. His tone was firm but not unkind. "Better if you go to them first. Shows cooperation."

For a moment, Cressida thought the reverend might argue. Deny. Deflect.

Instead, he nodded—defeated, like a man who'd been carrying a burden too long and was almost relieved to finally set it down.

Cressida stood, smoothing down her skirt. The gentleness in her own voice surprised her. "Don't worry. Blackvale is good at keeping secrets."

She wasn't entirely sure if that was meant to be comforting or damning.

From the look on Carlson's face, he wasn't sure either.

The hallway outside Carlson's office was dim, fluorescent lights casting shadows across worn carpet. Cressida was still processing the reverend's confession—decades of blackmail, systematic exploitation, forty years of secrets—when they turned the corner.

Nearly collided with Dianne Carlson.

The woman clutched a stack of hymnals against her chest, spines aligned with military precision. Her smile bloomed too quickly. Too brightly.

"Oh!" That breathless quality Southern women perfected when vulnerability served them better than strength. "Miles, Cressida. I didn't realize you were still here." The hymnals shifted. "Is everything alright? Did you need anything? I could make coffee, or—"

"We're fine, Mrs. Carlson," Miles said. "Just finishing up a conversation with the reverend."

Cressida studied her face. Eyes darting past them toward her husband's closed door. Coral-painted lips tightening. Something calculating in that glance—something that didn't match the concern in her voice.

"About poor Henrietta, I imagine." Dianne's expression shifted. Might have been grief. "Such a tragedy. Now, Henrietta may have been sharp, but she was *a child of God*. We must remember that. We all have our rough edges, don't we?" She adjusted the hymnals. Her wedding ring caught the light—a modest band, probably on her finger for decades. "Frederick has been taking it so hard. Every loss in the congregation affects him personally. That's just the kind of man he is."

Defense before attack. Cressida filed that away, along with how Mrs. Carlson's voice had gone harder on the word "sharp."

"When was the last time you saw Mrs. Dodd?" Cressida kept her tone casual. Two women chatting in a church hallway.

"Oh, let me think." Dianne tilted her head, blonde hair catching the light like spun sugar. "I delivered a casserole to the Dodd house a couple of days before her death. Tuesday, I believe. Or was it Wednesday?" A pause. "No, Tuesday." She nodded. "Part of the Ladies' Ministry schedule. We take turns bringing meals to the elderly and shut-ins. Henrietta wasn't either, of course, but she'd mentioned Willard had been under the weather, so I thought..." The smile went soft around the edges. "It's what we do in Blackvale. Take care of our own."

That slight emphasis on "our own." As if Henrietta had been part of some sacred circle. But something beneath the words didn't ring true.

A piano with one string out of tune.

"That was kind of you," Miles said.

"Well." Dianne's shoulders lifted in a modest shrug. "Anyone who'd marry someone like her must have known what they were getting into." The words slipped out before she seemed to catch herself, her eyes widening slightly as if she'd surprised herself with her own candor. "I mean—Henrietta and Willard had such a *cold* marriage. Everyone knew it. Not that it's any of my business, of course. But you couldn't help but notice."

Then she blinked, and the moment passed. Her expression softened again, tears suddenly welling in her eyes. "I'm sorry. I shouldn't speak ill of the dead. It's just—she was so *difficult* sometimes. But she didn't deserve what happened to her. No one deserves that."

The tears looked real enough. Maybe they were. Or maybe Dianne Carlson had just spent so many years performing public sympathy that the mechanics of it had become second nature—salt water summoned through muscle memory rather than genuine grief.

"We should let you get back to your work," Miles said, gesturing toward the hymnals.

"Oh, these." Dianne glanced down as if she'd forgotten she was holding them. "Yes, I need to get them sorted before evening service. But please, if you need anything—anything at all—don't hesitate to ask. Freddy and I are always here to help."

They exchanged goodbyes—the kind of polite, empty phrases that Southern culture had perfected over generations. But as they walked away, Cressida couldn't shake the feeling that Dianne Carlson knew more than her husband thought she did. The question was: what exactly did she know, and how long had she known it?

She glanced back once before they reached the exterior doors. Mrs. Carlson was still standing in the hallway, hymnals clutched to her chest, watching them with an expression Cressida couldn't quite read. Something in between fear and calculation—like a woman who'd spent forty years keeping secrets and had just realized the locks might finally be breaking.

Blackvale's secrets always found new custodians, Cressida thought as she pushed through the church doors. *The trick was deciding who still believed in forgiveness.*

Outside, the afternoon had started its slow slide toward evening. The sky was that shade of blue-gray that meant rain was coming—clouds gathering over the mountains like old bruises. Cressida could smell it on the wind, that metallic tang that always preceded a storm.

They reached Miles's Bronco in the parking lot, and she paused with her hand on the door handle. "Drop me off at the library."

Miles raised an eyebrow. "The library?"

"I need to print out the pictures I took the day of the competition." She pulled out her phone and scrolled through her photo gallery. "I still haven't set up my computer yet, and I want hard copies. Something I can spread out, look at properly." She glanced up at him. "You know we've lost two suspects in the past two days and gained nothing new on the others. Willard Dodd, Susan Mitchell, Jordan Quinn—we're missing something. I need to see it all laid out."

Miles studied her for a moment, then nodded. "I'll let your aunt and sister know you'll be late."

"Thanks." She climbed into the passenger seat, still scrolling through the photos she'd taken. The crowd shots, the competition tent, Henrietta's face as she examined the entries. Somewhere in those images was a detail they'd overlooked—she was sure of it.

The drive to the library took less than ten minutes. Miles pulled up to the curb outside the ivy and brick building with its American flag snapping in the pre-storm wind.

"You sure you don't want me to wait?" he asked.

"I'll walk back to my car when I'm done. It's not far." She grabbed her bag. "Besides, you should go visit your parents. I'm sure your dad will have questions about our church visit."

Miles's expression suggested he was already mentally preparing for that conversation. "Call if you need anything."

"Always do."

She watched him drive away, then turned toward the library. Nearly empty this late in the day—a different librarian behind the circulation desk, a handful of students hunched over laptops. She logged in with her aunt's library card and spent the next hour transferring photos from her phone, sending everything to the printer.

The images emerged one by one. Crisp. Detailed. Henrietta's hand reaching for the lavender garnish. Willard standing apart from the crowd, that pharmacy bag clutched in his fingers. Jordan Quinn's camera angled toward the judges' table. Susan Mitchell's expression as she watched Henrietta claim her Golden Spoon—not quite anger, not quite resignation.

She laid them out on the table, rearranging them like puzzle pieces. Looking for the pattern. The connection. The detail that would make everything else fall into place.

By the time she finished, darkness had settled over Blackvale like a blanket. The library's fluorescent lights felt too bright against the windows, which reflected her own image back—tired, determined, obsessed with a mystery that kept expanding the more she pulled at its edges.

Exhaustion pooled behind her eyes. The fear crept in: chasing shadows while a killer walked free. She'd come home to heal and instead found herself drowning in other people's secrets.

But then her gaze fell back to the photos spread across the table, and her chest tightened with renewed purpose.

She gathered the photos into a manila folder and stepped outside. The air tasted of rain and ozone. The storm had arrived while she'd been working—not a downpour yet, but that heavy mist that warned of worse to come. She pulled her coat tighter and started toward the parking lot where she'd left her car that morning.

The streets were empty, most of Blackvale's residents already home for dinner. Streetlights cast pools of yellow across wet pavement. She navigated the familiar route—past the antique shops with their darkened windows, past Hollow Creek Tavern where warm light and laughter spilled onto the sidewalk.

Halfway to her car, she saw it.

A sedan rolling through the intersection ahead, headlights cutting through the mist. The way it moved caught her attention—too careful, too deliberate. The rental company sticker visible even in the dim light.

The driver passed beneath a streetlight.

Jordan Quinn.

Her heartbeat kicked up. What was he still doing in Blackvale? He should be heading back to whatever city had spawned him. Yet here he was, driving through town on a rainy Tuesday night like he had somewhere specific to be.

Cressida didn't stop to think it through. She just moved, jogging back toward her car, the manila folder clutched against her chest to protect the photos from the rain. Her heels unsteady on the wet pavement—impractical for the sprint, but she pushed through anyway.

She reached the Mini. Yanked open the door. Tossed the folder onto the passenger seat.

The engine turned over with a familiar purr. She pulled out of the parking lot just in time to see Jordan's rental turn onto Maple Street.

She followed, keeping enough distance that she wouldn't be obvious but close enough not to lose him. The rain picked up—from mist to proper drops drumming against her windshield. Her wipers swept back and forth in a steady rhythm as she trailed the sedan through Blackvale's winding streets.

Part of her brain—the rational part, the part that sounded suspiciously like Miles—screamed that this was reckless. That she should call the sheriff's office, let them handle it. But the rest of her was already running scenarios, already calculating what Jordan Quinn might be doing out here on a night when he should have been miles away.

The sedan turned again.

She followed, her pulse thrumming with electricity. Whatever she was about to discover, it was going to crack this case wide open.

The rain fell harder. The darkness pressed closer. And somewhere ahead, Jordan Quinn drove toward a destination she was suddenly desperate to see.

Chapter Twenty

THE TAILLIGHTS AHEAD BLURRED into twin red smears through the rain-slicked windshield. Twenty minutes of following Jordan Quinn's rental sedan through increasingly treacherous roads. Cressida eased off the gas, letting the Mini fall back another car length. Then another. The distance felt both too close and not close enough—that precarious balance between losing him entirely and announcing herself like a neon sign screaming *I'm following you.*

Her wipers swept back and forth in a rhythm that was already starting to feel inadequate. The rain had shifted from steady drumming to something heavier, more insistent. Mountain rain that arrived with purpose and settled in for the night.

He knows something, she thought. *Too many questions. Too many details for a food blogger just passing through.*

Streetlights gave way to gloom as Jordan's car suddenly veered right, turning onto a road Cressida almost missed—narrow, unmarked, swallowed by trees on both sides. Oaks and pines that had been growing since before Blackvale became the kind of place people came to for weekend getaways and Instagram photos.

"Where are you going?" she muttered, yanking her wheel to follow.

The houses thinned out. Then disappeared entirely.

Asphalt faded beneath her tires, replaced by something rougher. Gravel? Packed dirt? The car juddered as she hit the first pothole, and she gripped the wheel tighter, her rings pressing into her palms.

The storm hammered the roof now, a relentless percussion that drowned out everything—including the small voice telling her to turn back. Water sheeted across the glass faster than the blades could clear it, turning the world into a warped, streaming blur of shadow and motion.

Jordan's taillights were barely visible now. Two red ghosts flickering through the curtain of downpour. Cressida leaned forward, as if those extra six inches would somehow improve her visibility.

"Come on, come on," she hissed at the windshield, as if sheer will could cut through the deluge.

The road twisted sharply—left, then right—climbing steadily upward into darkness so complete it felt like driving into a cave. Trees crowded closer on both sides, their branches forming a tunnel overhead that blocked what little moonlight might have filtered through. Her beams caught fragments: wet bark, hanging moss, the occasional reflective eyes of something watching from the undergrowth. Then potholes appeared like dark mouths, and she had to swerve hard to avoid one that looked deep enough to swallow a tire.

Another jarring bump sent her phone sliding across the passenger seat. She grabbed for it instinctively, then forced her hand back to the wheel. *Not now. Eyes forward.*

Jordan's taillights flickered ahead, there and gone through the downpour. He was maintaining speed despite the conditions, which meant either he knew these roads or he was running from something.

Or toward something.

The thought settled cold in her stomach.

They were climbing deeper into the mountains now—she could feel the angle of ascent in her ears, the pressure building as elevation rose. The woods pressed in darker, older, the kind of Appalachian treeline that swallowed sound and held onto secrets. Blackvale proper was miles behind them. Out here, there were no streetlights, no houses, no witnesses.

Just storm and gloom and two cars climbing toward something Cressida could only hope she'd return from.

For half a second the view cleared enough to see Jordan's brake lights flare bright red.

Then they vanished around another curve, and Cressida pressed the accelerator, following him deeper into the woods. Her beams swept across dense pines that looked like something out of a fairy tale—the unsettling kind where children got lost and never found their way home.

One moment Jordan's taillights were steady crimson beacons ahead, the next the road twisted sharply left and Cressida's wheels hit a slick patch of mud that sent the car sliding sideways with a stomach-dropping lurch.

"No no no—" Her hands flew across the wheel, overcorrecting, then correcting again as the backend fishtailed. The headlights swung wild across tree trunks and darkness before she managed to wrestle the car back into something resembling control, heart hammering against her ribs like it was trying to escape.

The car straightened. The tires found purchase again. She sucked in a breath that tasted like adrenaline and rain.

Maybe I should slow down.

The thought barely had time to settle before she rounded the bend and found—nothing.

Just empty road splitting into a Y-junction ahead, both paths swallowed by trees and endless night. No taillights. No sign anyone had driven through here at all.

"You've got to be kidding me."

Cressida eased her foot off the accelerator, letting the car roll to a stop at the fork. Left path or right path. Both equally dark, equally uninviting, equally likely to lead absolutely nowhere.

She killed the engine. Silence rushed in to replace it, broken only by the rain and her own breathing, still too fast, still catching up to the near-wipeout.

Think. Where am I?

Cressida pressed her palms against her eyes, trying to pull up mental maps from childhood summers. County Road 14, she was pretty sure—which meant left was the old logging road that wound toward the abandoned Thornwood quarry. She'd been there once, maybe twice, on teenage dares with Miles that ended with mosquito bites and poison ivy. Right, headed up toward—what was it called?—Shadewood Hollow, if memory served. The workers' cottages from when the quarry was still operational. A place where kudzu grew thick enough to hide whole buildings and locals only went if they were lost or stupid or both.

Her fingers drummed against the steering wheel again. *One-two-three. One-two-three.*

Logically speaking—if logic could even be considered at this point—he'd most likely head toward Shadewood Hollow. The quarry was played out, picked clean by scavengers and time. But the Hollow? That had structures still standing. Places to hide. Places to meet someone, if meeting someone was the plan.

Cressida's hand moved to the gearshift.

"Right it is." She turned the key.

The engine turned over with a reluctant grumble. Cressida eased the car right, tires crunching over gravel and exposed roots as the path narrowed. The rain kept up its assault for another ten minutes—relentless, punishing—before it began to ease. First to a steady drum, then a patter, then finally to scattered drops that felt more like afterthought than intention.

"Thank you, God," Cressida muttered, her shoulders dropping half an inch as visibility improved.

The woods pressed closer here, a canopy so dense that even the moonlight struggled to penetrate. Her headlights carved a pale tunnel through the darkness, illuminating glimpses of what Shadewood Hollow had become: mailboxes leaning at broken angles, wooden fences swallowed by kudzu, the skeletal remains of porches that had given up their fight with gravity years ago.

She drove slowly now, hyperaware of every pothole, every branch scraping against the car's undercarriage. The road—if it could still be called that—twisted between cottages that looked more like memories than structures. Empty windows stared at her like hollow eyes. Nature was winning the war here, reclaiming what industry had stolen and people had abandoned.

Then she saw it.

Taillights. Red brake lights flaring bright against the night, maybe fifty yards ahead.

Cressida's pulse kicked up again. She eased off the accelerator, letting her car roll forward at barely more than idle speed. Through the trees she could make out Jordan's rental sedan pulling off the path, parking beside a thick cluster of pines that partially obscured it from view.

"Got you," she breathed.

She pulled over about thirty yards back, tucking her car behind an overgrown thicket of wild rhododendron and honeysuckle. Killed the engine. Killed the lights. Sat in sudden, complete darkness broken only by the faint glow of her dashboard clock.

10:47 pm.

Her phone sat in the passenger seat where it had slid earlier, screen dark. She grabbed it, checked the signal—one flickering bar, barely there—and pocketed it anyway.

Her hands moved on autopilot. Phone secured. Keys held silent in her palm. The door latch released with the softest click she could manage.

Cool air rushed in—damp and alive. Dripping water. Rustling leaves. Somewhere in the distance, an owl called out, low and mournful, raising the hair on her arms.

The air up here was different. Thicker. Heavy with rot and wet earth and something else she couldn't name. Old smoke, maybe. Or just abandonment settling into every molecule.

She eased the door shut with both hands, holding her breath until the latch caught. Barely a whisper.

Then she was moving.

Low. Keeping to the path's edge where pine needles and wet leaves muffled her footsteps.

Ahead, Jordan's car sat empty, the driver's door hanging open. She could see him now—a tall silhouette moving through the trees with purpose, heading toward one of the larger cottages set back from the path. Most of its roof was still intact. The porch sagged like a broken promise. Windows just dark rectangles punched into weathered wood.

Cressida's fingers found her phone. She pulled it out, swiped to the camera, adjusted the settings for low light.

Her heart was doing that thing again—that rapid-fire rhythm that meant she was either about to connect dots in real time, or have a heart attack.

What are you doing here?

She crept closer, using tree trunks and overgrown bushes as cover. Hidden roots, broken glass, decades of accumulated forest debris—all threatened to trip her with every step. She'd done this before, back in Charlotte, following leads through construction sites and abandoned warehouses. But this was darker. Quieter. More isolated than anywhere she'd tailed someone.

Jordan reached the cottage and paused at the base of the porch steps. A quick scan—Cressida froze behind a thick oak—then he climbed up. The steps creaked under his weight, loud enough to make her wince. He didn't seem concerned about stealth. He moved like someone who expected to be alone out here.

The doorway swallowed him whole.

Cressida counted to ten, then moved forward, circling to approach from an angle that would give her a view through the side window. Her oxfords—oxblood leather chosen for style, not substance—sank into soft earth with every step. Water seeped through. *Great. Just great.*

Then she was there. Wood rough and damp against her palms as she pressed against the cottage's exterior wall. She edged toward the window, slow and careful, until she could peek inside.

Jordan stood in what might have once been a living room, illuminated by his phone's flashlight. The beam swept across bare walls, exposed beams, a floor littered with leaves and broken plaster. Searching for something—moving methodically, checking corners, running his hand along the wall like he was looking for a hidden switch or panel.

Cressida raised her phone, framed the shot, and took a photo. The camera made the softest click. Another. Jordan crouched down, examining something on the floor. Another photo. He stood, moved deeper into the cottage, disappearing through an interior doorway.

The phone lowered. *What is this place? What's he looking for?*

A branch snapped somewhere behind her.

Cressida whirled around, heart leaping. The forest stared back—dark, shifting, full of shadows that might be nothing or might be anything. Wind through pine needles. Water dripping from leaves. The distant call of that same owl, closer now.

Nothing else.

Get it together.

She turned back to the window—and froze.

Jordan was gone.

The living room stood empty, phone light extinguished, just darkness and decay visible through the grimy glass. She pressed closer, scanning the interior, but there was no sign of him. No movement. No light. He'd vanished as completely as he had on the road.

"No," Cressida whispered. "No no no, where did you—"

Another sound. Not behind her this time. To her left, maybe twenty feet away, something moving through the underbrush with deliberate steps.

Cressida's breath caught. She backed away from the window, mind racing. *Did he see me? Did he hear the camera? Is he circling around?*

The footsteps stopped.

Silence pressed in, thick and expectant. She could hear her own heartbeat, her own shallow breathing, the blood rushing in her ears. Every instinct screamed at her to run, to get back to her car, to get out of these woods before...

Before what?

She forced herself to think. *You've been in worse situations than this, Cressi. Actually, I have not been in worse situations than this, Cressida.*

Okay, different situations. Just breathe. Think.

Time to go.

Cressida backed away slowly, keeping her eyes on the cottage and the surrounding trees, every sense straining for any sign of where Jordan Quinn had disappeared to. The woods offered no answers—just shadows and whispers and the feeling of being watched by something she couldn't see.

She made it three steps before her boot caught on a hidden root and she stumbled, catching herself against a tree trunk with a gasp that sounded too loud in the listening quiet.

Somewhere in the darkness, something moved again.

And this time, Cressida ran.

Her oxfords slammed against wet earth, breath tearing through her chest in sharp gasps. Branches whipped at her face—she didn't care, didn't slow, just ran. The forest blurred into shadow and reaching limbs, every root a threat, every low branch a trap.

Get to the car. Get to the car. Get to the freaking car.

The mantra pounded in time with her footsteps. Behind her—or beside her, or *everywhere*—something moved through the underbrush. She couldn't tell if it was Jordan or wind or her own panicked imagination, but she wasn't stopping to find out.

Her phone bounced against her thigh. She wanted the flashlight, but her hands were busy keeping branches from her eyes and her feet were busy not breaking an ankle.

Then she saw it—the pale shape of her car materializing through the trees.

"Thank God," she gasped, stumbling the last few yards and yanking open the door. She threw herself inside, slammed it shut, hit the locks. The *thunk* of them engaging was the most beautiful sound she'd ever heard.

For a moment she just sat there, chest heaving, staring out at the dark forest pressing against her windows. Nothing moved. No Jordan. No mysterious footsteps. Just trees. Shadows. And the fading rain.

Her hands were still shaking when she shoved the key into the ignition and twisted.

The engine turned over—once, twice—then caught with a rattling purr that made her shoulders drop with relief. She threw the car into reverse, pressed the accelerator—

The tires spun.

"No." Cressida pressed harder. The engine whined. The tires spun faster, spitting wet earth and pine needles. The car rocked slightly but didn't move backward. Didn't move at all. "No no no, come *on*—"

She shifted to drive. Pressed the gas. The tires spun again, digging deeper into whatever soft earth she'd parked on. She could smell burning rubber mixing with the scent of wet forest.

"You have *got* to be kidding me."

Cressida killed the engine and leaned forward, pressing her forehead against the steering wheel. Her heart was still racing, her breath still coming too fast. Stuck. She was stuck in the middle of the woods at almost midnight with

Jordan Quinn somewhere out there and her car buried axle-deep in mud.

Of course. The universe really does have taste.

"Perfect," she muttered. "This is just *perfect*."

She sat up, wiping rain and sweat from her face, and pulled out her phone. One flickering bar of signal mocked her from the corner of the screen.

There was really only one option.

Cressida swiped through her contacts, and pressed Miles's name before she could talk herself out of it. The phone rang once—

"Cressida?" His voice came through immediately, alert despite the hour. "Everything okay?"

She closed her eyes. "You have to promise not to laugh."

There was a pause. When Miles spoke again, she could hear the smile in his voice. "You know that's not a promise I can make."

"My car is stuck."

Miles laughed—a warm, rich sound that would have been comforting under literally any other circumstances. "Of course it is. Where are you and your clown car? I'll come get you."

"I'm—" Cressida hesitated, biting her lip. "I'm out past County Road 14. Up in Shadewood Hollow. Near the old cottages."

The laughter died instantly. The silence that followed was sharp enough to cut.

"Miles?"

"Damn it, Cressi." His voice had gone flat, serious in a way that made her stomach clench. "Stay in the car and lock the doors. I'm on my way."

"The doors are already locked—"

"Good. Keep them that way. I mean it. Don't get out, don't open the windows, don't do *anything* until I get there. Understand?"

The fear in his voice made her own anxiety spike again. She glanced out at the dark forest, suddenly very aware of how isolated she was. "Yeah. I understand."

"Twenty minutes. Maybe less. I'm leaving now." She heard rustling on his end—keys jangling, a door opening. "What the hell were you thinking going up there alone?"

"Long story. I'll explain when you get here." Cressida wrapped her free arm around herself, suddenly cold despite the car's lingering warmth. "And Miles? Don't tell Aunt Sylvia and Roz."

"That's a given." A car door slammed. An engine roared to life. "Stay put, Cressi. I'm coming."

The call ended.

Cressida let the phone drop into her lap and stared out at the darkness. The forest stared back, patient and knowing. Somewhere out there, Jordan Quinn had vanished into an abandoned cottage for reasons she couldn't begin to guess. And somewhere—maybe close, maybe not—something had been following her through the trees.

She checked the locks again. Still secure. Wrapped both hands around the steering wheel just to have something to hold onto. Started counting her breaths—*one-two-three, one-two-three*—trying to slow her racing heart.

Twenty minutes, Miles had said. Maybe less.

She could do twenty minutes.

She had to.

Chapter Twenty-One

THE FIRST FIVE MINUTES passed in tense silence. Cressida kept her eyes on the rearview mirror, then the side mirrors, then straight ahead through the windshield—a constant rotation of vigilance that did nothing to calm her racing heart. The forest pressed close on all sides, dark and patiently waiting.

One-two-three, one-two-three. Her fingers drummed against the steering wheel. *Miles is coming. He'll be here soon. You're fine. You're locked in the car. You're completely—*

Movement.

Her breath caught. There—between two pines about fifteen feet to her left—something shifted. A shadow darker than the surrounding darkness, vertical where it shouldn't be, too tall to be a deer, too solid to be branches swaying in wind that had already died down to nothing.

Cressida's hand found the door lock, checked it again even though she knew it was engaged. The shadow didn't move. Just stood there. Watching? Waiting?

It's Jordan, she thought, heart hammering. *He circled back. He knows I followed him. He knows I took photos and now he's—*

The shadow shifted again, angling slightly as if turning to face her more directly.

"Okay," Cressida whispered to herself. "You need to know."

Her hand was already on the door handle.

She eased it open—just a crack, listening. Cool air rolled in, damp and sharp with wet pine. Something else threaded through it. Something organic and old.

"Jordan?" Her voice came out steadier than she felt. "Jordan Quinn, I know that's you. I saw you at the cottage. We should talk."

The shadow didn't respond. Didn't move. Just stood there in that impossible stillness that made her skin crawl.

Cressida pushed the door wider and stepped out, one hand on the frame. Pine needles crunched underfoot—too loud in the quiet. "Look, I'm not here to cause trouble. I just want to understand what you were doing up here." She squinted into the darkness. "If you're in some kind of danger, maybe I can help."

Nothing. The silhouette remained motionless, a darker patch that refused to resolve into recognizable shape.

This is stupid, a voice whispered in the back of her mind. *This is how people die in horror movies. Get back in the car, Cressi.*

She'd never been good at listening to that voice.

Her phone came out, thumb hovering over the flashlight button. "I'm going to turn on my light now. Don't run. I just want to talk."

She tapped it. White light blazed out, cutting through the gloom, illuminating rain-slicked bark and dripping needles and—

Nothing.

The space between the trees stood empty. No Jordan. No shadow. Just forest and fog and the faint mist of her own breath in the sudden cold.

"What the hell?" Cressida swept the light left, then right, her heart climbing into her throat. The beam found nothing but more trees, more shadows, more darkness pressing in from all sides. "Where did you—"

A branch cracked somewhere behind her.

She spun, light swinging wild, and caught a glimpse of something moving through the underbrush about twenty yards back—something that moved wrong, too fluid, too quick, like it was gliding rather than walking.

"Jordan?" Her voice cracked on his name. "Is that you?"

The movement stopped. Silence crashed down again, thick and suffocating. Cressida's hand tightened on her phone until her knuckles ached. The light trembled, making shadows dance and twist into shapes that might be anything.

Get back in the car.

She took a step backward, keeping the light trained on where she'd seen the movement. Another step. Her heel caught on something—a root, a rock, she didn't know—and she stumbled, catching herself against the car's hood with a metallic thump that echoed through the hollow.

The forest erupted with sound.

Not footsteps—rustling. Multiple sources, moving through the trees with wrong fluidity. Circling.

"Oh God." She scrambled backward along the car, light swinging frantically. "Oh God oh God—"

Her back hit the driver's side door. She reached for the handle, fingers scrabbling—

Something breathed.

Right next to her ear.

Hot. Wet. Carrying the scent of rot and earth and things that should stay buried.

She screamed—a sharp, piercing sound that tore through the quiet—and whirled around, light blazing. Nothing. Empty air. Forest staring back with patient, knowing gloom.

Before conscious thought caught up, her legs were already moving.

Away from the car. Away from whatever had just breathed down her neck. Deeper into the forest where the trees might offer cover. Her phone light bounced wild, strobing the world into flashes—bark, shadow, reaching branches that snagged her clothes and hair.

Behind her—or around her, or everywhere at once—the rustling followed. Keeping pace. Never quite visible but always *there*, just at the edge of her light's reach.

"Help!" Her voice cracked, breath coming in ragged gasps. "Somebody help me!"

A low-hanging branch caught her across the forehead. Stars exploded behind her eyes. She stumbled, nearly went down, caught herself against a tree trunk slick with moss and kept running. Warm blood slid through rain and sweat.

Miles, she thought desperately. *Where are you? How long has it been? Ten minutes? Fifteen? Please be close. Please—*

The ground disappeared beneath her feet.

She was falling—sliding down a steep embankment thick with wet leaves and loose soil, phone tumbling from her grip, light spinning away into the gloom. Her shoulder slammed into something hard. Her knee twisted. The world became a chaos of pain and terror and the absolute certainty that whatever had been following her was right behind, right there, reaching out with hands or claws or something worse—

She hit bottom in a tangle of limbs and brambles, gasping, tears streaming down her face mixing with blood and rain.

"Cressida!"

The voice cut through her panic like a lifeline. Distant but getting closer. Familiar. Real.

"*Cressida!*" Louder now, urgent, edged with fear she'd never heard from him before. "Where are you? Answer me!"

"Miles!" Her voice came out as a sob. "I'm here! I'm—"

She tried to stand and her knee buckled, sending her back down with a cry of pain. Blood soaked through her torn pants. Her hands were scraped raw, embedded with pine needles and small stones.

"Keep talking!" Miles's voice was closer now—maybe fifty yards, maybe less. "I'm coming to you. Just keep talking so I can find you!"

"I'm in a—a ravine or something. Down a slope." Cressida dragged herself to sit against a fallen log, scanning the murk above her with wide, terrified eyes. The rustling had stopped. Everything had stopped. The silence was somehow worse than the sound had been. "Miles, there's something out here. There's something in the woods and it was chasing me and—"

"I know. I'm almost there. Stay put."

Light appeared at the top of the embankment—a strong, steady beam cutting through the dark. Then Miles himself, silhouetted against his flashlight's glow, tall and solid and utterly, impossibly real.

"Cressi." His voice cracked on her name. "Jesus Christ, what happened to you?"

Before she could answer, he was already moving—sliding down the embankment with the kind of muscle memory of someone who'd spent years navigating these woods in darkness. In seconds he dropped to one knee beside her, propped his flashlight against his shoulder, and began checking her over with quick, gentle hands.

"You're bleeding." His fingers brushed her forehead. "Head wound. Probably needs stitches. What else hurts?"

"My knee." Her hands shook so badly she could barely gesture. "I twisted it. And my shoulder. Miles, there was something—"

"I know." In the flashlight's glow, his jaw was set hard. "I saw your car. Saw the door open. Thought—" He stopped. "Never mind what I thought. Can you walk?"

"I don't know. Maybe with help."

Miles shrugged out of his jacket and wrapped it around her shoulders. The fabric held his body heat, smelled like cedar and something clean and human and safe. "My truck's on the road, maybe two hundred yards from here. Think you can make it that far if I support you?"

Cressida nodded, not trusting her voice.

He helped her up slowly, taking most of her weight, one arm locked around her waist. She leaned into him, legs trembling, and forced herself not to look back into the darkness behind them.

"Miles?" she whispered. "What is this place? What's out here?"

He was quiet for a long moment, guiding her carefully around obstacles she couldn't see, his flashlight cutting a narrow path through the trees. When he finally spoke, his voice was low and serious.

"Nothing good, Cressi. Nothing good comes to Shadewood Hollow after dark. Not anymore."

He didn't elaborate. And she didn't ask.

They just walked—slow, painful progress through the listening forest—until the distant glow of his truck's headlights appeared like salvation through the trees.

Rain drummed against metal. Inside Miles' truck, the heater cranked out warmth that made Cressida's torn clothes steam. She curled against the passenger door, hunkered down in his jacket, and watched fog-thick forest slide past. Every shadow between the trees made her flinch.

Her knee throbbed in time with her heartbeat. Someone had taken a bat to her shoulder—that's what it felt like, anyway. The cut on her forehead had mostly stopped bleeding, but dried blood crusted along her hairline.

Miles kept both hands on the wheel, jaw tight, eyes flicking between the road and her with a frequency that might have been funny under different circumstances. He hadn't said much since getting her into the truck. Three times he'd asked if she was okay. Three times she'd given shaky affirmatives. Then he'd started the engine.

The silence stretched between them—not quite comfortable but not hostile either. More like both of them were trying to figure out what the hell had just happened and coming up empty.

Cressida opened her mouth. She wasn't sure what she wanted to say—maybe an apology for being reckless, maybe a question about what he'd meant by *nothing good comes to Shadewood Hollow after dark.*

His phone rang.

The ringtone cut through the quiet like a gunshot. Miles glanced at the screen, then hit speaker.

"Aunt Marnie." Carefully neutral. "It's almost midnight."

"I know what time it is, Miles Stone." Marnie's warm contralto filled the cab, somehow managing to sound both exhausted and energized. "And I know you're still up because you're always still up when something's bothering you. Got some updates on the Dodd case."

Cressida straightened despite the protest from her knee. Miles caught her eye, one eyebrow raised in question.

She nodded.

"Go ahead," Miles said. "I'm listening."

"Susan Mitchell's alibi checked out." Papers rustled in the background. "Deputy Jensen went back to the fairgrounds this afternoon, talked to the organizers. Found a witness—actually found three—who all remember Susan was helping set up the children's tent when Henrietta collapsed. Specifically remembers her carrying boxes of ribbons because one of them split open and she had to chase down about fifty purple ribbons in the wind."

Another suspect, gone. The certainty of it settled in Cressida's chest like a stone.

"And the Reverend?" Miles asked.

"Called Danny himself about an hour ago. I've already confirmed he was at that meditation retreat in Asheville all last week. I spoke to the retreat coordinator too—Carlson was there for every session, every meal. No way he could have been in Blackvale planning anything."

"Okay." The steering wheel creaked under Miles's grip. "What about the lab results?"

"Now that's where it gets interesting." Marnie's voice shifted, took on that particular quality she got when she was putting puzzle pieces together. "State lab got back to us on those organic plant oils in Henrietta's system. No lavender oil, Miles. None at all."

Wait—no lavender? Despite the pull in her shoulder, Cressida twisted toward Miles.

"But the purple around her lips—" he started.

"Food coloring," Marnie said flatly. "Purple food coloring, to be specific. Along with traces of honey and blueberry jam. Most likely from Sylvia's tart, given the timing."

Miles glanced at Cressida, something sharp and questioning in his eyes. She shook her head slightly.

"What else?" The truck took a turn too fast. "What else was in her system?"

"No allergy medication whatsoever, which is interesting given she supposedly had severe allergies. That's why she was going to that specialist according to her husband." More paper rustling. "She did have a savory breakfast before arriving at the fair—traces of thyme and sage in her stomach contents, along with—hold on, let me get this right. Purple food coloring, honey, blueberry jam like I said. And that's it."

"That was all?" Miles's voice dropped to barely above a whisper. "Nothing else in her stomach or bloodstream?"

"Nothing else, sugar." Marnie sighed, long and weary. "Look, I'm heading home. My eyes are crossing and my dear Xavier's probably forgotten I exist. But Miles? Make sure that girl of yours comes to see me soon, hear? Or I'll come find her, and she won't like it when I do."

Despite everything, Cressida's mouth quirked. *That girl of yours.* Aunt Marnie had been trying to matchmake since Cressida was sixteen.

"Will do, Aunt Marnie." His voice softened. "Get some rest."

"You too, baby. Both of you." The call ended with a soft click.

Quiet rushed back in, heavier than before.

Miles kept his eyes on the road. Cressida stared at her scraped, bloody hands.

"That's another suspect lost," she said finally. Her voice came out flat, defeated. "Susan's out. Reverend Carlson confirmed. And all I have to show for tonight is broken nails and a bruised knee."

She laughed—a short, bitter sound that had no humor in it. Self-pity welled up, hot and shameful, but she couldn't quite push it back down. "Why did I think I could solve this? It's not the same as figuring out who stole Mr. Pittman's newspapers back when we were kids. Or even—"

"Stop." Miles's hand shot out, catching hers. His palm was warm, callused from years of outdoor work, and he squeezed once—hard enough that she felt the pressure through her fog of misery. "You didn't think you could solve it. You *knew* we could. And we still can."

Cressida looked at him. Really looked. His jaw was set, eyes steady on the road, but his hand was still holding hers like an anchor. Like he meant every word.

The tears came before she could stop them—hot, frustrated, exhausted tears that she didn't bother trying to hide. They tracked down her cheeks, mixing with the dried blood and dirt, and she didn't care.

"Miles." Her voice broke on his name. "Just... take me home. Please. I wanna go home."

He didn't argue. Didn't try to rally her spirits or talk her out of her defeat. Just squeezed her hand once more, then let go and drove.

The mountain road unwound beneath them. Through half-closed eyes, Cressida watched fog and darkness give way to the distant glow of Blackvale's lights—pinpricks of warmth against the black. She leaned her head against the cold window. Let the truck's steady motion carry her down from the hollow, away from whatever had been out there in those trees.

For the moment, it was almost like safety.

CHAPTER
TWENTY-TWO

FOG PRESSED AGAINST THE windows the next morning—thick, solid, weighted. From her corner in Aunt Sylvia's kitchen nook, Cressida watched it through glass that seemed too thin to hold it back. Miles's jacket once again draped over her shoulders. She couldn't quite bring herself to return it.

Her knee throbbed. Her shoulder ached. The cut on her forehead pulled tight every time she frowned, which was often.

Gray, heavy, obscuring—the fog matched her mood perfectly.

The Vale House Inn was empty. Blissfully, unusually so. All the guests had braved the weather for day trips or antiquing expeditions, leaving just the three of them: Cressida wedged into worn cushions, Aunt Sylvia at the stove, and Roz at the table with her laptop open and reading glasses perched on her nose.

From the windowsill, the radio played low—some gospel station Aunt Sylvia favored—and her great-aunt sang along in rich contralto, voice sliding over words like honey. Spatula in one hand, wooden spoon in the other, she moved between pans with the practiced choreography of someone who'd been cooking in this kitchen for forty years, silver curls bouncing with each step, crimson poppies bright against cream linen, enough jewelry to open a small boutique, jangling softly as she worked.

"—shelter in the time of storm—"

Cinnamon and butter layered the air with something savory and rich underneath. Cressida's empty stomach clenched.

"I still can't believe you went out there alone." Roz's fingers clicked across the keys—sharp, staccato, barely restrained. She didn't look up. "To Shadewood Hollow. At night. Without telling anyone."

Cressida shifted, knee protesting. "I had my phone—"

"Which you *dropped* when you ran from whatever the hell was chasing you through those woods." Roz looked up now, dark eyes piercing behind her glasses. "Do you have any idea what could have happened?"

"I know." The words came out small. Cressida pulled Miles's jacket tighter. Cedar and safety. "I know, okay? It was stupid—"

"You don't think, Cressi. You just leap." The laptop closed—soft click, final in the quiet kitchen. Roz leaned forward, gave her sister the full weight of her attention, the kind that felt like being held under a microscope. Then her hand shot across the table, caught Cressida's wrist—brief but fierce, conveying everything words couldn't.

I could have lost you.

"Dr. Wade said you were lucky. Very, very lucky."

Behind them, butter hissed in the pan. Through the window, fog muffled the distant sound of a truck passing.

Cressida touched the bandage on her forehead gingerly, feeling Roz's gaze tracking the movement. Dr. Wade had made a house call last night—she didn't think doctors still did that, but apparently small towns operated on different rules—and checked her over with gentle, efficient hands while Miles hovered in the doorway like a silent sentinel.

No concussion, thank God. No stitches needed. Her knee would be sore for a while, bruised deep where she'd slammed it against that tree root. Her clothes from last night would never be the same and she could kiss those vintage oxfords goodbye. All things considered, she'd come out better than she looked.

Which wasn't saying much, given that she looked like she'd gone three rounds with the forest and lost.

"I'm fine," Cressida said quietly, watching Roz's expression flicker between relief and residual anger. "Really. It looks worse than it is."

"Mmhmm." Aunt Sylvia turned from the stove, spatula pointed like a conductor's baton. "And that's why you're sitting in my kitchen looking like something the cat dragged through a bramble patch, wearing Miles Stone's jacket like it's a security blanket, flinching every time the fog shifts outside the window?"

Cressida opened her mouth. Closed it. Had nothing to say to that.

Aunt Sylvia's expression softened. She set down the spatula, crossed to the nook, and settled on the bench opposite Cressida with a small sigh. Up close, the worry showed—fine lines around her great-aunt's eyes, tension beneath the usual bright smile.

"Sugar-lamb." Aunt Sylvia reached across the table, took Cressida's hand. Her thumb stroked over scraped knuckles. "You scared us. You scared Miles half to death—I've never heard that boy sound like that on the phone. And you scared yourself, didn't you?"

Cressida's throat tightened. She nodded.

"Good." A firm squeeze. "Fear keeps us honest. Keeps us from doing fool things twice." Her eyes crinkled. "Usually."

The gospel song shifted on the radio, something slower and sweeter. Roz's typing slowed—she was listening.

"Maybe—" The crack in her voice made Cressida stop, clear her throat. "Maybe I should let the authorities handle it from now on. Sheriff Stone, the state police. They have resources, training. They know what they're doing." She gestured at herself—bandages and bruises and borrowed jacket. "I'm just making things worse."

Something in her chest tightened even as she said it. A stubborn, gnawing hunger that refused to be satisfied by the sensible choice. Her mind still cataloged what she knew, sorting through suspects and motives and inconsistencies like shuffling cards, unable to stop even when she wanted to.

The kitchen went quiet except for the soft sizzle from the stove and the radio's distant harmonies.

Roz's voice came gentler now. "Let the professionals handle it, Cressi. You've done enough. More than enough. You found things they missed, asked questions they didn't think to ask." She gestured at the injuries. "But this isn't worth it."

Cressida nodded slowly. It made sense. It was the smart thing to do. The *safe* thing.

So why did it feel like giving up?

Aunt Sylvia studied Cressida with sharp, knowing eyes that saw too much and always had. A long moment passed. She rose with a soft rustle of linen and jewelry, crossed to the stove, and began plating something that smelled like salvation itself.

When she returned, the bowl made Cressida's mouth water instantly—crispy chicken nestled against golden waffles, butter melting into syrup, powdered sugar dusted over everything. Comfort food made sacred.

Aunt Sylvia set the bowl down, then settled back into her seat. Her voice came quiet but clear—the tone that meant something important was coming.

"You should do what your heart tells you to do, sugar-lamb." She folded her hands on the table, rings glinting in the foggy morning light. "But we Vale women..." A small smile touched her lips, something fierce and proud underneath the gentleness. "Well, we've never been ones to let the universe tell us we can't do something."

She said nothing else. Just patted Cressida's hand once more and rose, returning to her stove and her singing.

Cressida stared down at chicken and waffles and the weight of a legacy she'd been carrying her whole life.

Outside, the fog pressed close. Inside, the radio played on.

And Cressida picked up her fork, tasted syrup and butter and something that might have been hope, and wondered what the hell she was going to do next.

A low creak sounded from the back door—hinges protesting as it swung open. Then footsteps, heavy and deliberate, more than one set crossing the threshold. The fog swirled in with them, bringing cool mountain air and the earthy scent of damp wood and smoke.

Miles appeared first through the doorway, shoulders broad in charcoal flannel, dark hair dampened by fog. His parents followed: Sheriff Stone in his perpetually worn uniform, badge catching the overhead light, and Dr. Mae Stone with copper curls escaping a loose bun, canvas tote slung over one shoulder—probably full of therapy dog treats and homemade cookies, knowing her.

"Morning," Miles said quietly, finding Cressida's eyes immediately. Relief and worry flickered across his face. *You okay?*

She nodded. *I'm okay.*

Aunt Sylvia turned from the stove, spatula still in hand. She gave Sheriff Stone a long, measured look—the kind that could strip paint off walls or make grown men confess to crimes they'd forgotten they committed. The radio played on in the background, something about grace and mercy, while the silence stretched tight as a wire.

Her aunt's expression softened, just a fraction. "Your plate will be ready in a moment, Dan." Cordial, warm even, with that particular Southern hospitality that meant all transgressions were temporarily forgiven but absolutely not forgotten. "Roz, honey, pour the poor man some coffee."

Roz rose smoothly, laptop closed, and crossed to the coffee pot. "Cream and sugar, Sheriff Stone?"

"Black's fine, thank you." His voice was gravel-rough, worn smooth by years of delivering bad news and taking hard calls. He nodded once to Aunt Sylvia—acknowledgment, respect, maybe even apology—then moved further into the kitchen.

Dr. Mae touched her husband's arm briefly before heading straight for Cressida. "How are you feeling, sweetheart? Dan told me what happened. I brought some arnica gel—it'll help with the bruising." She dug through her tote, producing a small tin with practiced ease.

"I'm okay, really." Cressida accepted the tin. "Dr. Wade checked me over last night. Nothing serious."

"Mmhmm." Dr. Mae studied the bandage on Cressida's forehead. "And I'm sure you're following all his instructions about rest and elevation."

Cressida had the grace to look sheepish.

Miles crossed to where she sat, holding a manila folder—slightly damp from the fog, edges worn. He set it on the table with careful pre-cision. "Your photos. You left them in your car. Found your phone too."

Cressida's heart stuttered. Her car. She'd completely forgotten about it in the chaos of last night, abandoned on that dark mountain road—

"We got your car," Miles continued, reading the panic before she could voice it. "It's parked out back. No damage. Keys are in the folder."

Relief washed through her, sharp and sud-den. "Thank you," she said quietly, meeting his eyes. "I mean it. Thank you."

His expression softened. "Always."

Aunt Sylvia cleared her throat with point-ed emphasis. "Everyone sit. Food's ready and I didn't spend my morning cooking so y'all could admire my tile work."

They settled around the table with the choreography of people who'd done this be-fore: Sheriff Stone at the head (out of habit, probably, or maybe because Sylvia pointed him there with her spatula), Dr. Mae beside him, Miles next to Cressida, Roz back at her laptop with coffee in hand. Aunt Sylvia began distrib-uting plates—chicken and waffles for everyone, because apparently she'd been cooking for an army—and the kitchen filled with the comfort-able sounds of cutlery and gratitude.

For a few minutes, no one spoke. Just ate. Outside, the fog had begun to thin, pale gray giv-ing way to hints of watery sunlight that filtered through the kitchen windows. The warmth inside seemed to push back against the cold—Aunt Sylvia's cooking, the quiet companionship, the sense of being held by people who cared. Cressida let herself exist in this moment: safe, warm, surrounded by people who'd come running when she needed them.

Sheriff Stone set down his fork and cleared his throat. "I know the two of you are going to ask." He looked between Cressida and Miles. "It's a matter of public record, and you'd just file a request and make my life difficult until you got it. So I'll tell you anyway."

Cressida straightened. Her shoulder protested. Beside her, Miles glanced over with a frown before returning his attention to his father.

He pulled a folder from the leather satchel by his chair—not as thick as she'd expected, but substantial. He slid it across the table to Miles, who caught it with one hand and opened it, angling it so Cressida could see.

Papers. Official letterhead. *Blackvale Savings & Loan.* Columns of numbers, highlighted sections, notes scrawled in tight handwriting.

"Findings on the irregularities at the bank," Sheriff Stone said. "State auditors went through their records after we flagged some concerns following Henrietta's death."

Miles flipped through the pages. Cressida leaned in, scanning. Her brain sorted information automatically—building patterns, connecting dots.

There was something surreal about this, she thought distantly—sitting here bruised and bandaged, still wearing Miles's jacket, discussing financial crimes over chicken and waffles like it was the most natural thing in the world. Like she hadn't spent last night running blind through fog-thick woods with something breathing down her neck.

"Creative accounting," Sheriff Stone continued, voice flat and professional. "Several business accounts showing small discrepancies over the past four years. Amounts that wouldn't trigger automatic flags—nothing over a thousand dollars at a time. But when you put them all together..." He gestured at the papers. "Paints an interesting picture."

"How much total?" Miles asked quietly, finger tracing down a column of numbers.

"Around a hundred and forty-seven thousand, give or take."

Cressida's eyebrows shot up. Nearly forty grand a year. For four years someone was able to siphon off that much without anyone knowing.

"But," Sheriff Stone added, and his tone carried a warning, "there's no conclusive proof that Willard is the culprit. Just a lot of coincidences. He had access to these accounts in both of his roles—assistant branch manager and senior loan officer. The discrepancies started around the time he was promoted to those positions. But so did system upgrades, staff turnover, and a merger with a smaller credit union that complicated the bookkeeping."

"Convenient," Roz murmured from her laptop.

"Very," Sheriff Stone agreed. "But coincidences aren't evidence. The state's still investigating, but unless they can prove direct access and intent, Willard walks. And from what I've seen..." He shook his head. "The man's careful. If he did this, he did it smart."

Cressida studied the papers. One hundred forty seven thousand dollars. Not enough to retire on, not enough to run away with—but enough to matter. Enough to change things. Enough to be desperate about.

Desperate enough to kill?

Miles had gone very still beside her, his attention fixed on something in the folder. She watched his eyes narrow slightly, that little crease appearing between his brows that meant he'd caught something.

"What?" she asked quietly.

He tapped a line near the top of one page. "Willard's full name is listed here. Willard V. Dodd." He looked up at his father. "What does the V stand for?"

Sheriff Stone took a long sip of coffee, like he was fortifying himself. "Vern. Willard Vern Dodd. Family name—his grandfather was Vernon Dodd, owned a tobacco farm up near the Tennessee border before it went under in the eighties."

"Vern," Miles repeated slowly, testing the word.

And something in Cressida's brain went *ping*.

Sharp. Sudden. Like a notification sounding on her phone from an app she couldn't identify, buried somewhere in the folders she never organized properly. That feeling of *this matters* without knowing why, the sensation of two puzzle pieces that should fit together but she couldn't quite see how yet.

Vern. Willard Vern Dodd.

Why did that feel important?

She stared at the papers, at Willard's name typed in neat official font, and tried to chase down the thought skittering just out of reach in the back of her mind. Something about names. Something about—

The radio shifted to a commercial break—someone advertising fresh lavender wreaths at the farmers' market—and Cressida barely heard it. Her hand had moved automatically to Miles's jacket, fingers worrying at the fabric while her brain worked.

Vern. V. Why does that matter? Where have I seen—?

"Cressi?" Miles's voice, quiet and close. "You okay?"

She blinked, looked up to find everyone at the table watching her with varying degrees of concern. Aunt Sylvia with her fork paused mid-air. Roz with her coffee cup halfway to her lips. Dr. Mae with that therapist's gentle patience. Sheriff Stone with cop's eyes that missed nothing.

And Miles, dark eyes searching hers, reading every flicker of thought across her face like he always had.

"I don't know," Cressida said slowly, honestly. "But something about that name... it feels important. Like I should know why it matters."

She pressed her fingers to her temples, trying to force the connection. But the thought stayed just out of reach, maddeningly close but refusing to crystallize into something solid she could grab onto.

Vern. V. Willard V. Dodd. Why does that—

"Give it time," Dr. Mae said gently from across the table. "Sometimes our minds need to work through things in their own way. The answer will come when it's ready."

Cressida nodded, but she couldn't quite let it go. The thought kept circling in her mind. Insistent and impossible to ignore, even as conversation resumed around the table and Aunt Sylvia refilled coffee cups. The fog outside shifted and swirled like her own confusion—hiding something just out of reach, then revealing a glimpse before obscuring it again. Her brain was playing hide and seek with a fact that refused to stay still long enough to be caught.

CHAPTER TWENTY-THREE

SHERIFF STONE SET DOWN his fork with deliberate movement, the clink of metal against ceramic cutting through the comfortable breakfast sounds. His dark eyes fixed on Cressida with an expression she recognized from childhood—the one that preceded lectures about climbing too high in trees or "borrowing" his department-issued flashlight for midnight cemetery investigations.

"What were you thinking," he said, and though his voice stayed level, something raw flickered beneath it—worry bleeding through the professional calm like ink through wet paper. The kind of fear a father feels when his daughter does something reckless and survives it. "Going out to Shadewood Hollow at night? Alone?"

The kitchen went quiet except for the radio's soft crooning and the howl of the wind outside the windows—a howl like something alive.

Cressida opened her mouth, but Mae beat her to it.

"Dan." One word, gentle but firm, the tone of a woman who'd spent three decades redirecting her husband's protective instincts into something approaching reasonable. "Don't lecture the poor girl. She's already been through enough."

Stone's jaw tightened—not anger, but the physical effort of swallowing back words that wanted to spill out. Words like *you could have been killed* and *when will you ever learn* and *what would I do with Miles if something happened to you.* He subsided with a grunt that might have been agreement or just strategic retreat, but his hand gripped his coffee mug a little tighter than necessary.

Mae turned to Cressida, blue eyes soft with concern, and reached into her ever-present tote bag. When her hands emerged, they held—

Cressida blinked.

Coloring sheets. A box of crayons, the big 64-count kind with the built-in sharpener.

"These are for later," Mae said, setting them on the table beside Cressida's plate. "Remember, it's important to process feelings. And it's easier to do that when your hands are busy."

Miles made a sound somewhere between a laugh and a sigh. "Mom. We're not kids anymore."

Aunt Sylvia snorted from across the table, fork raised like a scepter, her expression brooking no argument. "You'll always be our babies, and don't you forget it."

"Amen to that," Mae said, reaching over to pat Miles's hand with the serene confidence of maternal truth.

Cressida felt something warm and complicated twist in her chest—affection and exasperation and the bone-deep comfort of being known, even when that knowing came with coloring sheets and lectures.

She wrapped both hands around her coffee mug, letting its heat seep into her palms and forced herself to meet Sheriff Stone's gaze. "I wasn't thinking," she admitted, the words coming slower than usual, more careful. "But something about Jordan..." She paused, searching for the right words. "Something about him makes my brain cells itch with wrongness. Like when you see a picture and one detail is off but you can't quite place what it is."

Sheriff Stone's expression shifted—still serious, but with a flicker of understanding. The look of someone who'd felt that same itch and learned to trust it.

"I'll look into the cottage you saw him searching," he said finally, reaching for his own coffee. "But trying to find out who owns it will be tricky. Property records out in Shadewood are a mess—generations of informal transfers, family disputes, tax sales that were never properly documented."

"There's still a handful of people who live out there," Aunt Sylvia offered, returning to the table with the coffee pot for refills. Her voice had gone softer, touched with something that might have been sadness. "Mostly transients now. But most of those families moved on or died out. Sad, really."

She poured coffee with the careful attention of someone buying time to think. "Used to be a proper community once. Back when the mines were running, before they went too deep and things turned... strange. But after the accidents, after the families started leaving..." She trailed off, shaking her head.

The radio shifted to something instrumental—piano and strings, melancholy and sweet.

Roz's chair scraped against the floor as she stood, closing her laptop with a decisive click. "I should head to work. City Council has a budget meeting at nine, and the mayor gets cranky when I'm not there to translate his rambling into actual policy."

Sheriff Stone rose too, fishing his keys from his pocket. "I should be going as well." He glanced at Mae, who was already gathering her tote. "I'll drop you off at your office."

"Thank you for breakfast, Sylvia," Mae said, moving to hug Aunt Sylvia with the ease of old friendship. "It was wonderful as always."

Sheriff Stone paused at the door, one hand on the frame, and turned back. His expression was almost shy. "Friday night's game still on?"

Aunt Sylvia's laugh rang through the kitchen, bright and wicked. "Sure is. And I'm not gonna go soft on you anymore, Dan Stone. My competitive spirit demands vengeance."

"Looking forward to it," he said, and the smile that crossed his face made him look years younger.

Then they were gone—Roz first with a wave and her laptop bag, then the Stones in a flurry of final goodbyes and reminders to rest. The door closed behind them, muffling the sound of engines starting and gravel crunching under tires.

The kitchen felt bigger in their absence. Quieter, despite the radio and Aunt Sylvia humming as she cleared plates.

Miles turned to Cressida, dark eyes searching her face with that particular intensity that meant he was reading her the way he always had—every flicker of thought, every shift of emotion written plain as text for him to decode.

"What do you want to do?" he asked quietly.

Cressida looked at the foggy morning pressing against the windows, at the coloring sheets Big Red had left like a promise of safety, of processing and normal healing. At the manila folder with her recovered car keys. At Miles, steady and patient and waiting for her to leap wherever her restless mind would take them next.

She thought about Henrietta collapsed across her prize-winning cake, purple-lipped and gasping. About Willard's blank affect and that pharmacy bag. About Jordan searching a dark cottage in Shadewood Hollow with methodical, desperate purpose. About the notification still pinging in her brain—*Vern. Willard V. Dodd. Why does that matter?*

About one hundred forty-seven thousand dollars siphoned in careful increments and secrets buried in property records and families that moved on or died out.

About truth hiding in plain sight, waiting for someone restless enough to find it.

"I want to take some painkillers and solve this," Cressida said, and her voice came out steady despite the ache in her knee and the fog in her thoughts. She met Miles's eyes, saw understanding flicker there, saw the agreement before she even finished speaking. "Let's go find Jordan."

CHAPTER TWENTY-FOUR

THE MAGNOLIA INN SAT on the western edge of Blackvale—a three-story Victorian converted sometime in the 1980s with all the charm of a tax write-off. White paint peeled like scabbed skin. A neon VACANCY sign buzzed in the fog.

Miles pulled the Bronco into the gravel lot, the crunch too loud in the muffled quiet. He killed the engine and drummed his fingers against the steering wheel. Cressida stared at the house while her mind spun through possibilities like a roulette wheel that hadn't landed yet.

"You sure about this?" Miles asked, dark eyes tracking the second-floor windows like he was already cataloging exits and blind spots.

"Nope." Cressida grabbed her phone—pink glitter case catching what little light penetrated the fog—and shoved it into her purse. "But when has that ever stopped me?"

Miles made a sound that might have been a laugh or a sigh or both. "Never once in the twenty-four years I've known you."

They took the narrow stairs to the second floor, the wood creaking under their feet like the building itself was gossiping about their presence. Her knee protested the whole time. Room 207 sat at the end of the hallway, door painted a shade of beige that aspired to nothing and achieved it perfectly.

Miles knocked. Three sharp raps that echoed down the empty corridor.

Silence. Then cautious footsteps and the metallic scrape of a chain lock being tested.

The door opened six inches. Jordan Quinn's face appeared in the gap, hair disheveled, eyes sharp with the wariness of someone who'd been expecting trouble and here it was, right on schedule.

"Cressida." Jordan's voice came out flat, but his eyes widened as he took in her appearance—the bandage stark white against her forehead, the careful way she shifted her weight to favor her injured side. "What happened to you?"

"Jordan!" Cressida offered her brightest smile, the one that preceded uncomfortable questions. "Got a minute?"

"I have nothing left to say to you." Jordan started to close the door, but Miles shifted his weight forward—not threatening, just *present*, filling the space with quiet authority that made the air feel heavier.

"Fine," Miles said, his tone conversational but edged with something harder underneath. "You can have this conversation with Sheriff Stone instead."

The door froze.

Cressida tilted her head, studying the calculation flickering across Jordan's face. "I wouldn't advise that, though. Relatively speaking—" she nodded toward Miles, "this is the nicer Stone."

Jordan's gaze cut to Miles, taking in the crossed arms and steady dark eyes that promised patience but also consequences. The kind of look that said I *will wait as long as it takes, and you will not enjoy what happens after.*

A beat. Two. Then Jordan stepped back and opened the door wider, resignation settling over his features like fog rolling down the mountain.

"Come in," he said quietly.

The hotel room matched every generic expectation—bland prints, clashing patterns, the ghost of cigarette smoke beneath industrial cleaner. But Jordan's details told a different story.

Cressida's focus narrowed. Miles called it her "Sherlock mode"—that hyperfocus state where everything else faded and the world became nothing but data points waiting to be connected.

The unmade bed. Tumbled sheets. Stack of receipts spread across the comforter—Hollow Creek Tavern, the bakery on Main Street, that little tea shop run by the Shongs. All dated from the past month. All carefully preserved. People don't keep receipts unless they're building a case or covering tracks.

The camera on the desk. Memory card slot conspicuously empty. That kind of absence screams intention.

And the laptop. Open. Glowing.

Cressida drifted closer, angling her head to read the screen without seeming to. A draft post, half-finished, the header visible at the top of the browser window.

Truth in the Kitchen.

Not *Mountain Flavors.*

Wrong name. Wrong website. Why lie about which blog he writes for?

Miles stayed just inside the doorway, arms crossed. A wall. Jordan couldn't leave without going through him, and they both knew it.

Cressida drifted through the room. Hands clasped behind her back. Museum tour energy.

The suitcase in the corner—half-unpacked. Expensive clothes, practical cuts. Someone who moved often but paid attention to quality.

The notepad on the nightstand. Tight hand-writing crammed across the page. Names, dates, question marks clustering like constellations.

And there, tucked between two tourism brochures on the desk. A photograph.

Color. High-resolution. Professional equip-ment, the kind that cost more than her last three cameras combined.

Henrietta Dodd.

Not at the competition. Not collapsed across her cake. This was from *weeks ago*: Hen-rietta laughing at some outdoor event, her sig-nature pearl necklace catching sunlight. Her ex-pression unguarded in a way Cressida had never seen in person.

She picked up the photo with two fingers. Evidence.

Which, she supposed, it was.

"So." Cressida turned, holding the photo be-tween them like an accusation. Her voice stayed light. Almost friendly. Her eyes weren't. "Want to tell us what a food journalist is really doing in Blackvale, Mr. Quinn?"

Jordan's jaw worked. "I came to cover the Golden Spoon competition and interview Hen-rietta Dodd."

"Try again," Miles said from the doorway. Still hadn't moved. Didn't need to.

Jordan's tells were loud. The flicker toward the laptop screen—twice now. The coiled spring tension in his shoulders. The way his expression tried too hard to look casual, which meant it wasn't.

"That's fine," Cressida said. "I can go first and you can just fill in the blank spots."

Cressida pushed off the desk, her voice shifting into the cadence she used when piecing a puzzle together out loud: half theory, half accusation, all momentum. "Let's start with the obvious. Henrietta knew you." She gestured toward the photograph still lying on the desk. "I saw it the day of the competition. That moment of recognition when she spotted you in the crowd. Not surprise—*recognition*. Like she'd seen you before."

Jordan's jaw tightened but he said nothing.

"Then there's the documentation," Cressida continued, pacing now, her hands moving as she talked. She gestured toward the notepad and the receipts. "Those notes aren't about restaurant reviews or recipe features. You weren't documenting the Golden Spoon Competition. You were documenting *Henrietta*. Specifically. Which means you didn't come to Blackvale as a food blogger covering an event." She stopped, turning to face him directly. "You came here for her."

Miles shifted his weight, his voice cutting through the room with quiet authority. "Ms. Vale told us you came to her house. Asked questions that felt less like casual curiosity and more like..." He paused, letting the silence stretch. "Probing."

Cressida stopped mid-pace, turning to face Jordan directly. Her expression now edged with something darker. "Was that when you planted the poison?"

"Hold on—" Jordan shot to his feet, hands raised in defense. "I haven't planted any poison. I haven't *killed* anyone."

Jordan's gaze cut to her—sharp, direct. The detachment he'd been projecting splintered.

"Is that what you really believe?" Wounded. Quiet.

Miles moved before she could answer, positioning himself between her and Jordan. "Then explain how you know details about Henrietta and Willard's finances. Their household. Things someone who's supposedly never been to Blackvale before wouldn't—*shouldn't*—know."

Jordan's shoulders sagged. He sank back onto the bed, head hanging low, fingers threading through his dark curls. The mini-fridge hummed. Traffic buzzed somewhere outside.

"Okay." Jordan's voice came out flat. "Fine. But this is all off the record."

Miles opened his mouth—Cressida could see the protest forming, the instinct to never agree to conditions before hearing the truth—but she elbowed him sharply in the side and pushed past, moving closer to Jordan.

"Keep talking." Her tone gentler now. She technically hadn't agreed to anything.

Jordan looked up, dark eyes moving between them. Then he exhaled—long, resigned, like he'd been holding that breath for weeks.

"I haven't been to Blackvale before," he said slowly. "But my mother grew up here."

Her brain fired like a starting pistol. Eyes wide. "The house I saw you at last night...that used to belong to your family."

Jordan's head snapped up. "That was *you*? Following me through Shadewood Hollow?"

"Was it *you* who chased me through the woods?" Cressida gestured at her bandaged forehead. "Because you owe me for a pair of 1930s Sommer & Kaufman oxfords and about three years off my life expectancy."

Miles cleared his throat. "Cressida. The *point*."

Jordan shook his head, bewilderment crossing his face. "I didn't chase anyone. I heard someone moving around outside and I *booked it* back to my car. Left Shadewood entirely."

Her certainty rippled and broke. She'd been so sure—*someone* had been hunting her through those trees. If not Jordan, then who?

"Yeah, the house belonged to my family." Jordan's voice dropped into that softer register of memory. "My grandfather worked at the old Thornwood Mines. Then his son after him."

The air changed like pressure building behind the eyes. That familiar tightening in her chest when a puzzle piece clicked into place but revealed something darker underneath.

"My grandmother," Jordan continued, his voice softening with memory, "was one of those cooks who didn't need recipes. Everything she made came from *here*." He pressed a hand to his chest. "She taught my mother everything—how to fold dough until it was light as clouds, how to coax flavor from nothing, how to make a kitchen feel like love."

Cressida watched his face as he spoke, cataloging the shift in his expression—the way grief and pride warred for dominance. She'd seen that look before, on others left behind. The weight of inherited pain.

"My mom dreamed of opening her own shop someday," Jordan said. "Not some fancy restaurant—just a small place where she could share what she loved with people. Make them feel the way my grandmother's kitchen made her feel." He paused, jaw working. "Safe. Understood. *Seen*."

Miles shifted his weight—a tell Cressida caught immediately. The way his shoulders angled forward, the tightening around his eyes. *Lawyer mode activated.*

"Let me guess," Miles said. "She knew Henrietta."

Jordan's laugh came out wrong. Bitter edges, hollow center—the kind of sound that meant *yes, and it destroyed everything.*

"They went to culinary school together. Asheville Institute of Culinary Arts. My mom was top of her class—until Henrietta accused her of cheating. Said she'd stolen recipes right out of Henrietta's personal notebook."

The mini-fridge hummed. Outside, a car door slammed. The silence stretched taut as wire.

"My mother was kicked out three months before graduation," Jordan continued, his voice flat now, stripped of inflection. "No hearing. No chance to defend herself. Just... gone. And she was never the same after that."

Cressida's brain fired—*click-click-click*—connections snapping into place like dominoes falling in perfect sequence. Stolen recipes. Henrietta's rise while someone else's dream burned to ash. The pattern was *there*, stark and unmistakable. How many times? How many other Jordan Quinns were out there, carrying their mothers' ghosts, their fathers' quiet grief, their own inherited rage? How many dreams had Henrietta crushed on her way to fame, stepping on backs like they were rungs on a ladder she'd kick away once she reached the top?

"For as long as I can remember," Jordan said quietly, "my mother never stepped foot in the kitchen. She'd try sometimes—I'd catch her standing in the doorway, staring at the stove like it was a stranger. But the moment she'd reach

for a mixing bowl or pick up a knife, she'd just..."
He made a helpless gesture. "Break down. Completely fall apart."

Cressida moved closer, perching on the edge of the desk. Her voice came out softer than usual, careful. "When did things get worse?"

Jordan's hands curled into fists on his knees. "My great-grandmother—my mom's grandmother—passed away when I was five. That's when my mom just... sank. Into this depression she never came back from."

He looked up, dark eyes meeting Cressida's, and she saw it there—the hollow ache of a child who'd watched someone disappear while still physically present.

"By the time I was seven she was in a hospital bed that smelled of disinfectant," Jordan said. " By ten, she was gone."

Cressida felt something tighten in her chest—that dangerous edge where curiosity sharpened into something closer to caring. Filed under: *reasons I'm terrible at keeping distance.*

"But by then," Jordan continued, voice hardening again, "I knew all about 'the great Henrietta Dodd.' Every time she released a new cookbook, every time her face showed up on some morning show or magazine cover, something inside me grew. Something dark. Angry."

Grief hardening into something sharper. Shoulders pulled back, jaw set. She'd seen it before—people who nursed wounds until they calcified into weapons.

"Is that why you killed her? Revenge for your mom?"

"No." Too loud, too fast. Jordan shot to his feet, hands raised, fingers curling and uncurling. "I didn't—I *didn't* kill her."

Three uneven steps to the window. One palm pressed flat against the glass. His reflection ghosted in the fog-streaked pane. When he spoke again, his voice dropped lower, steadier—but underneath it ran something frayed.

"I came here for her. I've spent *years* on this—tracking down everyone she'd burned, collecting their stories, building something that couldn't be ignored." A pause. "I wanted the whole world to see it."

He turned back. Exhaustion carved deep around his eyes, the weight of carrying someone else's ghost for too long. But there was something else. Just a flicker. A coldness in the set of his mouth. The kind of steely resolve that didn't match *journalist seeking truth. Filed under: people who blur the line between justice and revenge.*

"But now she's dead." His laugh came out thin, hollow. "So what's the point? The truth doesn't matter if there's no one left to—" He broke off. "Who even cares anymore?"

His face shifted—grief first, expected, the tightness around his eyes. But underneath it: something sharper. The flicker of someone watching their carefully scripted ending get rewritten by someone else's hand.

She filed it away. Not conclusive—grief did strange things to people, twisted their expressions into shapes that looked like guilt when it was just loss processed sideways. But worth noting.

Miles cut through the silence: "To right the wrong that was done to your mother. Her legacy should still be shared. Her story should still be heard. Truth doesn't stop mattering just because the villain's gone."

Jordan stared at Miles like he'd spoken a language Jordan had forgotten he understood. Something cracked in his composure—raw, unguarded—then shuttered closed again behind that neutral mask.

Cressida stood, sharp pain from her knee making her smooth her skirt to cover the wince. Jordan's story tracked cleanly: tragic backstory, clear motive, the kind of narrative that explained almost everything. *Almost.* Not quite murder. Revenge fantasies and actual violence sat on different shelves—and Jordan's grief read too fresh, too unprocessed for someone who'd already crossed that line. People who killed didn't usually look disappointed that their victim was dead. They looked relieved. Or terrified. Or coldly satisfied.

Jordan looked frustrated. Like someone had stolen the ending he'd been working toward for years.

Not a killer. Not *the* killer, anyway.

But definitely suspicious.

"I need a copy of your research," she said. "Everything you've collected on Henrietta—her history, the people she hurt, the pattern of how she operated."

Jordan's eyes narrowed. "Why?"

"Because it'll help us find who actually killed her." She held his gaze—let him see the sincerity there, not all of it. Not the part still cataloging the micro-expressions that didn't quite line up. "Henrietta deserved to pay for her crimes. She deserved to face the consequences of what she did to your mother and God knows how many others. But no one—*no one*—deserves to be murdered."

The mini-fridge hummed. Jordan's shoulders dropped half an inch. Miles shifted his weight. The air shifted again—not tension lifting, not trust forming. Just a door cracking open where before there'd been a wall.

Jordan wasn't their killer. But his research? That was a potential map to who might be.

He closed his eyes for a second, like he was closing a door on something in himself, then nodded.

"Okay," he said. "I'll share everything I have."

Outside, the fog slid down the mountain like a hand pulling curtains. Inside, the door to who killed Henrietta Dodd cracked open—just wide enough to let the truth slip through.

CHAPTER
TWENTY-FIVE

BACK IN THE BRONCO, Cressida spread Jordan's research across her lap. Papers rustled with each bump in the road, photographs sliding against manila folders stuffed with printouts and handwritten notes. Miles navigated the winding mountain route back toward the east side of Blackvale, his focus split between the fog-thick curves ahead and the occasional sidelong glance at her furious page-turning.

Cressida's fingers moved fast, pulling folders, scanning contents, discarding what didn't matter. Connections snapped into place—disparate facts magnetizing toward each other.

Then she saw it again.

Willard Vern Dodd.

The name jumped off the page—handwritten in Jordan's neat block letters across the top of a document about Henrietta's early career. Something pinged in Cressida's head, bright and insistent, like a bell struck at just the right frequency.

"Hold on," she muttered, more to herself than Miles. Her hands dove into her messenger bag, fishing past her glitter-covered phone case, past half-empty notebooks and loose pens, until her fingers closed around the manila envelope she'd tucked there this morning.

She pulled out her photos, spreading them across Jordan's papers. Her eyes hunted for something she couldn't name but would know on sight.

There.

Her finger hovered over one particular photo. A layered tart with lattice crust work and what looked like purple-blue filling peeking through the woven dough. She searched for the photos of Aunt Sylvia's entry and placed them side by side on her lap, angling them toward the dashboard light.

Aunt Sylvia's tart—golden-brown crust crimped with decades of precision, deep purple-blue jam catching the light like stained glass, studded with lavender buds. The honey-gold glaze made the whole thing shine, crystallized flowers scattered across the top like edible confetti.

Pride swelled in her chest. *That's my aunt. That's what real artistry looks like.*

Then she shifted her attention to the other tart.

At first glance, nearly identical—same lattice pattern, same ceramic dish, same crystallized flowers. Someone had gone to considerable effort to make it a replica.

But the longer she stared, the more the differences emerged. The color was off—lighter, more lavender than the deep twilight purple of real blueberries cooked down with honey and time. The lattice less precise, edges not quite as crisp, weaving slightly uneven. And there was no honey-bourbon glaze—no liquid-gold shine, no sticky sweetness.

"It's a copy," she said aloud, her voice tight. "A *bad* copy."

Miles glanced over, eyebrows lifting. "What's a copy?"

"Anyone who knew Aunt Sylvia's work would spot it immediately." Cressida's finger stabbed at the photo of the knockoff tart. "Wrong filling color. No glaze. Lattice crust work is amateur hour compared to hers."

Cressida's pulse kicked up. She squinted at the label beneath the tart.

Entry #47: "Lavender-Honey Jam Tart" by Vernald D. Dowd

"Oh my God," Cressida breathed.

"What now? I can't read your mind, remember."

Her brain was already spinning letters around like Scrabble tiles, rearranging them with manic energy. Her finger stabbed at the photo, then at Jordan's notes, then back again.

"Vernald D. Dowd," she said, each word coming out faster than the last. "It's an anagram."

"No clue what you're talking about, but anagram for what?"

"*Willard Vern Dodd.*" Cressida looked up at him, eyes bright with the thrill of connection. "He entered this tart under a fake name—just scrambled the letters around like some cryptic crossword puzzle."

The Bronco slowed slightly as Miles processed that, his jaw working. His voice came out measured but threaded with growing interest.

"That must have been what he was doing," Miles said slowly. "When Summer Patton heard him in the kitchen. He was making a *replica* of Sylvia's tart."

"But *why*?" She stared at the photo like it might suddenly explain itself. "Why make a knockoff and enter it under a fake name?"

Miles didn't answer. Neither did the photo.

Cressida chewed her bottom lip and pulled out her phone. She navigated to her contacts with one hand, then hit the number saved as *Aunt Sylvia* (*Goddess of All Things Delicious*).

Three rings. Four. Then that familiar warm voice, bright with curiosity.

"Cressida-honey, what's wrong?"

"Nothing's wrong," Cressida said quickly. "I just need you to tell me something about your tart."

A pause. Then Aunt Sylvia's voice sharpened with the kind of focus that made her terrifying at poker. "What kind of something?"

"Ingredients," Cressida said. "The specific ones."

"Well." Aunt Sylvia's voice took on that rhythm it always did when she talked about her craft—part pride, part poetry. "It's not just lavender and blueberry, sugar-plum. There's honey from Blackwood Apiary, the kind that comes from bees that feed on mountain wildflowers. And I use a hint of lemon thyme. Fresh, not dried, to balance the sweetness. Then the glaze is honey-bourbon, made with that Blackvale Reserve bourbon from Hollow Creek Distillery. Burns your nose if you get too close while it's reducing."

Cressida's pen flew across her notebook, scribbling shorthand. "Lemon thyme. Honey-bourbon glaze. Got it."

"Cressida Vale, what in heaven's name are you doing?"

"Solving a murder," Cressida said cheerfully. "Thanks, Aunt Sylvia. You're a lifesaver. We're on our way back now."

Cressida ended the call before Aunt Sylvia could waylay her with questions. She immediately opened her browser, fingers flying across the screen as she typed search terms with the kind of focused intensity that made the rest of the world fade into white noise.

Lemon thyme poisonous lookalike plants
Honey bourbon glaze toxic substitutes
Lavender similar purple flowers deadly

Miles kept driving, but she could feel his attention on her even as he navigated another hairpin turn. The Bronco's engine hummed. Fog rolled over the truck. And Cressida scrolled, scanning articles and botanical guides and toxicology databases with the speed of someone who'd spent years learning to sift signals from noise.

Then she found it.

Her screen showed a botanical identification page, complete with side-by-side photos that made her stomach flip. The leaves looked almost identical to an untrained eye. Same color. Similar shape. Easy to mistake if you weren't paying attention or if someone *wanted* you to mistake them.

"Jackpot," Cressida whispered. Then louder, pumping her fist in the air hard enough to make the papers on her lap scatter. "*Jackpot!*"

Miles glanced over, eyebrows lifting. "Okay. So you've got the Who and the What, I'm guessing." His voice stayed level. "But we still need the How."

That stopped Cressida mid-celebration.

She looked at him, shoulders sagging slightly, the adrenaline rush cooling into something more complicated. Her voice came out flat, resigned.

"You are *such* a party pooper sometimes, you know that?"

Miles's mouth twitched—not quite a smile but close. His eyes stayed on the road but his voice carried warmth that meant he was enjoying himself.

"Actually," he said, "I'm an *incredibly handsome* party pooper. All the time. Thank you very much."

Cressida laughed—real and bright, the sound bubbling up without permission in that way Miles always managed to pull from her, the sound filling the Bronco's cabin as they descended through fog toward Vale House.

Toward answers. Toward justice. Toward whatever came next.

By the time they crested the ridge, the fog had thinned and the town unfurled below—quiet, unknowing.

The back door of Vale House swung open with its familiar creak—wood on wood, the sound of home—and Cressida stepped into warmth that smelled of cinnamon and butter. The kitchen glowed golden in the afternoon light, copper pots hanging from hooks above the butcher-block island, herbs drying in bundles near the window.

But it wasn't the kitchen that stopped Cressida in her tracks.

It was Rosalind.

Her sister stood at the far end of the island, surrounded by cardboard boxes and bubble wrap that looked wildly out of place against the Southern country charm of Aunt Sylvia's domain. Rosalind's chestnut hair was pulled back in its usual sleek updo, but her hands moved as she gestured, voice pitched with an enthusiasm Cressida rarely heard outside of election season.

"I picked the most discreet ones I could find." Rosalind held up what looked like a small wooden birdhouse, turning it over like a QVC host. "See? From the street, it'll just look decorative. No one will know it's recording."

Aunt Sylvia stood beside her, arms crossed but expression softening at the edges—the way it always did when one of her girls was trying to take care of her. She wore a floral apron over a cream blouse, silver curls catching the light, red lipstick perfect.

"Rosalind-honey, I appreciate this, but I don't want this place looking like some kind of surveillance compound. Vale House has *charm.*"

"Which is exactly why I got covers." Rosalind reached for another package. She pulled out something that looked like a vintage doorbell—brass and ceramic, with delicate floral detailing that could have come straight from an antique shop. "I found a small shop in Asheville that specializes in decorative security equipment. This one mounts beside the door and no one will ever know it's anything but period-appropriate hardware."

Miles stepped in behind Cressida. The door fell shut with a soft thud. He scanned the room with that quiet analytical focus of his—taking in the boxes, the equipment, Rosalind's uncharacteristic energy.

Cressida stood frozen.

Something had snagged in her brain like fabric on a nail. The world blurred into background noise. The birdhouse camera in Rosalind's hand. The doorbell. The *concept* of hidden surveillance disguised as everyday objects.

Then she said it. Loud. Sudden. With the kind of volume that made both Rosalind and Aunt Sylvia jump.

"Why didn't I think of that?!"

Rosalind blinked. "Think of what?"

But Cressida was already moving—spinning on her heel, grabbing Miles's arm with both hands, pulling him back toward the door they'd *just* walked through. Her fingers wrapped around his forearm like a vice, her eyes bright with the manic energy that meant she'd connected dots no one else could see yet.

"Come on," she said, already dragging him. "We have to go."

Miles planted his feet, resisting with the patience of someone who'd spent years managing Cressida Vale's sudden bursts of inspiration. "We *just* got back."

"I know—"

"We've been going for hours."

"I *know*—"

"And I'm *starving*." His voice took on a note of long-suffering that somehow managed to be both exasperated and affectionate. "Cressida, what about *lunch*?"

Cressida stopped pulling—but only because she needed both hands to gesture wildly at nothing and everything. "Lunch can wait. This can't."

"This being—?"

"I'll explain outside." She grabbed his arm again, tugging insistently. "Trust me."

Miles sighed—long and resigned and entirely predictable. But he let her pull him back out the door, away from Rosalind's confused expression and Aunt Sylvia's knowing smile.

Fog clung to the ground in patches, misting around the old oaks lining Vale House's driveway. Golden light filtered through leaves, woodsmoke drifted from somewhere down the valley.

Down the gravel driveway she went, loafers crunching stone, breath misting. Her pulse thrummed too fast, stomach twisting with too much coffee and not enough sleep. Her knee ached—dull, persistent—but momentum carried her forward. At the end, where Vale House's property met the quiet residential street, she stopped.

And turned.

Across the street: a row of houses facing Aunt Sylvia's property. Colonial revival. Craftsman bungalow. Victorian with gingerbread trim. Older homes, well-maintained. The kind of places where people cared about property values and neighborhood watch.

Left. Then right. Searching for something she couldn't quite name yet.

Miles stood beside her, hands in his pockets, watching with that expression he got when he was waiting for her brain to finish its acrobatics.

"Okay," he said. "What are we doing now?"

Cressida swept her hand toward the houses across the street. "Aunt Sylvia might not want cameras disrupting her house's charm, but her neighbors might care more about protecting their property."

Miles's eyebrows lifted. Understanding clicked into place. "With security systems."

"Exactly." She turned to face him fully. "What if one of them caught whoever planted that stuff in Sylvia's kitchen?"

He tilted his head, following her logic. "Then we'd have our proof."

She pointed at him like he'd just won a prize. "Exactly."

The objection was forming—she could see it in the way his jaw worked, the slight furrow between his brows. The voice of reason preparing to speak. She cut him off.

"Yes, I know it's a long shot." Her gesture encompassed the quiet street. "But right now we have loose threads and—"

She trailed off, letting the gesture finish the sentence.

Miles sighed. Not frustrated. Resigned to the inevitable. "No clue where this is going, but I trust that look in your eye."

"Good."

"So." He pulled his hands from his pockets, scanning the neighboring houses. "Which door are we knocking on first?"

Fog curled around the mailboxes. The street went still, like it was listening.

CHAPTER TWENTY-SIX

CRESSIDA STUDIED THE HOUSES across the street. Most were historic—charming, well-maintained, presenting the carefully preserved gentility that defined Blackvale.

Three doors down, something stood out.

Newer construction. Maybe fifteen years old. Designed to blend with its historic neighbors but clearly built for modern sensibilities. The siding too uniform, the roofline too clean. Windows caught the afternoon light differently than old wavy glass. Landscaping precisely trimmed—boxwoods shaped into perfect spheres, mulch edges sharp as knife cuts.

A sleek SUV sat in the driveway. Metallic gray. On the back window, a stick-figure decal—two adults, two small figures, and a dog.

"There," she said, pointing. "Three doors down."

Miles followed her gaze, squinting against the sun. "What makes you so sure?"

She gestured with both hands, building her case through layers of observation stacked until they formed something solid.

"Newer build means they were probably wired for security from the start. Young family with small kids—" She pointed at a plastic playhouse visible in the side yard, bright primary colors faded by sun and weather. "—means they're worried about safety. And that level of maintenance?" Another gesture at the perfectly edged lawn, the pristine mulch, the absence of fallen leaves or stray branches. "People who care tend to protect."

Miles ran her logic through his mental checklist. Head tilted. Then he nodded slowly. "That's... actually solid reasoning."

"I have my moments."

She was already moving toward the crosswalk.

Miles fell into step beside her with that easy rhythm they'd developed over decades. Her theory proved accurate. A small camera sat mounted at the corner of the roofline, angled to capture both the driveway and a generous slice of street.

The doorbell was one of those video models. Sleek black plastic with a lens that caught the afternoon light.

"Told you," Cressida murmured, a grin tugging at her lips. She glanced at Miles. "Quick, get your wallet out."

Miles was already reaching for his back pocket, pulling out his wallet.

Cressida reached out and rang the bell.

A chime sounded from inside—digital and cheerful. Then immediate chaos: a dog barking and small feet thundering across what sounded like hardwood floors. A voice called out something indistinct but maternal in tone.

The door opened after a moment to reveal a woman in her early thirties, brown hair pulled into a messy ponytail that suggested she'd given up on anything fancier around breakfast time. She was wearing yoga pants and a shirt with what might be dried oatmeal on the shoulder. A toddler—maybe three years old, with wide brown eyes and a juice-stained mouth—peeked out from behind her leg, gripping her mother's pants with one chubby fist.

Her expression shifted: confusion, wariness, then—after her eyes flicked from Cressida to Miles and back—something brighter. Stranger danger versus neighborhood concern versus the obvious excitement of being part of something interesting.

"Hi," she said, friendly but cautious. The voice of someone interrupted mid-parenting. "Can I help you?"

Cressida's smile was warm as she gestured between herself and Miles. "Hi, I'm Cressida Vale, and this is Miles Stone—Sheriff Stone's son. I'm staying with my Aunt Sylvia at Vale House Inn just down the street." She pointed vaguely behind them. "We noticed you have security cameras. Someone broke into my aunt's house recently, and we're hoping your cameras might have caught whoever did it."

Miles flipped open his wallet, holding up his driver's license.

The woman blinked. Her gaze darted past them—toward Vale House, visible through the gap in the trees—then back to their faces. The cautious politeness flickered. Curiosity won.

"Oh my god, really? At Vale House?" A pause. Another assessing look. "I'm Amanda Olsen. Come in, please. This is Oliver."

She stepped aside, pulling the door wider. One hand on her hip.

The toddler remained planted directly in the doorway like a tiny, juice-stained sentry. He stared up at them, thumb halfway to his mouth.

Amanda glanced down. "Ollie, honey, move." She nudged him gently with her knee, affectionate but firm.

Oliver shuffled sideways about six inches, still staring.

"Say hi, Ollie," Amanda prompted.

"Hi," Oliver said solemnly, his voice small and serious.

Cressida leaned forward slightly, meeting his eye level. "Hi, Oliver. Nice to meet you."

Oliver considered this gravely, then turned and bolted deeper into the house.

Amanda sighed—long-suffering and fond. "He's shy until he's not. Then you can't get him to stop talking." She gestured them inside. "Come on in."

They followed her into a living room that looked like childhood had exploded across every available surface. Board books—worn and colorful—were scattered near a wicker toy basket overflowing with stuffed animals and plastic blocks. A baby swing sat in the corner, gently rocking on its own, still moving from some recent disturbance. Foam floor tiles in primary colors formed a soft play area near the coffee table, which was covered in half-assembled puzzles and a sippy cup lying on its side.

A newborn in a pink onesie slept in a bouncer seat nearby, face turned to the side, tiny fist curled near a chubby cheek. The soft rise and fall of the infant's chest was the only movement in that corner of the room.

Cressida felt the warmth of a home actively *lived* in, the kind of organized chaos that came from small humans and not enough hours in the day. It was so different from Vale House's curated elegance, from the careful preservation of antique charm and historical integrity.

"I'm actually a huge mystery fan," Amanda said as she led them toward a desk tucked in the corner of the room. A computer sat there—desktop model, slightly outdated but clearly functional—surrounded by scattered papers and a coffee mug with a cartoon cat on it. "I've read every Agatha Christie novel at least twice. Some of them three times, actually. *Murder on the Orient Express* is probably my favorite, though *And Then There Were None* is a close second—" She caught herself, laughing a little self-consciously. "Sorry. I don't get to talk to adults much during the day. This is just—this is so exciting. I mean, not that your aunt's house was broken into, that's terrible, obviously terrible, but that I might actually help solve something real."

Amanda woke the computer. The monitor flickered to life, bathing her face in blue-white light.

"When did it happen?"

Miles spoke before Cressida could. "We're not entirely sure. Sometime in the last few days. Probably evening or night."

"Okay, let me pull up the footage." Amanda clicked through menus. "The cameras save everything for two weeks. After that it auto-deletes to save space."

She double-clicked something. A security interface appeared—split-screen views of the driveway, the front door, the street.

"I'll set you up so you can scroll through. What dates do you need?"

Cressida's hands were already moving toward the keyboard, that restless energy humming under her skin. "These past two weeks should work."

Amanda adjusted parameters. The interface responded with little confirmation beeps.

"There you go." She stepped back, gesturing toward the chair. "I'm going to grab some coffee—would you like some?"

"That would be great, thank you," Miles said. "I take mine black, she likes cream and sugar."

Amanda's footsteps faded toward the kitchen, accompanied by the distant sound of cabinets opening.

Oliver materialized between them like a tiny, curious ghost. He planted himself directly in front of the desk, craning his neck to see the computer screen. His juice-stained mouth formed a small O of concentration.

"Whatcha looking for?" The question came with that brand of child-curiosity that demanded real answers.

"Someone who maybe walked past your house a few days ago."

Cressida started scrubbing through the footage. The video timeline scrolled beneath her cursor—hours compressed into minutes, the street outside transforming through cycles of light and shadow. Day bleeding into evening bleeding into night.

"Like a bad guy?"

"Maybe," Miles said.

Oliver considered this with the gravity of someone who'd clearly given significant thought to the concept of bad guys. Then his expression shifted—brightening with the kind of enthusiasm that came from having important information to share. "We have a monster in our backyard," he announced with complete seriousness. "He likes chicken."

Cressida glanced at Miles, catching the way his mouth twitched at the corners—fighting amusement and losing—before turning back to Oliver. "That sounds scary," she said, keeping her voice appropriately concerned while her attention returned to the footage.

"He's nice though. He just makes loud noises sometimes at night. Mommy says he's 'maginary but I seen him." Oliver's pronunciation of "imaginary" came out compressed, confident despite the missing syllable.

"What does he look like?" Miles asked, indulging the kid while Cressida continued scanning footage—cars passing in accelerated time, a neighbor walking a dog in fast-forward, the sky darkening and lightening in rhythmic cycles.

"Big and fuzzy. Orange. He has pointy ears and a really long tail." Oliver spread his arms wide to demonstrate size, nearly whacking Miles in the process. "And he sleeps in the shed sometimes."

Cressida paused the footage mid-scroll. "Orange and fuzzy?"

"Uh-huh. And he goes—" Oliver made a strange yowling sound that was probably supposed to be menacing but came out adorable—somewhere between a squeaky toy and a very small dinosaur.

"Does he meow?" Cressida asked carefully.

Oliver considered this with the seriousness of a scholar contemplating a particularly thorny philosophical question. "Sometimes. But really loud. Like—MEOW!" He demonstrated at full toddler volume, the sound ricocheting off the walls and probably audible three houses down.

Miles's eyebrow lifted fractionally. "Maybe we'll add orange monsters to the suspect list," he said.

Amanda returned with two mugs—ceramic, mismatched, steam rising. She stopped mid-stride. "Oliver, are you bothering them?"

"He's fine," Cressida said, accepting the mug with both hands. The ceramic was warm against her palms, the coffee smelling rich and slightly bitter. "He was just telling us about the monster in your backyard."

Amanda sighed, exhaling equal parts affection and chagrin. "The imaginary monster, yes. He's very insistent about it. I keep telling him it's probably just raccoons getting into the garbage."

"Mom, it's *not* raccoons." Oliver's voice climbed with indignation. "Raccoons are gray. This is orange."

Cressida's attention returned to the footage, the conversation fading as her focus narrowed. The camera angle captured a good portion of the street, including the edge of Vale House Inn's property—the Victorian roofline catching late afternoon light in one frame, shrouded in fog in another.

She sped through hours of quiet suburban evening. Cars passed in fast-forward blur. A neighbor walked a dog that moved like a stop-motion puppet. Street lamps flickered on in accelerated twilight. Nothing unusual. Just ordinary rhythm, compressed and replayed at double speed.

Then, on the sixth night back, she spotted it.

A figure moving down the sidewalk. Hood pulled up despite the warm evening. Hunched slightly, as if carrying something beneath their jacket.

Wrong posture for a casual stroll. Too deliberate. Too aware.

Her pulse kicked up, that familiar electric tingle spreading through her chest. She leaned closer, one hand hovering over the mouse, the other drumming against the desk.

The figure paused at the edge of Vale House's driveway. Stopped mid-stride, head swiveling left and right.

Checking. Looking for witnesses.

Then the person cut across the lawn, moving with purpose now, heading toward the back of the house. The direction of the kitchen entrance. Victorian gingerbread trim cast shadows across the figure's face, making features impossible to distinguish.

"There," she said quietly.

Miles leaned in immediately, his shoulder brushing hers. The timestamp in the corner read 11:47 pm, numbers glowing pale green against the grainy footage.

They watched in silence as the hooded figure disappeared around the side of the house, swallowed by shadows and the camera's limited angle.

Cressida held her breath without meaning to, counting seconds in her head. *One Mississippi, two Mississippi...* Her fingers tightened on the mouse.

Roughly twelve minutes later, the figure reappeared—moving more quickly now, no longer pretending to be casual. The hunched posture was gone, replaced by something that looked almost like urgency. The person cut back across the lawn at an angle, heading toward the street, and within seconds had vanished from the camera's frame entirely.

"Can you zoom in?" Miles leaned in closer. So did Amanda.

Cressida clicked through the interface's zoom controls. The image pixelated immediately—blocky artifacts obscuring more than they revealed. She adjusted settings, tried different angles. Nothing helped. The resolution wasn't good enough. The figure had kept their head down throughout, clearly aware of potential cameras.

But there *was* something.

The build. The gait. How the shoulders moved, the length of stride, the weight distribution.

"That's a man," Cressida said, sitting back. "Look at the way he moves."

Miles studied the footage, tracking the figure's movements with the attention he usually reserved for case precedents. He replayed the sequence. Once. Twice. Three times.

"Circumstantial," he said finally. "But the shoulder width, the gait pattern—definitely male."

"Can't see if he's carrying anything." Miles rewound the footage.

Cressida squinted at the screen. The figure's jacket bulged slightly at the front—something tucked beneath it, maybe—but the darkness made specifics impossible. Her fingers drummed against the desk. "Not clearly. But it would have been small enough to fit under a jacket." The rhythm of her tapping accelerated. "We need to show this to your dad."

"Yeah." Miles straightened, reaching for his phone. "This is actual evidence. Time-stamped, documented, showing someone actively trespassing."

Amanda vibrated with barely contained excitement. "Did you find something?"

"We did." Cressida turned in the chair. "Would it be possible to get a copy of this footage? The sheriff's office will probably want the original file."

"Of course! I can email it, or put it on a USB drive—I think I have one somewhere." Amanda pulled open the desk drawer, rummaging through random office supplies before producing a small flash drive. "Aha!"

CHAPTER
TWENTY-SEVEN

WHILE AMANDA NAVIGATED THE file transfer interface, Cressida's attention drifted back to Oliver. The kid had retreated to the corner of the room, crouched over his toy truck, making soft engine noises under his breath. But his eyes kept flicking toward the adults, toward the computer screen, lingering on the frozen frame of the hooded figure with the kind of fascination children reserved for things they sensed were important even if they couldn't articulate why.

An idea had been crystallizing in Cressida's mind since his monster story.

She pushed herself up from the desk chair and crossed the few feet to where Oliver was staging what looked like an elaborate truck rescue mission involving a plastic dinosaur and a Lego person.

"Hey, Oliver," she said, crouching down to his eye level. Her knee protested the position immediately but she ignored the discomfort, focusing instead on the kid's upturned face. His eyes were wide, curious, still holding remnants of juice around his mouth. "Before we go, could you show me where your backyard monster likes to nap? I'm really curious."

Oliver's face lit up like someone had flipped a switch—pure, unfiltered joy radiating from every feature. His mouth formed a surprised O, his sticky fingers abandoning the truck mid-rescue. "Really? You believe me?"

"I believe you saw something orange and fuzzy," Cressida said diplomatically. "And I'd like to see where it sleeps."

"Okay!" Oliver grabbed her hand with the kind of sticky toddler enthusiasm that came from recent juice consumption and questionable hand-washing practices. His fingers were warm, gripping with surprising strength. "Come on!"

Miles raised an eyebrow but followed without protest as Oliver dragged Cressida toward the back of the house.

Amanda trailed behind, USB drive clutched like a trophy. "He's going to be impossible after this," she said, acknowledgement threading through her voice—the maternal amusement of watching her kid's wild imagination get validated by adults who should know better.

They passed through the kitchen's lived-in chaos—dishes stacked in the sink, high chair crusted with dried cereal, refrigerator covered in alphabet magnets and finger-painted masterpieces.

Oliver yanked open the back door and burst into the backyard with the kind of energy that made Cressida wonder where toddlers kept their batteries.

The backyard was small but well-maintained, carved from the mountain slope. A wooden play structure dominated one corner—primary colors faded by weather, slide warped but functional. Near the back fence sat a storage shed, painted robin's-egg blue, with a small window set high and a door that hung slightly crooked.

Oliver made a beeline for it, pointing with theatrical flair. "In there! That's where he sleeps sometimes."

Cressida approached carefully, loafers crunching against crispy grass. The door wasn't quite closed—a gap just wide enough for something cat-sized to slip through.

She peered through the dusty window, cupping her hands against the glass. Inside, curled on a folded tarp, was a large orange tabby. His fur was thick, magnificent despite being slightly matted. One ear was tattered and his tail—wrapped around his body like a scarf—was indeed *really long*, just as Oliver had described.

The cat was asleep, or pretending to be, his sides rising and falling with the slow rhythm of feline contentment. Unbothered. Unrepentant. Living his best life in someone else's shed.

"Well," Cressida said, straightening up and turning to Oliver with complete seriousness, "your monster is definitely real."

Miles came up beside her and peered through the window, his height giving him a clearer view. Recognition flickered across his features. "Is that—"

"Kennard," Cressida confirmed, satisfaction settled warm in her chest. Another piece clicking into place. "Mrs. Buckner's missing cat." She turned to Amanda, who was standing a few feet back with one hand on Oliver's shoulder. "Would you mind if we removed your backyard monster? I know someone who's been very worried about him."

Amanda's hand flew to her mouth. "Oh my god, that's someone's *cat*? I had no idea—Oliver kept talking about it, but I thought he was just being imaginative. I've heard something out here at night, but I figured it was strays or raccoons..."

"Not a stray," Cressida assured her, already reaching for the shed door. The metal was cool under her palm, slightly rusty. "Just a very adventurous cat who has excellent taste in sheds."

She opened the door slowly, hinges creaking. Inside, Kennard regarded her with the supreme indifference of a cat who knew he'd been found but wasn't particularly concerned about the implications. His yellow-green eyes blinked once, slowly, the feline equivalent of *And?*

"Hey there, fancy meeting you here," Cressida murmured, extending her hand with deliberate patience. Kennard considered her offering with regal evaluation, then leaned forward and sniffed. His whiskers twitched. His pink nose touched her knuckles.

Then he simply leaped towards her.

The weight surprised her—solid muscle beneath magnificent fluff, substantial and warm. Her shoulder protested faintly, a reminder that she wasn't fully healed, but she adjusted anyway. His purr started immediately, rumbling through her chest. Something about his easy trust—this cat who'd been missing for days, now settling into her arms without protest—made her throat tighten unexpectedly. Small victories. They mattered more than she'd admitted to herself lately.

"Good boy," she said softly, adjusting her grip to support his considerable bulk. His tail draped over her forearm like a luxurious scarf.

She backed out of the shed carefully; Kennard made no move to escape, perfectly content to be carried like the royalty he clearly believed himself to be.

Oliver's eyes went saucer-wide, his whole face lighting up with wonder. "You caught him!" The words came out in a breathless rush, half-shout, half-whisper, as if he couldn't quite believe what he was seeing.

"I did." Cressida turned to face him fully, letting Oliver get a good look at his backyard monster in all his orange tabby glory. Kennard's ear—the tattered one—twitched as he tracked the movement of the kid's pointing finger. "And now I'm going to take him home to his person, who really misses him. Thank you so much for telling us where he was hiding."

Oliver beamed and his chest puffed out slightly, shoulders squaring. "I helped solve the mystery!"

"You absolutely did," Miles confirmed, reaching over to ruffle the kid's hair. "Without you, we never would have found him."

Oliver preened under the attention, practically glowing. Amanda's hand on his shoulder tightened slightly—maternal pride and relief mixing in equal measure across her features.

They made their way back inside, retracing their steps through Amanda's house. Cressida adjusted her grip on Kennard as they navigated the doorway—the cat had started kneading her shoulder with his front paws, claws catching slightly in the fabric of her blouse in that rhythmic motion cats made when they were content.

It was uncomfortable and endearing in equal measure.

Amanda met them at the front door, the USB drive held in her outstretched hand. "I really hope it helps."

"It will," Cressida assured her, shifting Kennard's weight as he continued his shoulder massage with increasing enthusiasm. The purr had intensified, vibrating through her entire upper body. "Thank you so much, Amanda. And Oliver."

"Anytime," Amanda said warmly. "If you need anything else, I'm right here. And if you solve this thing, I want to hear all about it."

"Deal," Cressida promised, meaning it.

Miles carried the USB drive like precious cargo as they made their way back to Vale House. Cressida managed an increasingly squirmy Kennard, who'd decided that riding in her arms was acceptable but staying still while doing so was apparently optional. He shifted position every few minutes, trying to drape himself over her shoulder, then deciding her arms were better, then reconsidering the shoulder option.

The walk back felt shorter with purpose driving their steps. The mountain air had warmed considerably, the fog burned off in patches to reveal glimpses of valley and ridge beyond. Birds called from the pines lining the road, their songs bright against the rustle of wind through needles.

"So," Miles said as they walked, his stride easy beside her, "we've got footage of our suspect, and you've solved the Case of the Missing Cat. Not bad for a day's work."

"Mrs. Buckner is going to be thrilled," Cressida said, wrestling Kennard back into a more secure position as he attempted to climb onto her head. "But first—"

"First we need to show this footage to my dad," Miles finished, his tone shifting slightly—still conversational but edged with awareness of what that conversation would entail. His jaw tightened almost imperceptibly, and he looked toward the mountain ridge ahead rather than at her. "Yeah. I know." A pause. "You ready for that?"

Cressida thought about Sheriff Stone's reaction to them investigating—the resigned exasperation mixed with what she'd guess to be paternal concern. About Deputy Nash's discovery of those receipts at Aunt Sylvia's house, the implications still spinning out in widening circles. About the hooded figure on camera, moving with deliberate purpose, planting evidence while the house slept around him.

About the tart that had started this whole tangled mess—innocent pastry turned murder weapon, or frame job, or both.

Kennard chose that moment to headbutt her chin affectionately, his skull solid against her jaw. She laughed despite herself, despite the weight of what came next.

"Ready or not," she said, meeting Miles's gaze with determination settling firmly in her chest, "it's time to see a man about a tart."

CHAPTER TWENTY-EIGHT

THE DRIVE BACK TO High Glen Estate felt shorter than it should have—a compression of time that came with momentum, with purpose solidifying into action. Miles navigated the winding mountain roads with practiced ease, his hands steady on the wheel as they traced the familiar route back to where this particular thread of investigation had started. Kennard had settled into a contented loaf position on Cressida's lap, his purr a constant rumble that vibrated through her thighs.

The USB drive sat between them in the center console like a talisman, a small rectangle of plastic and circuitry containing evidence that could crack this case wide open. Or at least provide the leverage they needed to push it in the right direction.

As they approached the turnoff to High Glen Estate, Cressida spotted them immediately—three official vehicles parked in a neat row along the circular drive like a cavalry waiting for the charge. Two county explorers, their white and blue paint schemes crisp against the manicured lawn, and Sheriff Stone's aging Bronco sitting between them like a patriarch among his offspring.

Miles pulled his own Bronco up beside his father's, the similarity between the two vehicles almost comical if the circumstances weren't so serious. Same make, same basic shape—just separated by two decades and approximately a million miles of philosophical difference about how to approach the law they both respected.

"Showtime," Miles murmured, cutting the engine.

Sheriff Stone stood near the front steps of High Glen Estate, his posture a blend of relaxed authority and coiled readiness that came from three decades of wearing the badge. Deputy Jensen was beside him, arms crossed, her military bearing evident even in casual stance. Deputy Nash hovered slightly behind them both, his young face creased with concentration as he reviewed something on his notepad.

All three turned as Miles and Cressida emerged from the Bronco—Cressida still clutching Kennard, who'd chosen this moment to drape himself over her shoulder like a very large, very orange fur stole. Her shoulder grumbled under his weight, but she shifted slightly to accommodate him.

Nash's reaction was immediate and visceral. "Ah, *shit*—" The word burst out before he could stop it, his face flushing red as his hand flew up in an aborted gesture of apology. "I mean—sorry, ma'am. Sorry for cursing in front of ladies."

Cressida bit back a smile, adjusting her grip on Kennard who'd started kneading her shoulder again with renewed enthusiasm. "I've heard worse, Deputy."

"I'm sure you have," Jensen said dryly, her dark eyes tracking Cressida with the kind of assessment that missed nothing—the cat, the bandage on her head, the slight limp. "I told you to be careful." A pause, weighted with meaning. "That's the opposite of what you did."

"That's how they operate," Sheriff Stone said, his voice carrying that particular tone of resigned exasperation Cressida had learned to recognize as his version of grudging respect. He shifted his weight, thumbs hooked in his belt. His gaze moved between her and Miles with the precision of someone reading a situation in real time. "Jensen, Nash—conduct the search while I talk to Mr. Dodd." His attention fixed on them both, hard and unwavering. "You two are silent bystanders. Understood?"

Cressida met his gaze with a slight smile. "Don't steal your thunder. Got it."

Miles sighed—affection, exasperation, and the weariness of someone who'd spent years translating between Cressida's irreverence and his father's authority all compressed into that single sound. "We understand." He threw her a look. *Please don't make this harder than it needs to be.*

She gave him her most innocent expression. *Would I do that?*

His expression suggested he knew exactly what she'd do, but he'd love her anyway.

Sheriff Stone approached the massive front door with the deliberate stride of someone who'd knocked on a thousand doors in his career—some in mercy, some in duty, all with the same unwavering commitment. His knuckles rapped against the dark wood.

The door opened after a moment, revealing the same maid who'd greeted them during their previous visit. No tears today—her eyes were clear, her posture professional, though something in her expression suggested wariness at the sight of so many official vehicles crowding the drive.

"Sheriff," she said. "Mr. Dodd is with his roses again."

The garden stretched out before them like something from a country estate magazine. Geometric beds of prize-winning roses in graduated shades from cream to deep crimson. Espaliered fruit trees trained against stone walls. Gravel paths raked to perfect uniformity. Every bloom positioned just so, every leaf disease-free, every stem properly staked.

Decades of careful cultivation and obsessive attention.

Except for one section.

Willard Dodd stood among his prized roses near the western wall, methodically pruning. But something was wrong—fundamentally, viscerally wrong in a way that made Cressida's chest tighten even before her brain caught up to catalog the specifics.

He was cutting blooms that didn't need cutting. Destroying perfectly healthy canes with deliberate snips of his shears. A 'Queen Elizabeth' hybrid tea in full glory—the kind of bloom that would have won ribbons at any county fair—fell to the ground, its pink petals already bruising against the dirt. Another cut, another perfect rose sacrificed. His movements were mechanical, purposeless, the rhythm of destruction steady as a metronome.

Snip. A 'Double Delight' with cream and crimson petals tumbled onto the growing pile at his feet.

Snip. A butter-yellow 'Peace' rose joined it, stem severed mid-cane.

The garden smelled like green things dying—that sharp, bitter scent of sap bleeding from fresh wounds mixed with the sweet perfume of roses that would never finish blooming. Kennard's claws pricked through Cressida's blouse.

Sheriff Stone's boots crunched on gravel. "Mr. Dodd." His voice carried across the garden. "I need to ask you some questions about your wife's death."

Willard didn't answer. The shears kept moving—snip, snip—through stems that didn't need cutting. A deep red bloom, heavy-headed, years old judging by the cane's thickness, tumbled to the ground.

Cressida watched the mechanical movements, the blank expression. The roses at his feet represented more than flowers. They were time. Effort. Proof that someone could nurture beauty while their life crumbled.

She stepped closer. "Mr. Dodd..." Kennard's purr rumbled against her neck. "Do you want to tell us what happened?"

"It's time to stop hiding the truth." Miles's voice was firm but soft.

Only the shears answered. Another rose fell—delicate apricot 'Just Joey,' three seasons to bloom. The petals landed face-up, still beautiful in destruction.

Willard's hands stilled.

The shears hung loose, tips pointing groundward. He stared at the ruined blooms—years of cultivation destroyed in minutes. His shoulders sagged.

When he spoke, his voice came from somewhere distant. "Henrietta came home from visiting Sylvia three days before the competition." A swallow, throat working. "She was gloating. Told me about Sylvia's entry—elaborate tart, lavender, crystal flowers. Said it didn't matter how good it was. She'd make sure Sylvia lost again."

Footsteps on gravel—Jensen and Nash approaching. The sheriff's palm came up. *Don't spook him.*

Willard's knuckles went white on the shears. "I'd already purchased the porpheyne. Used Sylvia's debit card information—accessed it through the bank, through a subordinate's credentials." Matter-of-fact now, reciting details. "The original plan was slow poisoning. If anyone detected it, it would trace to Sylvia. I'd been preparing. Months. Maybe longer."

Premeditation. Months of it. The kind of calculated patience that spoke to desperation wearing the mask of strategy.

Miles tensed beside her. His hand twitched—started toward her arm, then stopped. His father was watching.

"But you didn't use it that way, did you?" Miles asked.

"No." Willard's laugh was bitter, hollow. "Because that day—the day before the competition—Henrietta came home and she was crueler than ever." His voice cracked slightly, the first real emotion bleeding through the flat recitation. "Demanding I take even more money from the bank. Said we needed to move, start fresh somewhere else. Didn't matter that the house was mortgaged to the hilt, that we'd get nothing for it. She wanted what she wanted."

He dropped the shears then, the metal clattering against the gravel at his feet. His hands came up to cover his face, pressing against his eyes like he could block out the memory through sheer force. "I found her emails. To an attorney, planning the divorce. To investigators, ready to sell me out for the embezzlement she'd been pressuring me to commit for *years*. I'd overheard her arguing with Ayita, taking credit for that poor girl's work. Like she'd done so many times before, to so many people."

"So you made a similar dish," she said softly. "To what Henrietta had described from my aunt's entry."

"Yes." Willard's hands dropped, revealing eyes that were red-rimmed but dry, like he'd cried himself out days ago. "She'd already paid someone to make her entry—some professional pastry chef from Charlotte who owed her a favor. She never baked a damn thing herself, not in twenty years. But she described Sylvia's entry in such detail, so pleased with herself for knowing the 'competition.'" His voice dripped bitterness. "A tart with lavender. But I used a different herb mixed in. I had to add food coloring to get the right color."

Sheriff Stone stepped forward, brows scrunched with confusion over a confession that still needed more. More details. "Why a different herb?"

"Russian Sage," Willard said flatly. "Looks almost identical to culinary lavender. Henrietta was severely allergic to sage." He laughed again, that same hollow sound. "The porpheyne amplified that reaction. Quickened it."

The pieces were falling into place now, the full picture emerging. Not a simple poisoning but something more elaborate—a frame within a frame, insurance policies layered on top of organic opportunity.

"I entered my tart under a false name," Willard continued, his voice barely above a whisper now.

"Vernald D. Dowd." Cressida supplied.

He nodded.

"I knew she'd go after Sylvia, and would want to twist the knife." His smile was grotesque, a rictus of grief and satisfaction. "She couldn't help herself. She never could."

The garden was silent except for the distant call of a mockingbird and the rustle of wind through the roses Willard hadn't yet destroyed. Kennard's purr had stopped, the cat perfectly still on Cressida's shoulder as if even he recognized the weight of this moment.

Willard's hand moved then—slow, deliberate—and reached for the pruning shears lying at his feet.

The reaction was instant, trained, visceral. Sheriff Stone's hand dropped to his service weapon, fingers wrapping around the grip without drawing. Miles moved closer to her. Deputy Jensen's posture shifted, weight forward, her own hand hovering near her holster. Nash was slower—half a beat behind—but his hand found his weapon too, uncertainty flickering across his young face even as muscle memory kicked in.

Cressida's breath caught. Kennard's claws dug deeper into her shoulder, sending a sharp jolt through her still-aching joint. The cat hissing as if sensing that crackling moment.

But Willard just picked up the shears with the same mechanical precision he'd been using all along. His fingers curled around the handles, metal catching the afternoon light, and he went back to pruning. Snip. Another 'Chrysler Imperial' fell—deep crimson petals scattering across the dirt like drops of blood. His voice continued as if nothing had happened, flat and distant, reciting facts with the same rhythm as his destruction.

"I snuck out one night," he said, cutting through a perfectly healthy 'Fragrant Cloud.' The orange-red bloom tumbled to join the growing pile. "Planted the porpheyne receipts in Sylvia's kitchen. The poison too—tucked it behind her spice jars where it'd be found easily enough. After I put a couple of drops in her tart." Snip. Another rose sacrificed. "Used the spare key Sylvia kept in her safe deposit box at the bank."

"I left Henrietta's medication in the car on purpose." His laugh was bitter, hollow. "Knew she'd get angry. She always got angry when things weren't exactly as she wanted them. Sent me back for it right before the judging started—made a whole scene about it because that's what she did."

The mockingbird called again from somewhere in the garden, its song incongruously cheerful against the weight of confession hanging in the air.

"While everyone was focused on the judging," he continued, his voice taking on a dreamy quality, "I switched the labels. Mine and Sylvia's entries."

The roses smelled stronger now—that sweet, cloying scent of blooms cut too early mixed with the bitter green of wounded stems.

"Then when everyone was focused on her dying—" Willard swallowed hard, Adam's apple bobbing. "When she collapsed across that table with her face in the cake she'd been so proud of, when everyone was screaming and panicking and trying to help—I made sure Sylvia's entry was Sylvia's again, and mine was just... some random dish from a person nobody would remember."

A butter-yellow 'Graham Thomas' fell, its perfect spiral of petals already browning at the edges.

"It wasn't enough to be the best in Black-vale—she needed to be famous. National. International." The words came faster now, spilling out like he couldn't hold them back. "Equipment, marketing, consultants, travel to auditions—it costs money. So much money. She was going to discard me. As if I was just another stepping stone."

The shears dropped again. Both hands came up to cover his face, shoulders shaking—not with sobs exactly, but with something deeper and more broken.

"I thought she loved me." His voice was raw and vulnerable in a way that made Cressida want to reach out with unwilling sympathy. "Honestly and truly loved me. That's why I endured it—the public humiliation, the demands, the cruelty. I believed underneath it all, there was something real. Something worth saving."

That bitter laugh again.

"But she didn't know how to love. Not really. Not anyone except herself and what people could do for her."

Afternoon light slanted through the garden, catching on scattered rose petals and turning them into drops of colored glass.

"I loved her though." Willard's gaze was distant now, focused on something only he could see. "Still do, despite everything. Despite knowing she was going to destroy me. I thought it would be painless—the allergy would look like a mistake, like she'd accidentally used the wrong herb. Quick. Merciful, even."

His eyes found Cressida's then, pleading and desperate.

"Tell your aunt it wasn't personal. Sylvia was just... convenient. The perfect scapegoat because Henrietta had already set her up by bragging about her entry. But I never had anything against her. This was never about her."

Sheriff Stone stepped forward, his voice carrying the weight of ritual. "Willard Dodd, you're under arrest for the murder of Henrietta Dodd." He pulled handcuffs from his belt. Metal clicked softly. "You have the right to remain silent. Anything you say can and will be used against you in a court of law. You have the right to an attorney. If you cannot afford an attorney, one will be provided for you."

Willard didn't resist. Just held out his hands, wrists together, with the same mechanical compliance he'd shown throughout the entire confession.

The cuffs clicked shut.

Final. Irrevocable.

As they passed Cressida and Miles on their way toward the house, Sheriff Stone paused. Looked at them both with those dark eyes. "Good job, you two."

His gaze lingered on Miles. Held there a beat longer. Something shifted in his expression. Recognition maybe.

Miles's jaw tightened. He watched his father guide Willard forward, Jensen and Nash falling into formation behind them.

Cressida and Miles stood in the ruined garden, surrounded by scattered rose petals and the sweet-bitter smell of dying things. The afternoon light was fading now, casting long shadows across the geometric beds and espaliered fruit trees. Everything looked the same as it had an hour ago—the stone walls, the gravel paths, the careful cultivation of decades.

Except for one section, where perfect blooms lay scattered like casualties, where years of care had been destroyed in minutes by hands that had built them up with just as much precision.

Kennard purred against Cressida's neck, the vibration steady and grounding. She reached up absently to scratch behind his ears, her gaze still fixed on the retreating figures—the sheriff's measured stride, Willard's shuffling compliance, the deputies flanking them like an honor guard for the condemned.

"Love," she said quietly, more to herself than to Miles. "It makes people do terrible things."

Miles didn't answer right away. Just stood beside her, solid and steady, his presence the kind of anchor she needed after watching a man confess to murdering the wife he claimed to still love.

When he finally spoke, his voice was soft but certain. "Not love. The absence of it."

CHAPTER
TWENTY-NINE

THE BACKYARD OF VALE House had transformed into something out of a fever dream—half Southern hospitality, half organized chaos. Cressida navigated through the crowd with two sweating glasses of lemonade, her progress slowed by the sheer density of bodies packed into every available inch of grass. Neighbors, Inn guests still in casual wear, Aunt Sylvia's garden club—half of Blackvale had descended on Vale House.

The news had spread with small-town velocity. *The Sheriff's office had arrested Willard Dodd for murdering his wife.* The words had rippled out from the station, each retelling widening the circle until truth blurred into folklore. By the time Cressida and Miles had pulled up to

Vale House, an impromptu cookout was already in full swing.

It was like the entire town had received a summons written in invisible ink: *Sylvia Vale has been vindicated. Attendance mandatory. Bring food.*

The crowd itself was a fascinating cross-section of Blackvale society. Old families mingling with newer residents. Shop owners talking to Inn guests. Members of different churches forming temporary alliances around shared potato salad. Cressida recognized faces from the Midsummer Feast and Fair—people who'd been in the competition tent when Henrietta died, witnesses who'd given statements, bystanders who'd become unwitting participants in tragedy.

Mismatched tables had materialized from garages and church basements—folding tables with metal legs, card tables with wobbly corners, even someone's repurposed door laid across sawhorses. Each one laden with dishes that represented a cross-section of Southern culinary tradition. Potato salad in three different variations. Deviled eggs on crystal platters. Coleslaw ranging from vinegar-sharp to mayo-heavy. Baked beans in slow cookers still plugged into extension cords that snaked back toward the house.

Chairs appeared with practiced speed—lawn chairs with faded fabric, folding chairs from the church fellowship hall. Identified by the barely-visible *Blackvale First Baptist Church* stamped on the back support. Even a few weathered Adirondack chairs hauled from someone's front porch.

Cressida suspected—no, she was *certain*—that at least some of the people bearing casseroles and pies were offering them as a particularly Southern form of apology. The kind that didn't require actual words but communicated *I may have doubted your innocence but here's my grandmother's secret-recipe banana pudding so we're good now, right?* Food as absolution. Covered dishes as penance.

Near the makeshift buffet line, Ayita stood beside her father. Craig's Butcher Shop had donated enough meat to feed half the county—thick steaks, racks of ribs glistening with marinade, packages of hot dogs for the kids, what looked like half a pig's worth of pork shoulder. Ayita's turquoise-streaked hair caught the late afternoon light as she waved. Relief softened her features. She'd been under suspicion too. Had felt that same weight.

The real surprise was Sheriff Stone and Deputy Nash at the grills—two massive, industrial-sized affairs wheeled in from somewhere. The Sheriff worked his with the focused intensity he probably applied to crime scenes. Nash handled the other with less confidence but genuine enthusiasm, his face flushed from heat and what looked like attention from several younger women lingering nearby.

Sheriff Stone had shed his uniform shirt for a plain white t-shirt already sporting grease stains. An apron reading *Kiss the Cook* in fading letters circled his waist. He wielded tongs like a weapon, flipping ribs with precision while smoke billowed around him.

Near the patio, Aunt Sylvia held court. She'd claimed one of the good chairs—wrought-iron with actual cushion padding—and attracted an audience like a flame drawing moths. Mayor Whitfield sat to her right, suit jacket draped over his chair back. Rev. Carlson occupied her left, clerical collar loosened. Mae Stone perched on someone else's chair arm, copper curls catching light like a halo. Others clustered around, focused on Sylvia with the attention usually reserved for keynote speakers.

Her aunt was in her element. The flowing purple caftan with gold embroidery, the matching turban over silver-streaked curls, the signature red lipstick unsmudged despite an hour of continuous talking. Her hands moved as she spoke, gesturing with theatrical flair. From this distance, Cressida couldn't hear the words, but she saw the reactions—gasps, laughter, shocked expressions, knowing nods.

Willard's confession was being retold. Probably with embellishments. Definitely with Aunt Sylvia's gift for narrative drama. By tomorrow, the tale would be legend—polished, refined, ready to join Blackvale's oral tradition alongside Civil War skirmishes and that panther someone claimed to see up on Widow's Peak.

Roz had stationed herself near the drink table with strategic positioning that suggested military training. She looked impeccable—navy blazer, cream blouse, chestnut hair in that effortlessly smooth updo Cressida had never mastered. But there were cracks in the composure. Sharper movements. An edge to her smile when redirecting someone from the low lemonade. Alert eyes cataloging every person, every interaction, every potential problem.

Roz directed foot traffic with the energy of someone who'd spent years herding city council meetings. *"Drinks are over here. Food line starts at that table, please don't block the path to the house. Yes, there's sweet tea. No, the bathroom line isn't that long if you use the one upstairs."* Her voice carried across the yard—not shouting, just projecting with authority that made people automatically obey.

Deputy Nash kept gravitating toward Roz's station. He'd make an excuse—checking the ice, refilling the tea, asking if she needed anything. Roz would respond with Southern belle manners while straightening, her movements becoming just a fraction more precise. Nash would linger a moment too long before remembering his grilling duties and hurrying back to the Sheriff's side.

Children ran between the tables, their laughter high and clear, occasionally earning gentle reprimands from parents too relaxed to really enforce anything. Someone had set up a cornhole game near the back fence. Music drifted from a bluetooth speaker somewhere—classic country, the kind that everyone knew the words to even if they wouldn't admit it.

Miles appeared at her side just as she nearly collided with Mrs. Henderson from the post office, his hand shooting out to steady the glasses before lemonade could drench anyone. His fingers wrapped around hers for just a moment—warm, solid, grounding—before he took one of the sweating glasses.

"Half the town," he murmured, his voice carrying that familiar note of mild exasperation tempered with warmth that she'd heard a thousand times growing up. His gaze swept across the crowded yard with the kind of careful assessment that was pure Sheriff Stone training, even if he'd never admit it. "And I'm pretty sure the other half is still grabbing their casserole dishes."

"We're going to run out of backyard soon." The words came out lighter than she felt. "Maybe we should start directing people to the front lawn. Or the roof."

"Community processing," Miles observed, taking a sip of lemonade. "Collective ritual. When something disrupts the social order, people gather. Break bread. Reaffirm bonds. It's anthropologically predictable."

"You sound like your mother."

"Guilty." His lips quirked in that almost-smile. "She's the one who taught me about grief rituals and communal healing. Though I don't think she anticipated it applying to impromptu cookouts."

Cressida watched Sheriff Stone flip a rack of ribs without breaking a sweat. "Your dad's really committed to the grill master role."

"He's been manning community events since I was a kid," Miles said. His voice was carefully neutral, but something flickered in his expression—pride maybe, or old complicated family dynamics temporarily set aside. "Fourth of July, church picnics, fundraisers. He's the unofficial official grillmaster of Blackvale County."

"Deputy Nash looks like he's about to pass out from heat and nerves."

"He's also trying very hard to impress your sister."

"I noticed." Cressida grinned. "Roz is pretending not to notice him noticing her. It's adorable and painful to watch."

Movement caught her eye near the back gate—two figures entering with the kind of purposeful stride that spelled trouble. Mrs. Buckner in one of her signature pastel pantsuits, this one a particularly aggressive shade of lavender that caught the late afternoon sun. And beside her, moving with that unhurried grace that somehow made everyone else seem frantic by comparison, Aunt Marnie.

Behind them, tail high and expression judgmental, stalked Kennard. The elderly tabby's torn ear twitched as he surveyed the gathering with the air of a general inspecting troops he'd already deemed inadequate.

Cressida's hand shot out, fingers closing around Miles's arm with enough force to make him grunt in surprise. "Nope. No. Absolutely not."

"What—" he started, but she was already moving, pulling him backward through the crowd with the kind of desperate urgency usually reserved for avoiding exes at weddings.

They made it to the back of the shed before Miles dug in his heels, using his superior weight to halt their retreat. "Cressida—"

"Saving you," she hissed, pressing herself against the weathered wood and pulling him into the narrow shadow beside her. Close quarters—close enough that she could smell the faint scent of his soap, something clean and simple that reminded her of pine needles and rain. "Trust me."

He followed her gaze back toward the gate where Mrs. Buckner was already scanning the crowd with predatory focus, her oversized handbag swinging from one arm like a weapon. Aunt Marnie stood beside her, hands clasped, that knowing smile playing at the corners of her mouth that meant she'd already spotted them and was choosing to let them think they'd escaped.

"Good call," Miles said quietly, his breath warm against her temple. They stayed pressed against the shed, hidden in the narrow gap between weathered boards and overgrown hydrangeas that Aunt Sylvia kept meaning to trim back.

The crowd noise washed over them—laughter, conversation, the sizzle of meat on the grills, children's shrieks of delight. But here in their makeshift hiding spot, everything felt muffled. Separate. Like they'd found a pocket of quiet in the middle of chaos.

"So," Miles said after a moment, his tone shifting into something lighter, teasing. "Our first solved case." He held his lemonade up in a mock toast, the glass catching fragments of sunlight filtering through the hydrangea leaves. "Should we celebrate? Get business cards printed? *Vale & Stone Investigations—We'll Eventually Figure It Out.*"

She laughed despite herself, the sound breaking free before she could stop it. "Technically it was your dad's arrest. We just did the legwork." But even as she said it, she felt something warm unfurl in her chest. Pride, maybe.

Or satisfaction. The kind that came from seeing something through to the end.

"That's literally what investigation means," Miles pointed out, that dry humor threading through his voice. "The legwork is the whole job. The arrest is just paperwork."

He wasn't wrong. They'd been the ones to connect the dots—to see what everyone else had missed because they were too close, too convinced of their own narratives. She and Miles had looked at the evidence without the weight of decades of assumptions.

"It feels surreal," she admitted quietly, her gaze drifting past the shed toward the crowd. She could see Aunt Sylvia holding court, see the Sheriff and Deputy Nash at their grills, see all these people who'd lived this tragedy and were now processing it through potato salad and sweet tea. "Like we accidentally stumbled into being exactly what we used to pretend to be as kids."

Miles was quiet for a moment, his shoulder warm against hers where they stood pressed together in the narrow space. When he spoke, his tone had gone quieter, more thoughtful. "Maybe that's not an accident."

She turned to look at him, found him already watching her with those dark eyes that saw too much. "What do you mean?"

"Just—" He paused, seeming to consider his words. "Maybe we've been growing into this all along. Those games we played, all those mysteries we invented because Blackvale was too small and too boring... maybe we were practicing. Preparing."

"For what? A murder investigation in our hometown?" But even as she said it, she knew what he meant. Felt it in her bones—that sense of rightness that came from finally doing something that fit.

"For finding what we're supposed to do." His voice was soft but certain.

Something tightened in her chest—not uncomfortable, but insistent. Like her ribs had suddenly remembered they were supposed to protect something fragile. She didn't trust herself to speak yet, so she stayed quiet, letting the weight of his words settle between them.

"You with your instincts," he continued, "your ability to see patterns in chaos. Me with—whatever it is I do."

"Logic," she supplied, finding her voice again. "Reason. The ability to keep me from climbing through windows without checking if they're alarmed first."

His mouth quirked. "That too."

They fell into comfortable silence, watching the party unfold beyond their hiding spot. The celebration felt earned but hollow somehow. Justice served, case closed. But the why of it all—the darkness that had driven Willard to poison his wife—that lingered like smoke.

"Henrietta's vanity killed her," Cressida said quietly, voicing the thought that had been circling since they'd left High Glen Estate. "Not the poison. Not really. Her need to be perfect, to be celebrated, to win at all costs—it created the prison Willard lived in. Day after day, year after year, until he couldn't see any other way out."

Miles nodded slowly. "And Willard's despair killed them both. He couldn't imagine a future where he left. Where he chose himself over the life they'd built, the image they projected. So he chose murder instead of divorce."

"Because divorce would have been public failure," she continued, the pieces still settling into place even now. "Would have meant admitting defeat. Showing weakness. Everything Henrietta had trained him never to do."

"Darkness hiding in ordinary kitchens," Miles said softly. "In morning routines and dinner conversations. In marriages that look perfect from the outside but are rotting from within."

She shivered despite the summer heat, despite the warmth radiating from the crowd and the grills and Miles beside her. Because he was right—that was the truly terrifying part. Not that murder happened, but that it happened in spaces that looked so normal. That people could smile and wave and bake prize-winning cakes while plotting death.

Her gaze drifted past the party, past the fence line, toward the dark ridge of mountains rising in the distance. Somewhere out there, hidden in the folds of the hills, was Shadewood Hollow. She couldn't see it from here—couldn't see anything but the familiar silhouette of peaks against the darkening sky—but she knew it was there. Waiting.

A gust of wind cut through the backyard, sudden and sharp. Cold in a way that had no business existing in the middle of summer. It raised goosebumps along her arms, sent the hydrangea leaves rustling with a sound like whispered warnings.

Miles felt it too—she could tell by the way he tensed beside her, his head turning toward those distant mountains with the kind of instinctive wariness his father had probably taught him in childhood. Listening for what the wind carried. Reading signs most people missed. And for the first time all day, she didn't feel safe.

The party continued around them, oblivious. Laughter and conversation, the sizzle of meat, the clink of glasses. Celebration of justice served, of mystery solved, of their small town returning to its careful equilibrium.

But Cressida stood in the shadow of the shed with that cold wind still prickling her skin, staring at mountains that suddenly seemed closer than they should be, darker than the fading light warranted. And she knew—felt it in her bones with the same certainty that had brought her back—that Blackvale wasn't done whispering yet.

Not even close.

About J.P. White

J.P. WHITE IS A librarian and writer based in the United States, born and raised in Winston-Salem, North Carolina. By day, she helps readers discover the stories meant just for them; by night, she writes the ones she once searched for herself.

A lifelong creative, J.P. enjoys digital art, watercolor painting, and visiting museums and libraries wherever their travels take them. Her work is deeply inspired by everyday life and the countless people she encounters through her work in libraries-each conversation, question, and recommendation offering a glimpse into the quiet mysteries of human connection.

Though surrounded by books professionally, J.P.'s path to writing didn't begin with a love of reading so much as a love of helping. She entered librarianship to guide others toward stories that resonated with them-stories that felt like home. When those same stories proved elusive for her own younger self, J.P. began writing instead. What started in high school as a search for belonging has grown into a lifelong vocation.

Under the pen name J.P. White, she writes cozy and gothic-tinged mysteries that center atmosphere, character, and emotional truth-stories where found family matters, curiosity is rewarded, and justice often arrives with a teacup nearby.

Want more Vale & Stone mysteries?

Join my email list and get A *Haunting at Angelwood* **FREE**

SCAN ME

Scan here or visit: https://bit.ly/inkbound-blackvale

www.ingramcontent.com/pod-product-compliance
Lightning Source LLC
Chambersburg PA
CBHW051939240626
47153CB00005B/1555